TELLING LIES ONLINE

TELLING LIES ONLINE

MIRANDA MACLEOD

Apple Blossom Press
Boston, MA

Telling Lies Online

Copyright © 2016 Miranda MacLeod

All rights reserved. No part of this publication may be reproduced, distributed, or transmitted in any form or by any means, including photocopying, recording, or other electronic or mechanical methods, without the prior written permission of the publisher or author, except in the case of brief quotations embodied in critical reviews and certain other noncommercial uses permitted by copyright law.

Find out more: www.mirandamacleod.com
Contact the author: miranda@mirandamacleod.com

ISBN-13: 9781530355792

This is a work of fiction. Any resemblance of characters to actual persons, living or dead, is purely coincidental.

Apple Blossom Press
PO Box 547
Bolton MA 01740

ALSO BY MIRANDA MACLEOD

Telling Lies Online

Holly & Ivy (cowritten with T.B. Markinson)

Love's Encore Trilogy:

A Road Through Mountains

Your Name in Lights

Fifty Percent Illusion

Americans Abroad Series:

Waltzing on the Danube

Holme for the Holidays

Stockholm Syndrome

Letters to Cupid

London Holiday

Check mirandamacleod.com for more about these titles, and for other books coming soon!

ABOUT THE AUTHOR

Originally from southern California, Miranda now lives in New England and writes heartfelt romances and romantic comedies featuring witty and charmingly flawed women that you'll want to marry. Or just grab a coffee with, if that's more your thing. She spent way too many years in graduate school, worked in professional theater and film, and held temp jobs in just about every office building in downtown Boston.

To find out about her upcoming releases and take advantage of exclusive sales, be sure to sign up for her newsletter at her website: mirandamacleod.com.

TELLING LIES ONLINE

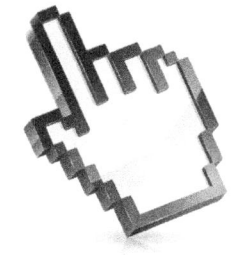

ONE

BLINKING WITH URGENCY, the unfamiliar message glowed red against the black background of the computer screen. Jamie's brow furrowed in confusion. She'd only been gone a few minutes and the Tech Cupid chat window had been active when she left.

MAINTENANCE MODE.

What did that mean? Her fingers raked through her cropped blond tresses, trying to work out what had caused it.

"Paul?"

The door to the kitchen swung open, revealing a tall man with a shining bald head. "Hey, Jay. You change your mind and want me to fix you a plate?" he asked.

"Are you kidding? I don't know how you can eat this late at night. I just wondered if you did something with the router."

"Uh uh, why? Is the Wi-Fi still not working?"

"It was fine until a minute ago. Now something's not

right." She smacked the side of her laptop repeatedly but the message remained unchanged.

"I see percussive maintenance isn't working," Paul said. His ivory teeth sparkled in a goofy grin. "Have you tried the old gold standard, turning it off and then on again?"

Jamie glared at him like she would an annoying little brother. Though the contrast of his ebony skin alongside her pale Nordic features made it pretty unlikely that they were actually related, Paul was the closest thing to a sibling she'd ever had. But at the moment, his lack of technological prowess was not inspiring feelings of brotherly love. Rolling her eyes, Jamie shut down her browser, then restarted it. The Tech Cupid chat window popped back onto the screen, good as new.

"Oh. Never mind." She felt her cheeks burn as Paul's teasing laughter echoed from the kitchen.

Unfortunately, the gray dot next to PortlandProf's avatar indicated she was currently offline. Jamie's body had been tingling in anticipation of continuing their chat, but now she slumped in disappointment. She glanced at the clock. It was past midnight, which meant she'd probably gone to bed. Jamie knew she should do the same, but was too excited to sleep.

She stole a final glance at PortlandProf's profile picture, lingering one last moment before clicking her mouse to close the chat window. A faint smile teased her lips as it disappeared. At barely an inch square, there was still something about the woman's candid expression in her icon that Jamie found utterly captivating, like she had been captured in the middle of a heartfelt laugh.

I'll bet she has a great laugh. She certainly had a great sense of humor. Jamie couldn't remember ever laughing as much as she had since she started corresponding with PortlandProf.

Or rather, Claire. *Claire.* That was her name, Claire.

They'd exchanged their real names tonight. Just first names, of course, at least for now. You couldn't be too careful about how much personal information you shared on an Internet dating site. But instinct told Jamie that she might have finally found *the one.* She wanted to pinch herself! Was it really possible that such a charming, beautiful woman lived only an hour away, and was actually as interested in Jamie as Jamie was in her?

Given her disastrous track record in dating, it seemed like a miracle.

The clinking of silverware against porcelain broke Jamie's reverie. She looked up as Paul entered the dining room, balancing a heaping plate of leftovers in one hand. Jamie shuffled a pile of papers aside so Paul could sit beside her at the long mahogany table.

"Come, join me," she said. "The dining room table makes a great desk, but I hear you can eat on them, too."

"So, I take it the Wi-Fi upstairs is still not working?"

Jamie shook her head. "Not a single bar."

"Sorry. You know me and technology." He gave a self-deprecating shrug. "I'll get someone to look at it."

"No rush. I really don't mind." Despite their chat being cut short, Jamie's spirits were soaring so high after her evening with Claire that she doubted anything could bother her right now.

"You're sure looking pleased with the world," Paul said, nudging Jamie in the ribs with his elbow. "Did someone send you some free porn or something?"

"Ewww," she replied, wrinkling her nose in disgust. "Seriously, Paulie, why is porn the only thing a guy can think of that might make someone look happy?"

"Uhhh." He gave his head an exaggerated scratch, clearly at a loss for a better answer. "Okay, so, if it's not that, what else could it possibly be?"

"Well, if you must know, I took your advice."

"Which advice?" Paul's forehead wrinkled. "You bought those leather pants? You finally signed up for salsa lessons?"

Jamie raised her eyebrows. "Dream on, my friend."

"Wait!" Paul clapped his hands. "Oh my God. You decided to host one of those naughty toy parties for my birthday and you're inviting the hot diving instructor from the Marine Institute as my present!"

Jamie rolled her eyes. While her position as one of the Institute's principle climate researchers didn't leave a lot of time for Caribbean vacations, one of the perks of the job was that employees could sign up for the occasional demonstration dive in their massive ocean tank. The instructor for her dive had been a particularly good looking man whom Paul was convinced gave off some sort of strong "gaydar" vibe. He'd been trying to get the guy's number for months.

"Paul, do you want to know why I don't take your

advice more often than I do? Because nine times out of ten, you give really bad advice."

"Ah, come on. Everyone needs at least one pair of leather pants!"

"See, that's what I'm talking about. But I guess signing up for Tech Cupid must have been lucky number ten, because I'm only a few days into my free trial and I already met someone who's perfect for me."

"Oh yeah? Congratulations, Girly!" Paul paused to swallow a bite of his dinner. "So, when you moving out?"

Jamie cringed. "Shut up, Paul," she said, smacking the back of his bald head playfully. "You can't get rid of me that easily this time."

"Yeah, well, I guess I just remember how it went last time you met *the one*. Was it even a whole month before you moved in with Naomi? And then, let me think," he continued, tapping his finger against the patch of hair on his chin, "it was your eight week anniversary when it all fell apart, right?"

Jamie pursed her lips, her eyes narrowing. She was a practical person by nature but she had an impulsive side when it came to love. So many times she'd been convinced a new relationship was the real deal. So many times she'd been proven wrong. Sometimes even before the unpacking was complete. If he planned to run through the complete history of her relationship failures, she might need to go heat up a plate of food for herself, just to keep up her strength.

"Eight weeks," he repeated, shaking his head slowly and clicking his tongue as if to scold her. "And then who got stuck living with your sorry ass again? Oh, right. That was me."

"Come on. You've loved every minute of it. You jump for joy every single time I move back in with you. But fine," Jamie said with a shrug. "Point taken. Maybe I've rushed things a little too much in the past."

Jamie glowered as Paul broke into a mock coughing fit in response.

"Ha, ha," she said when he was done. "I've learned my lesson."

"Uh huh. Repeatedly," Paul responded, clearly unconvinced. "And this time will be different why?"

"For one thing, I don't have a choice. I've got to take it slower this time. Claire lives in Maine."

"Maine? Is she a lumberjack or something?" He thought for a moment. "Well, that *is* different. Usually you're the one rocking the flannel and hiking boots, not your dates."

Jamie glanced self-consciously at the threadbare flannel shirt she had tossed on after work. Even in the summer heat, she rarely went without it, like a security blanket. "No, she's not a lumberjack. She's an English professor at some liberal arts college in Portland. So, it's not like either one of us can just pick up and move." Jamie paused, a dreamy expression softening her emerald eyes. "Not right away, anyway."

"Uh huh," Paul responded. "Somehow I know you'll find a way." He gestured toward her laptop. "You might as well show me a picture of this Claire person so I'll recognize her when I see her."

Jamie glared at her friend. "What, the moving van she'll show up in won't be enough of a clue for you," she quipped. She pulled up Claire's profile page and slid the laptop toward him.

Anyone who knew Jamie at all would have to admit that everything about the woman in the profile, from her curly brunette ponytail and golden brown eyes to her love of the ocean and obsession with all things British, screamed that she was *the one*. It was like someone had just delivered a big bag of Jamie-catnip. Paul continued to scroll, his brow furrowing as he approached the bottom of the screen.

"Hey, Jay, have you seen this?" he asked. "There's an urgent notice here from the Tech Cupid IT department."

"What? No, I didn't see it," Jamie replied. "What does it say?"

"Uh, it says: Dear Valued Customer, yada yada... problems with demographic information on some new profiles... now resolved... please refresh your account for updated information."

"Huh. Maybe that's what that maintenance screen was about."

"Should I go ahead and do the update?"

Jamie shrugged. "Sure."

Paul hit the refresh button and then clicked back to Claire's profile. His eyebrows shot up in alarm. "Uh, Jay? There's maybe a, um... did you say Claire lives in Portland, Maine?"

"Yeah, why?"

"Because I refreshed the page like the message said to, and now her profile says Portland, Oregon."

"What?" Jamie shrieked, dragging her fingers through her hair. "No, that can't be right, Paul. Oregon is on the other side of the country! You did something wrong, obviously. You said it yourself, you suck at technology."

"Hey, I just did what the instructions said!"

"Paul, you don't understand. I really like this girl. All those emails and chats we've exchanged..." Jamie's voice trailed off in a tone of desperation. "Just fix it, okay?"

"Yeah, okay. I'll fix it. Just calm down, Girly." Paul clicked, typed, and clicked some more.

Recalling a detail from an earlier chat session, Jamie released her tortured hair from its death grip and smiled. "Paul, it has to be another glitch. There's no way she's in Oregon."

"Why's that?" he asked.

"In our very first chat, she asked me where I lived. I said north of Salem, and then she said she was just outside Portland, and we figured out it would take about an hour's drive to meet up. You know," she added sheepishly, "if we ever decided to meet. Not like we're rushing into it."

Jamie paused in frustration as Paul failed to respond. His face appeared troubled. "Paul, just pull up the first couple of messages, okay? You'll see what I mean. She's in Maine. No doubt about it."

"Jamie Lee," he said softly.

Jamie froze. No one called her that any more. She'd been just plain Jamie, or Jay to her friends, for as long as she could remember. Even her own mother hadn't called her Jamie Lee since around the time she'd stopped scolding her for forgetting to bring her lunch box home from school. Whatever Paul had discovered, it couldn't be good.

"Jamie Lee," he repeated when he had her full attention. "First of all, there's a Salem in Oregon, too. Or have you forgotten the state capital song we had to sing in fifth grade?" He started to hum.

"Stop!" she pleaded. "You don't have to sing me the song. I'll take your word for it. But, so what?"

"So, the Portland and Salem in Oregon are about the same distance apart as the Portland and Salem here. I just checked the map. So that chat you had doesn't prove anything."

"Oh, come on," Jamie whined in frustration. "What kind of bullshit is that, anyway?"

Why would someone go putting Portlands and Salems right next to each other all over the country? Did they run out of names? Jamie wasn't convinced that a supreme being existed in the universe, but if it did, sometimes it seemed like it was just looking for a way to smack her down. Well, Jamie wasn't going to let the universe win. Not this time.

"That's okay," she added, her voice filled with determination. "I'll just fly to Oregon. It's not like you have to take a covered wagon across the country and risk dying of dysentery any more."

Paul sighed heavily. "Jay, that's not all. In fact, that's the good news. Here. I'd better just show you."

Jamie felt a chilly lump form in her stomach. What could possibly be worse than finding out that the love of her life lived three thousand miles away? She leaned over Paul's shoulder, looking blankly at the screen.

"See, right here," he said, his index finger tapping a line near the top of Claire's profile.

Jamie's heart sank as she stared at the words. She blinked rapidly, hoping that if she blinked enough times the words would change.

Woman seeking man.

No way. Claire had been the one to message her first, so she obviously wasn't looking for a man. Why did Tech Cupid now insist that she was? Why would Claire be seeking a man, unless...no, it couldn't be...

"That can't be right, can it? I thought Tech Cupid was a gay dating site."

Paul shrugged. "It's what they're known for, but strictly speaking, they offer everything."

"Even so," Jamie said, "she's the one who wanted to talk to me. Why would she do that if she's not at least interested in women?"

"Well," Paul said, "what did you put for an answer on that line?"

Jamie groaned. "I think I left it blank. I thought they were joking. Still, she had to have noticed I'm a woman."

"Maybe she thought you were a dude?" Paul winced as Jamie's open palm made contact with the back of his head. "No, seriously. The tech glitch could have left off your gender. Let me see your profile." He chuckled. "Uh, yeah. She totally thought you were a dude!"

"That's ridiculous, Paulie. I know I'm not the world's most feminine person, but I'm positive no one has ever mistaken me for a guy."

He looked her up and down with a dubious frown. "Okay. I'll take your word for it."

Jamie crossed her arms and stared at the floor, her cheeks burning. She might not always take the time to polish her appearance, but she liked to believe women generally found her attractive anyway. Hell, she could look downright hot when she tried, even at the ripe old age of thirty-four.

"Just look at this profile pic," Paul said, pointing to the screen. "Observe that you are wearing some sort of khaki coveralls and a cowboy hat. A cowboy hat, Jay? Have you been reading those lesbian cowgirl romance novels again?"

Jamie shrugged, embarrassed. "Maybe."

"Your face is completely hidden by that ten gallon abomination. Who knows what's under there. A girl, a guy, a sheepdog..."

"Really? A sheepdog?" Jamie rolled her eyes. "It was the only picture I could find, okay?"

"For God's sake, Jay, I'm a professional photographer. If this is the best you can manage on your own, promise me you will never post another photo of yourself anywhere, ever, without consulting me first, 'kay?"

"I'll admit that it's not a great picture," Jamie said, her

voice clipped. "But I don't see how that leads to me being a guy."

Paul snorted. "Take a look at your description. Six feet tall, athletic build, and you told her your name was Jay."

"So? That's all true." She smiled, feeling especially proud of how lean and toned she managed to keep her body with bike riding and regular morning swims.

"I know it's not your fault that you're freakishly tall and have a boy's name, but that's a pretty masculine description." Paul glanced from the computer screen to his friend and then back again. "If they left out the part about you being a girl, hell, I might respond to your profile. If it weren't for that hideous hat."

"Lay off the hat, Paulie. I like the hat." Jamie tugged sharply at her hair, wincing as several follicles snapped under the assault. "Seriously, could Claire really think I'm a guy?"

Paul raised his eyebrows and remained silent.

"This is a disaster, Paulie. What am I going to do?"

Paul sighed. "Not much you can do. Maybe you could figure out a way around the Oregon thing, but the being attracted to men instead of women thing is kind of a deal breaker, don't ya think?" He paused and looked Jamie squarely in the eyes. "You have to tell her the truth."

Jamie whimpered. "But then she won't want to talk to me any more."

"She might still want to be friends," Paul suggested encouragingly.

Jamie gave him a withering look at this suggestion. "I don't want her to be my *friend*."

Jamie rested her head in her hands, defeated. Paul was right, of course. Some things in life you could change and some you just couldn't. And who you were attracted to was planted firmly on the side of things that couldn't be changed. Hadn't Jamie spent most of high school explaining this concept to her mother? If she couldn't choose to be straight to make her own mother happy, then a straight woman wasn't going to choose not to be straight just because they'd shared a couple of nice online chats.

Jamie stared at the tiny image of Claire on her profile page. *My dream woman*. She was three thousand miles away and wouldn't want to talk to Jamie ever again as soon as she knew the truth. Or worse, she'd want to be *friends*. That prospect wrung every ounce of joy from Jamie's heart.

Tomorrow, Jamie thought, *I'll deal with it tomorrow*. She needed to hold onto the dream a little while longer, even if it could only last for one more night.

TWO

"HEY, LI'L SIS," a woman's voice echoed from the hall. "You're in early today, *hermanita!*"

"*Hola*, Theresa!" Claire answered, brushing a stray curl behind her ear before looking up to see her sister standing just beyond her office door. "Yeah, I guess I am." Her gaze fell longingly on the steaming cup of coffee in her sister's hands. Her sleep deprived brain whimpered for caffeine. "I don't suppose you brought one of those for me?"

"Sorry, I didn't expect you'd be in so early." Theresa approached Claire's desk and offered her the cup anyway. "Are you teaching morning classes now or something?"

Claire took a grateful swig of the bitter liquid before handing it back. "No, I just had a little insomnia and figured I might as well grade some papers."

The truth was, Claire had barely slept a wink after reading the urgent message from Tech Cupid's IT department last night. *Massachusetts*? She still couldn't wrap her head around how one of the most popular new dating sites in the country could make such a colossal mistake. Claire had never expected to feel such a strong connection with any guy, let alone one she met on the Internet. The revelation that Jay lived clear on the opposite coast instead of just down the road had left her tossing and turning into the wee hours of morning.

The sight of her sister, though, gave Claire a flash of inspiration. "Hey, sis? Do you know people at any of the colleges around Boston?"

"Boston?" Theresa shrugged. "Probably. Why?" Claire's sister worked in the admissions office of Lovejoy College and had connections at most of the liberal arts schools across the country.

"Oh, it's nothing really," Claire replied with an attempt at nonchalance that was completely at odds with the desperation gnawing at her insides. "It's just, my current contract is up after the summer term and I thought maybe I should look into some other opportunities for next semester. That's all."

"Hold on a second. I thought you were basically guaranteed to get the tenure track position that's opening up when Dr. Grafton retires next spring."

"It's not a sure thing, believe me. I should be looking into all my options."

"Come on, everyone here loves you. You'll get the position. So why're you thinking about Boston? You've never even mentioned wanting to visit Boston before! Now you want to move there?" Theresa's eyes narrowed in suspicion. "Next semester is winter. Winter, Claire? You despise winter."

"I told you, it's nothing." Claire found another curl that had escaped her ponytail and twirled it around her finger. "And it would be fall, not winter. Fall in New England is supposed to be beautiful."

"So take a vacation there." Theresa studied her sister and shook her head. "The end of the term is only a few weeks away. There's no time to plan. And you're a planner. So what's this really about?"

"It's, well," Claire put her hand self-consciously in front of her mouth and mumbled, "I finally activated that Tech Cupid membership you bought me for my birthday last month, and..."

"And...?"

She burrowed her mouth deeper into her hand. "And, I think I might have met someone."

"Claire! Oh my goodness, really?" Theresa nearly leaped into the extra chair beside Claire's desk, propping her chin on her hands and staring intently at her with a wide grin. "I swear, I thought it would never happen. Tell me all about it! What is he, or she, like?"

"Well, his name is Jay, and—wait. What do you mean by *or she*?"

"What?" Theresa responded vaguely, suddenly much more interested in lining up a pile of paper clips along the edge of Claire's desk than in making eye contact.

"You said 'tell me what he, *or she*, is like.' What exactly are you trying to say? Theresa, you know I'm not gay!" The squeak of her voice made the strong denial sound like it came from a chipmunk.

"Sure, okay. Only, I mean, you know I love you no matter what, right? All I meant to say was that whatever makes you happy makes me happy." She gave her sister an awkward shrug.

"Theresa, just because I don't date a lot of guys or talk about my sex life all the time like some people do doesn't mean I'm hiding in the closet."

"No, of course not! It's just..."

"Just what?"

"Honestly, *hermanita*? In the past decade, I don't ever remember you going on a date, other than those two blind dates I set you up with that you claimed were disasters. And as far as a sex life goes—are you sure you even have one?"

"Oh my God, Theresa, yes, I've had sex. I study the nineteenth century, I don't live in it. You think I've never had sex?" She could feel her cheeks burning.

"I didn't say never, but recently? When, Claire? When was the last time you had sex?"

Claire thought for a minute. "London! When I went to that Jane Austen symposium in London," she announced in triumph.

"That Austen thing was seven years ago. Got something more recent?"

Claire's face fell. Had it really been that long? "Well, I've been busy. I was trying to finish a dissertation, in case you'd forgotten. That doesn't make me a lesbian." Her voice dropped to an uncomfortable whisper as she said the final word.

"No, you're right. *That* does not make you a lesbian. No one thinks you're a lesbian because you were writing your dissertation."

"Exactly. Wait—why did you say it that way? Like there's some other reason that you do. Or that other people do." A look of panic crossed Claire's face. "Do other people think I'm a lesbian, Theresa?" She drummed her fingers nervously on the top of the desk. "Who thinks that, Aunt Marisol? That woman's a fanatic. She thinks the statues in church talk to her. Has she been saying things about me?" Claire's voice squeaked again as she asked. "Why haven't you told me this before?"

"Relax, Claire. Calm down. Aunt Marisol hasn't said anything." Theresa drew a deep breath. "No one's said anything. It's just my own observations. Like how you're always telling me about some new girl you met at the coffee shop, or how you can go on forever about a hundred of your favorite actresses but can't name a single actor you think is hot." Theresa shrugged. "You just get a hunch about that sort of thing after a while."

"That doesn't mean anything! I like to meet new people, and I happen to like movies with strong female characters. You're reading too much into totally normal behavior, Theresa."

Claire's sister waved her hands in surrender. "Fine. You're probably right. It's just that ever since you were a kid, since right after Mom and Dad died, it's like you've been hiding something and it makes you sad. So I took a guess that maybe that's what it was. I'm sorry if I was wrong."

"Oh, Theresa." Claire's face softened as tears glistened on her lashes. Any mention of their parents always made her eyes well up. "Of course I've been sad. But not because— well, not because of *that*. I just miss Mom and Dad."

"That's all?"

"Of course! As for hiding stuff, you remember what it was like living with Aunt Marisol. I hid stuff from her all the time, and I know you did, too."

Theresa chuckled. "Yeah, well, the woman's like a bloodhound."

The expression on Claire's face turned serious. "You know that I want a family more than anything, right? Like we had with Mom and Dad. I've been waiting so long for a sign to know when I've met the right one. It's just never happened until now with Jay."

Theresa shook her head. "Signs again, Claire? I thought you'd grow out of that eventually." She threw her hands into the air. "Jay's in Boston. There's a sign for you. It looks exactly like an interstate sign that reads Boston: 3,000 miles. We're talking about the other side of the country, Claire!"

"You're telling me!" Claire replied. "It wasn't intentional, trust me. You wouldn't *believe* the disaster this is." Claire went on to explain the technical mix up in detail. "But, maybe it's fate," she concluded. "I really think Jay's the one, and if it hadn't been for this screw up, we never would have met."

"But you haven't met," Theresa pointed out, "and you're already thinking of moving to Massachusetts, sight unseen. It's not like you at all. What does Jay think of this plan?"

Claire sighed. "I don't know. I don't even know if he's aware of the problem yet. I only got the message last night. Then the server went down, and I haven't seen him online yet this morning to discuss it."

"Well, you might hold off mentioning the moving idea, okay? Guys freak out over stuff like that. Look, I'll check with some of my contacts and see what job openings there are, but don't get your hopes up. Even if you get an offer, it may not be half as secure as what you already have."

"Relax, sis," Claire said. "I value my career. I'm not going to do anything stupid. I just have faith that the universe wouldn't send me the sign I've been waiting for without delivering a way for it to work out."

"*Ay dios mio.* You're so stubborn. Has it occurred to you that the fact that everything got screwed up is a sign to keep looking?"

Claire laughed. "How about we make a bargain? You put in a good word for me wherever you can, and if the perfect offer comes along, then you'll agree that it's a sign from the universe that I'm right about this and you won't argue with me about going."

"Fine. Deal." Theresa stood, crushing her sister in a heartfelt embrace before heading to the door. "I doubt it's going to happen, but if the universe really does send that sign of yours, I'll even help you pack," she added.

Claire watched her sister depart, the heel of her right foot tapping rapidly against her battered metal desk. Despite her attempt at bravado and her talk of signs and faith, she wasn't delusional. She knew the odds were against her. With the ink barely dry on her PhD and only a handful of published articles to her credit, it would be hard to compete for a tenure track position against a city full of highly connected Ivy Leaguers. And Theresa was right. She would be a fool to give up the security she enjoyed at Lovejoy College for anything less.

Even with a fantastic offer, could she really just pick up and move across the country to a city she'd never seen before? Leave behind her friends, her sister, and the little bit of family she had left?

Deep down, though, Claire felt compelled. Ever since her parents had died in a car accident when she was nine, she'd had a clear vision of what her perfect future life would be. A husband, two kids, a nice little house, a dog—the ideal life, just like what her parents had. Actually, the dog was optional. She was more of a cat person. But the husband was essential. You didn't get the kids and the house without the husband. It was a package deal.

It's not like it hadn't occurred to Claire that she wasn't as boy crazy as the rest of her friends. When you spent prom night at home reading a book and were the only one in your dorm studying on the weekend instead of out on a date, you started to suspect that you might be a little different. But different as in serious and academic, not *different*. Sure, she found a lot of women attractive, objectively speaking. Didn't everyone? She'd read an article once explaining that all women were bisexual by nature. It was just normal. It didn't mean she had to act on it or anything.

She'd made a plan for her future, and she refused to be distracted from it. She had faith in that plan to make her happy, and she had faith in the universe to send her a sign when the time came.

She'd thought she'd received a sign once before. It was on that trip to London her senior year of college. There were six other women in her group and every single one of them had nurtured a lifelong obsession with Mr. Darcy. Apparently it was a requirement that all female Jane Austen scholars had to be in love with Darcy. Claire had never seen the appeal, not of the character nor, to be honest, of Colin Firth, the actor who was synonymous with Darcy for pretty much every woman in the western world. After all, Elizabeth Bennet was much more engaging as a character, and she could've done so much better than Darcy. It was the look on her colleagues' faces when she voiced that opinion after a few drinks the first night of the conference that made Claire realize that, even among serious academics like herself, she might not quite fit in. She'd laughed it off, of course, and gone along with them the rest of the week as they waxed rhapsodic over everything vaguely Darcy-related.

And then along came that guy at the hotel bar the

last night of the trip who started flirting with her. When one of the other women commented on how he looked just like Colin Firth, well, Claire was positive it was a sign. She was certain that if she took him up on the suggestion to join him in his hotel room that night, she'd finally figure out what all the fuss was—about sex *and* about Darcy, since she didn't really get either one.

It turned out to be a spectacular failure as plans went. Fifteen minutes of awkward groping under sheets that reeked of stale ale had done absolutely nothing to demystify the allure of sex. Or Darcy. She flew back to Portland with her faith momentarily shaken, until she realized she had just been wrong about the meaning of the sign. It hadn't been meant to teach her about guys or sex at all. It was simply a sign that Jane Austen wasn't really her true calling. If she didn't get something as fundamental as Darcy, she wasn't meant to be an Austen scholar. So she put the whole thing behind her, chose a new topic for her dissertation, and trusted that the sign she had really been waiting for would appear when it was time.

Then there was Jay.

Sure, it had taken a few years longer than anticipated, but better late than never. Jay was the first guy she'd felt genuine attraction for in her entire life. She loved the way he wrote, his jokes, how they enjoyed so many of the same things. As for physical attraction, well, his profile picture was a little hard to see but she thought he might be her type. If she had a type. She wasn't convinced she did. She had flipped through so many promising profiles only to move on because the pictures left her feeling a little hollow. But something about Jay's picture had caught her eye. Maybe it was the kind of dorky, adorable cowboy hat. Anyway, the emotional connection was what mattered, and once they met in person all of that physical stuff would fall into place, too, right?

Maybe I should ask for another picture, just to be certain.

A blinking box in the corner of the monitor caught Claire's eye. A new chat window popped open. *Jay.* A sign. This connection they shared was so intense that just by thinking about him, he appeared. Surely it meant that things were finally going to turn out the way they were supposed to be.

THREE

CLAIRE: So, you've seen the news about the screw up? That I'm on the west coast and you're on the east?

Jay: Yeah, I saw it. But what should we do about it?

Jamie stared at the screen, nerves jangling, dreading Claire's response. What if she said they should break it off now, that the distance would be too hard to overcome? It would be the safest answer, even ideal in a way. It would put an end to it without Jamie having to deliver the even more difficult news about her gender. It might break Jamie's heart for her to say it, but at least it would be a clean break. What if Claire said the distance didn't matter to her? Then Jamie was going to have to tell her the truth, and it would almost certainly be over anyway after that. *Almost* certainly. It was that damned optimism, telling her maybe it wouldn't be over after all, that kept Jamie tied up in knots awaiting Claire's reply.

CLAIRE: *I REALLY LIKE YOU. I WANT TO KEEP GETTING TO KNOW YOU. I DON'T CARE HOW FAR AWAY YOU ARE.*

Jamie beamed. Claire wanted to get to know her. She liked her. She didn't care about the distance.

This is wonderful! Jamie thought. *No, this is terrible.* Now Jamie was going to have to confess the rest of it. Maybe it wouldn't matter. Maybe Claire was into women, too, and just hadn't mentioned it. *Yeah, right.*

Contrary to popular wisdom, as well as a surprising number of articles in gentleman's magazines, most women were not secretly bisexual. It turned out that it wasn't actually a rite of passage for all freshmen girls to engage in experimental hanky-panky with their college roommates, nor were the vast majority of women inclined to be overwhelmed by sexual curiosity when placed in the vicinity of a few shots of tequila, some bikini-clad friends, and a hot tub. Jamie had enough experience in the real world to know this for an absolute fact. It was a nice dream, but the chances of Claire being the one woman to buck this well-established trend was remote. Might as well just get it over with.

JAY: *CLAIRE, THERE'S SOMETHING ELSE I SHOULD PROBABLY TELL YOU. SOMETHING IMPORTANT.*

CLAIRE: *NOT MORE BAD NEWS, I HOPE?*

Jamie's fingers froze above the keyboard. She could almost feel the tension radiating from her computer screen. This was it, the moment of truth. She braced herself for the horrible task ahead.

JAY: *NO. GOOD NEWS! I'M MOVING TO A NEW*

APARTMENT. IN THE CITY. IT'S A LITTLE PLACE IN BEACON HILL WITH A VIEW OF THE CHARLES RIVER. I CAN SEE THE SAILBOATS FROM MY WINDOW! BUT IT'S BAD NEWS, TOO, I GUESS, BECAUSE THE PLACE IS REALLY SMALL. JUST A STUDIO, IN FACT. SO I DON'T HAVE ROOM FOR GUESTS. I'M AFRAID THAT'S GOING TO MAKE MEETING IN PERSON ANY TIME SOON REALLY DIFFICULT.

Jamie's fingers trembled atop the keyboard. She told herself she hadn't meant to do it, to write that. Her pulse raced as she reread the words on the screen. Jamie often fantasized about moving to that part of Boston, but it was just that—a fantasy. And a fantasy that, while nice, had absolutely nothing to do with the matter at hand. It certainly wasn't something she had ever intended to post. But there it was, flashing back at her from cyberspace.

Somehow Jamie's fingers had taken over, and she'd had hit the enter key with her pinky almost by reflex. Now the lie had traveled all the way to Portland in a fraction of an instant. Thanks to technology, deception moved at lightning speed.

CLAIRE: *THAT SOUNDS WONDERFUL! I'VE HEARD OF BEACON HILL AND WOULD LOVE TO SEE IT SOMEDAY. JUST AS I WOULD LOVE TO SEE YOU. BUT I GUESS IT MIGHT BE A WHILE.*

JAY: *I GUESS IT WILL. I DON'T HAVE ANY VACATION TIME OR I'D COME SEE YOU SOONER...*

Another lie. Jamie hadn't taken a vacation in years. *I can't come see you right now because you're bound to figure out I'm a girl if we meet in person.* There was still time to address that particular elephant in the room before she got herself in too deep. She should just screw up her courage and start typing.

CLAIRE: *AND I HAVE THE REST OF THE SUMMER TERM AHEAD OF ME WITH NO BREAKS. IN FACT, I'VE GOT A CLASS TO TEACH IN A FEW MINUTES SO I HAVE TO GO. COULD YOU DO SOMETHING FOR ME?*

JAY: *OF COURSE, JUST NAME IT.*

CLAIRE: *SEND ME A BETTER PICTURE OF YOURSELF. THE ONE ON YOUR PROFILE WAS REALLY HARD TO SEE.*

A picture. Well, that was one way to break the news. *Just send her one of the ten thousand photos in which I actually look like a girl and she'll catch on, guaranteed. And never talk to me again.* Jamie sighed.

JAY: *NO PROBLEM. I'LL SEND IT TO YOU LATER TODAY.*

Now what? Jamie grabbed a CD labeled 'Esplanade' from a pile on Paul's desk. Those would be the photos Paul took when they went to the Fourth of July fireworks earlier in the summer. She popped the disk in her bag, then bolted out the door and hopped on her bicycle, pedaling frantically so she wouldn't be late to work.

When lunchtime arrived, Jamie slipped the photo CD into her work computer and opened a folder with her name on it. There were some good shots of her. Not a cowboy hat among them, so Paul would approve. She was smiling in most of them, looking cute and coy and not at all like a cowardly, deceitful liar. She chose one where her face wore a serious, soulful expression, and the afternoon sun glinted off her hair in just the right way so that it looked like a cloud of spun gold. It was a really good photo. Paul was a genius photographer. If any picture could make Claire decide to fall in love with Jamie even though she was not a man, this was the one that could do it. She should just type up her confession, attach the photo, and be done with it.

Only she couldn't. Not yet. Jamie poked around idly on her computer, buying herself some time. There was another folder on the CD and Jamie opened it to find a picture of a tall, athletic man with sandy blond hair standing on the Esplanade, only without the crowds and mayhem of the fireworks photos. It must have been from one of Paul's photo shoots in early summer. Probably for a catalog, if the model's generically preppy wardrobe was any indication.

Jamie opened a few more. They were all of the same model, wearing different outfits, sometimes with a sailboat behind him, sometimes walking a dog. A golden retriever, naturally. Preppy New England model-types always had golden retrievers. Jamie didn't care for dogs, didn't like they way they slobbered. She was more of a cat person. But she supposed the dog made a nice accessory for conveying that wholesome, all-American look.

Now, if only Jamie looked like this guy, she figured she could win Claire in a heartbeat. She didn't need to be attracted to men to know this guy was the type who made straight girls swoon. But Jamie wasn't that guy, or any guy. She wasn't even the type of girl who had ever wished that she *were* a guy. She loved being a woman. But for the first time in her life, she regretted the fact deeply.

A little part of Jamie's brain knew all along what she was going to do next and had the decency to be horrified about it. She was an honest person at heart. She wouldn't dare fudge the numbers on her taxes or look at another person's cards when they left for the bathroom in the middle of a poker game. In short, she was simply not the kind of person who would take a photo of a tall, blond model walking a golden retriever in front of a sailboat from her best friend's portfolio and try to pass it off as herself to some poor, unsuspecting woman on the other side of the country. No, Jamie just wasn't that kind of person. Which is why it came as such a surprise to her, at least to all but that little part of her brain that had seen it coming all along, when she attached the photo to her message and pressed send.

FOUR

JAMIE STARED AT THE COMPUTER, stunned. She couldn't believe she had actually just done what she'd done. Her hands shook and her heart raced with the adrenaline that coursed through her. Forget a morning at the gym—nothing could compare to perpetuating a big, fat lie when it came to raising the heart rate. Jamie massaged her temples with trembling fingers. She had gone too far and she knew it. But it was the only thing she could think of not to lose Claire. Not yet.

The universe had played a cruel trick, revealing her heart's desire one minute only to snatch it away the next. The universe was always messing with her like that where love was concerned. She wasn't going to let it win without a fight.

Is there any possible way I could get away with this? Absolutely not. No way. *What if Claire wants more pictures?* There were a few more in the file, she reasoned. She could send those at some point. But what about when Claire asked for a phone call or a video chat? Surely Jamie was in for it then. *Best not dwell on that.* More pictures, though. Jamie could do that and buy herself some time.

She took a look at the photos from Paul's file again. The trouble with catalog photos was, well, they looked like they came from a catalog. They were all so similar. Jamie wondered if her computer skills would be sufficient to make them look more natural. Too bad she couldn't call Paulie. He was a disaster at most technology, but an absolute master of photo manipulation. Still, Jamie knew her way around the basics well enough to give it a try, and she had plenty of time before lunch ended to get started.

She glanced out her office door and confirmed that her research assistant, Alan, had left for lunch. His desk was empty, and no one else appeared to be around. Jamie didn't think she was violating any company policies with what she was doing, but she didn't exactly want anyone to catch her doing it, either. She grabbed an apple from her drawer to stave off hunger, pulled up the first picture of Blond Model Man, and got to work.

Twenty minutes later, the first photo was coming along but she'd hit a roadblock. She'd removed the model from the Esplanade and placed him in front of her favorite diner, then applied a few filters to make it look more like a snap shot. Something was off, though. Maybe the shadowing? *Paulie would know how to fix it.* Absentmindedly, she reached for her phone. It was only on the fourth ring that she remembered that what she was attempting to do was completely and utterly indefensible. It defied reason, common sense, and at least a hundred other qualities that good, decent people were supposed to possess. Before she could manage to hang up, Paul answered.

"Jay? What's up, Girly?"

"Hi, Paulie. Nothing. I shouldn't even be bothering you at work."

"Well, since you're calling, it's got to be a Photoshop question. Anything else and you'd just text."

"How did you— um, yeah, it is." Damn. How did he do that? He could read her mind. She would never get away with this. "So, I've got a picture I wanted to use in, um, a big report. For the Board of Directors. And I'm trying to get the shadows right but something looks funny."

"Okay, well, send it to me."

"Um, I can't."

"What, is it some super top secret photo of a mutant three-eyed fish or something?"

"Uh, yeah. Something like that."

"You're lying."

Some master of deception she'd turned out to be. How would she ever keep up her charade with Claire if she couldn't manage to lie to Paul for even a minute?

"Oh, Paulie," she said with a sigh, "you don't know the half of it." Mortified, Jamie told Paul the whole story of sending Claire the first photo. "I tried to tell her, Paul. I really did. I just couldn't do it. I know this can't go anywhere, but I was really hoping to have a few more weeks. I like her so much. I'm not ready to let go."

"This might be the dumbest thing you've ever done, Jay. And I say this as your best friend who has seen you at your dumbest. Which picture did you send her, anyway?" Paul listened as Jamie described it. "Oh, yeah. That's Blake. Damn, Girly. You've got some healthy self-esteem if you think the male version of you would look even half as fine as Blake. But you can't use those pictures."

"I know, Paul. I know what I'm doing is wrong—"

"No. Well, yes, it is, but that's not what I mean. Those pictures belong to my client. I'll be in deep shit if anyone ever finds out they were circulated without permission." Paul hesitated. "Look, I've work with Blake a lot. I think I can find a few old candid shots, which I will let you use if you promise that you will only do so for the purpose of getting this girl out of your system. Got that?"

Jamie grinned into the phone. "Yes, Paulie, I promise."

"I'm serious, Jay. You're obsessed. So chat with this Claire girl and find out what's wrong with her, because when you like them this much, there's always something wrong with them. Then get over her, move on, find yourself a nice, local lesbian, and don't be stupid again any time soon, okay?"

"Okay. Thanks, Paul. Love you."

"Yeah, love you, too, Girly."

That had gone a lot better than Jamie could have

hoped. Sure, she was still a liar. And there was still no chance that she'd end up with Claire. But at least now Paul knew the truth and he didn't hate her. That was something. Jamie took a deep breath and felt the tension in her temples ease. At least coming clean had settled her nerves.

The staccato ring of her office phone nearly sent Jamie catapulting from her chair. Her nerves weren't as settled as she'd thought. The caller ID read *Diane Swenson*—her new boss. Jamie cringed. Her boss' voice sounded strained as she asked Jamie to come to her office.

The woman is inscrutable, Jamie thought. She could be pleasant enough when it suited her, but it always felt like she was holding something back. Maybe Jamie just noticed it more because of how different she was from Dr. Matthews. He'd been a large, jovial Brit, and a major reason that Jamie had been drawn to the Marine Institute. When he'd been diagnosed with cancer, his abrupt retirement had dealt quite a blow, both to the research team and to Jamie personally. He'd been an excellent mentor.

The jury was still out on Dr. Swenson. Jamie was eager to do whatever she could to make a good impression. It was hardly a secret that Jamie was on the short list to replace Dr. Matthews as Head of Research. If she wanted the promotion, she knew she needed to shine.

Jamie looked with chagrin at the photo of Blake on her computer. Playing around with Photoshop at work ranked low on the list of ways to do that. She closed the file and scurried down the hall to Dr. Swenson's office.

Jamie stepped through the door and waited while her boss spoke on the phone. She tried not to fidget, but the woman made her nervous. Dr. Swenson had a demeanor that was as cold as it was professional. She was the Institute's director, and her word was law. If she could ever get on her good side, Jamie knew it would do wonders for her career. She just wasn't sure where to start. When Dr. Matthews left, his projects had been divided between Jamie and a rival colleague, and she was convinced their boss had given him all the best ones. Jamie wanted nothing more than a chance to prove her skills.

Setting the receiver down, Dr. Swenson looked Jamie directly in the eyes and spoke in a solemn tone. "A grave deception has just been brought to my attention."

Could the woman be more cryptic? Jamie hadn't the slightest idea what her boss meant. *Wait, did she say deception?* An image of Claire's avatar flashed into her head, along with the photos of sandy-haired Blake. Jamie's eyes grew wide. *But how could she possibly know?* Surely they weren't monitoring the computers, were they? That was crazy. *Careful,* Jamie thought. *Don't let your guilty conscience run away with your imagination.*

"Jamie, I've just received very distressing information about the meta-analysis that Philip Matthews was working on before his departure."

"His work on global deep water ocean temperatures? That's one of the projects you assigned to Dr. Michaels." Jamie tried to hide the bitterness she felt. If the preliminary results held true, that study would prove that current calculations underestimated global warming rates by a factor of ten. She would've done anything to have her name attached to that research.

Dr. Swenson nodded. "Yes. And apparently Dr. Michaels has been telling anyone who will listen that the preliminary results were falsified."

"I'm sorry, what?" Jamie nearly bubbled with outrage. The idea was absurd, and an insult to Dr. Matthews' integrity.

"If this is true, it would be a disaster. When Dr. Matthews presented the preliminary findings at last year's UN climate change conference, it put our Institute on the map. We added several major donors as a result, and we're relying on that income."

"Are you saying you really believe he lied about the results?" Jamie was horrified.

"Even if he didn't, it might not matter. If the press gets a hold of it, we're ruined," Dr. Swenson replied. "Honestly, I can't imagine someone of Dr. Matthew's reputation deliberately manipulating results, but Dr. Michaels can't think of any other explanation."

"Apparently not. And what exactly is he trying to explain?"

"He had his research assistant rerun the simulations to check the original results, and nothing matches up. That's why I called you. This project needs a thorough review, and I'm an administrator, not a researcher."

"And Dr. Michaels, he gave it to an assistant to rerun? From *scratch*?" Jamie stifled a groan. Her colleague was both arrogant and lazy. Of course, he'd insist on starting from scratch, and then assign it to someone else. It was about a million times more likely that he had screwed up the variables than that Dr. Matthews had lied. But proving it would be a challenge.

"Dr. Matthews thought very highly of you. I shouldn't tell you that, perhaps. I know he was your mentor, but I need you to be objective, regardless of how it turns out."

"Of course." Jamie felt a thrill of pride. It was the closest thing to a compliment she'd ever received from Dr. Swenson.

Her boss' face softened into what nearly passed for a smile. "If you can fix this discreetly and we're successful in keeping our funding, this could absolutely make your career."

Jamie walked back to her office in a daze. Her boss had handed her the opportunity that could change the course of her career, if only she could solve this puzzle. She'd promised to be objective, but she couldn't accept that Dr. Matthews would deliberately falsify results. It had to be Dr. Michaels' screw up. Jamie sat at her desk and rubbed her temples, momentarily overwhelmed by the magnitude of the task ahead of her. *Better get to work.*

She jiggled the mouse and her computer hummed back to life. Jamie's eye was drawn to the corner of the screen where a Tech Cupid chat window sat open. A new message was waiting from Claire. Jamie sighed. She shouldn't be chatting with Claire right now. She had too much work to do. In fact, she shouldn't be chatting with her at all. Or sending her fake photos. Or continuing to lie to her. She shut her eyes tightly for a moment, pushing the thoughts back into the recesses of her brain. She closed the chat window without a reply.

No time for that now.

Jamie had a problem to solve and her mentor's name to clear. Dr. Matthews wasn't the type who would lie, Jamie was certain of it. *I bet people think that about me, too*, she chastised herself, thinking of Claire.

Oh, the irony.

FIVE

CLAIRE MANEUVERED her car into the driveway of her sister's house. The smell of charcoal smoke and cooking meat wafted across the flagstone steps as she approached the vintage Craftsman cottage. The family would be in the back yard, with Theresa curled up to read in her favorite Adirondack chair while Larry flipped burgers and Jesse and Ryan tumbled on the grass. It was the same every week, a tableau of domestic perfection.

Sunday dinner with Theresa was a time honored ritual that was not to be missed, even during those times when Claire struggled not to feel sorry for her lonely, single self. Happily, today was not one of those days, though her current relationship status wasn't exactly inspiring her to do handsprings across the lawn, either.

For starters, Jay had sent her another picture of himself and it'd made her very nervous. She had stared at that picture for hours, waiting for that giddy feeling she knew she was supposed to get, but so far it hadn't come.

There was no question that he was handsome. He could've been a model. And yet... the only thing she felt was nervousness that she hadn't been overwhelmed with attraction the way she had hoped. On top of that, teaching positions in Boston were turning out to be even more ruthlessly competitive than she had thought. And now some major problem at his work had kept Jay offline completely since Thursday afternoon. It was starting to feel like she would never catch a break in this relationship thing.

As soon as the backyard gate slammed shut, the boys dashed across the lawn and flung themselves at Claire. She traversed the distance between the gate and the back porch with one ragamuffin dangling from each leg. Theresa rushed down the porch steps to meet her, rescuing the foil wrapped platter in her outstretched hands just seconds before the boys succeeded in tackling their aunt to the ground.

"Aunt Claire, Aunt Claire, what did you bring uth? Ith it watermelon?" lisped Ryan, who was currently missing not one but both of his front teeth.

"Hey, *mijo*! Did the tooth fairy visit your house this week?" Claire asked as she struggled to sit up in the soft grass.

"Yeth! I got a dollar!" he replied with a toothless grin.

"Awesome! And yes, I brought watermelon. With those missing teeth, you're going to be the seed spitting champ for sure this time!" She turned to look at her older nephew. "Jesse, have you started football practice yet?"

"Nah, not yet. Coach is on vacation in Orlando. Can

you take us to Orlando, Aunt Claire?" the older boy asked while attempting his best pleading puppy dog expression.

"No, she cannot, young man!" Theresa interjected. "Your *tia* spoils you enough!"

"Sorry, *mijo*," Claire said. "You're mom's right, though. Orlando's kind of far. Tell you what, instead of Orlando, how about we go sailing one last time before school starts, huh?"

"Yes!" Jesse shouted, pumping his fist in the air. "Sailing's my favorite! Thanks, *Tia*." With that, he and Ryan raced off across the lawn, arguing over which one was going to help Aunt Claire more with the sails the next time they were on the boat.

The boys played until it was time for dinner, then everyone sat in the cool shade of the porch to eat their burgers and hot dogs. As promised, Claire led the boys in a watermelon seed spitting contest after they ate, cheering them on as they sent seeds flying over the porch railing and watermelon juice cascading down their fronts. Soon the sun was low in the sky and Theresa announced that it was time for the boys to get ready for bed.

"Aww, Mom," Jesse complained, "it's not even dark yet!"

"I don't care. It's almost eight thirty and you have camp in the morning. Now, go hop in the shower!"

"Aunt Claire?" Ryan asked with a yawn, "Will you help me with my shower?"

"You bet, *mijo*." She looked at her sister and

shrugged guiltily. "After all, the watermelon juice is kind of my fault."

"You're spoiling them." Theresa shook her head indulgently. "Fine. But once they're in bed, I want to hear the latest on the new boyfriend."

Claire nodded, trying to suppress the nervous flutter in her stomach. She took the boys by the hands and led them inside. She reemerged on the darkened porch an hour later, her tiny charges bathed and dressed in their superhero pajamas, with stories read and covers tucked. She pulled up a chair beside Theresa, propping her feet up on the coffee table where a trio of citronella candles burned to ward off the evening bugs.

"You don't have to exhaust yourself every week with them," Theresa said, stretching her arms lazily and turning her face toward her sister in the glowing light. "Those boys have their *tia* wrapped around their little fingers, and believe me, they know it."

Claire noted her sister's relaxed expression and smiled. Her back might ache in the morning from today's rough and tumble, but she wouldn't miss it for anything. She cherished the time spent with her nephews and it pleased her to give her busy sister a break now and then.

"I don't mind. I like to spoil them. Besides, it's only once a week. It's not like I've got kids wearing me out every night like you do." Though she tried to disguise it, the longing in her voice seeped through.

"Don't worry, *hermanita*," Theresa replied, "you'll have your own babies before you know it. And you'll be desperate for me to come over and rescue you for an evening, so you just remember that before you go running away to Boston for good, okay?"

Claire sighed. "Yeah, well, I don't think that's going to happen any time soon."

"What's wrong? Problems with Jay?"

"No, nothing like that." Claire replied, shaking her head. "Well, we haven't chatted much the past few days because of some work crisis he has going on, but that's not it. I'm just not having any luck finding a job."

"Well, maybe that's for the best." Theresa put up her hand to fend off Claire's protest. "This way you can get to know each other better, maybe meet up for a long weekend, no strings attached. There's no rush."

"Yeah, I know. I just thought—"

"You thought there would be a big, blazing sign from the universe." Theresa studied her sister quietly for a moment. "Claire, I think you're one of the last people I know who truly believes in magic."

"I don't!" Claire straightened her back in indignation. "Well, okay, maybe I do," she admitted, relaxing back against the cushion of her chair. "I don't know. When you say it out loud like that, it makes me sound like I'm some dumb kid."

"It's not dumb to want your life to be magical. Who doesn't want that? It's just usually not how it works. You have to plod along and figure things out over time." She gestured behind her toward the kitchen window where her husband was cleaning up after dinner. "Look at me and Larry. We dated off and on for years before we figured out what we wanted. But it turned out okay, right?"

"More than okay." Claire took a deep breath, appreciating the sweet scent of roses in the night air. She could hear crickets chirping from grass that was still strewn with toys, and through the kitchen window came a faint clinking as Larry loaded the dishwasher. "Honestly, it's perfect."

Theresa laughed. "It's far from perfect, but it works. And eventually you'll find what works for you."

"I want it now," Claire said with an exaggerated whine, which her sister rewarded with the same pretend punch to the shoulder she'd used since they were children. "But seriously, Theresa, haven't you heard anything from any of the people you contacted?"

"Just some polite rejections and a lot of promises to let me know if something comes up. A few possibilities if you can wait until next year. Here," Theresa added, reaching for her phone, "I'll forward the emails to you so you can follow up. Oh, wait." She squinted at the phone. "Here's one I didn't see before. It must've come in Friday after I left the office."

"What does it say?" Claire asked, sliding to the edge of her chair.

"Um, hold on. It's... oh, wow."

"Wow? Good wow or bad wow?"

"Good, maybe. It's from the head of the English department at Exeter College, just north of the city. She says my email was forwarded to her because they had something open up unexpectedly. They're already interviewing candidates and she could fit you—" Theresa's brow furrowed. "Oh, wait. It has to be this coming week because they need to make the decision by Friday. Oh, that's too bad."

"No it isn't. I could do that."

"You could get to Boston for an interview this week?"

"Yes!" Claire broke into a grin. "I can fly out tomorrow afternoon. As long as I'm home in time for Thursday's exam, I can do it. In fact, this is probably the only week this whole summer it would work because my Wednesday class was canceled. You know what that means?"

"Let me guess," Theresa said with a groan, "it's a sign, right?"

Claire laughed. "Absolutely! But I have to get home and look for tickets right now if I'm going to make this work." She jumped up and gave her sister a quick squeeze. "Thanks for dinner, sis, and tell Larry I'm sorry to rush off, okay?" She skipped down the porch steps and across the lawn, stopping to wave to her sister from the gate.

Back home, Claire sat in front of the computer reviewing her travel options. Her foot twitched anxiously against her chair leg as she studied the screen.

Am I really going to do this? There was a flight tomorrow afternoon that would get her into Boston late Monday evening. Her pulse raced at the realization that she could be there tomorrow night. Claire closed her eyes, breathing deeply to calm her shaky nerves. Hadn't every sign pointed her in this direction? *I have to have faith*, she thought.

Claire focused on the screen. The only return flight was overnight on Wednesday. It wasn't ideal. She'd have to drive straight from the airport to her Thursday class with no time to change or sleep, but it could be done. Claire looked at the note next to tomorrow's flight, blinking bright red to warn her that there were just two seats available. Her stomach clenched.

Should I do it? The cost was exorbitant, but she had enough to cover it if she used the money she'd been saving to go back to England. That dream never seemed to work out, but maybe this one would.

She pulled up a Tech Cupid chat window. She needed to see what Jay thought. Actually, she knew what Jay would think if she were foolish enough to mention signs to him again. She'd brought it up once. That had been a mistake. Jay was too pragmatic for signs, and he'd made his scientific disdain for the subject painfully clear. It was one of the few things about which they disagreed. *But he'd still want me to come, right?*

Claire chewed on her bottom lip, trying to decide what to do. Her browser refreshed and the blinking message now informed her that there was only one seat left on tomorrow's flight. She started to fill in the ticket form, keeping one eye on the chat window. It remained empty. It was well past midnight in Boston and Claire realized that she probably couldn't reach him until morning. She held her hand on the mouse, the pointer hovering over the buy button. Her finger twitched, then she clicked the mouse decisively. One seat left. Another sign.

She was going to Boston.

Claire sent Jay a quick message before heading to her room to pack. She slept soundly that night despite her excitement for the upcoming trip. There was still no response from Jay the next morning as Claire prepared to teach her first class, but she wasn't too concerned. She knew Jay was dealing with some serious issues at work and would respond when he could.

She'd hoped he might get back to her over his lunch break, but there were no new messages when she shut down her computer before heading to the airport. It was only on the plane, as Claire checked the Tech Cupid app one last time before switching her phone off for the flight, that she really started to worry.

In her rush to get to Boston in time, she'd forgotten one very important detail. Aside from her Tech Cupid account, she had no way of reaching Jay. She didn't have another email address, or a phone number. She knew where he worked, but had no idea where he lived, apart from it being somewhere on Beacon Hill. What if she didn't hear from him once she arrived? Were there a lot of apartments that overlooked the Charles? Could she just check mailboxes until she found his name?

And that's when it hit her. She was flying three thousand miles across the country to meet a man that she hoped to spend the rest of her life with, and she didn't even know his last name.

SIX

JAMIE FLOATED in the dimly-lit diving pool, savoring the feeling of weightlessness. Every muscle in her body ached with an intensity she had never experienced before in her life. She hadn't left her office in almost a week except for the occasional fast food run or to crawl into her own bed for a few hours of sleep. Even that hadn't been a guarantee.

She'd spent last night curled up on her office floor with a couple of sweatshirts from the lost and found bin as a makeshift pillow. Several muscles in her neck could attest to it providing a less than ideal sleep. But the long days and nights had paid off. She'd had to go all the way back to the original raw data, but she'd finally located the error. And, surprise, surprise, it was all Dr. Michaels' fault. The idiot had deleted all the variable names and decided to save a little time by just guessing what they were. He guessed wrong. If Jamie was promoted to Head of Research, the first thing she would do is put

Dr. Michaels on a project that even he couldn't ruin. Like making coffee.

The only thing was, though correcting those mistakes had yielded the desired results, Jamie had uncovered another problem in the process. Temperature measurements from some of the Greenland seas seemed surprisingly low, while others were unusually erratic. It could take months to double check the data, even if she could put every available research assistant on it immediately. It would delay the study's publication, probably past the point where they could present it at the next global climate summit. And after all that work, there was a chance it might not have a significant impact on the results.

It was the course of action she planned to recommend, but she knew her boss wasn't going to like it. Jamie squeezed her eyes shut behind her mask. She would think about that later. Right now, all she wanted to do was enjoy a peaceful dive.

There was no sound in the tank aside from the rhythmic rush of air and the bubbling of her breath as she took in oxygen from her tank and let it out into the surrounding water. The ocean tank exhibit was open to the public, and toward the surface she could hear a docent explaining the diving process to a crowd of tourists. It was still the height of the summer season and Jamie knew there must have been at least a hundred people watching from above. There were probably a few hundred more observing from vantage points around the towering glass walls of the tank. But once fully submerged, the environment became peaceful and serene. There were no phones ringing, no tense voices or urgent meetings. Just her and the fish. Heaven.

She gravitated toward the simulated coral reef in the center of the tank. When she neared the glass she could see the flashes of cameras and curious faces peering in, but toward the center it was like she was the only inhabitant of a private, magical world. She watched as a sea turtle passed just inches from her right arm, and a sting ray glided below her left foot. There were eels, and barracuda, and brightly colored reef fishes. A half hour dive in the ocean tank had all the healing properties of a trip to the Bahamas, with none of the expense or jet lag. It was the only thing Jamie had found that could take a bad day and instantly make it right. Well that, or a message from Claire. Yes, Claire had magical properties all her own.

Claire.

Jamie hadn't had the time to spare more than a fleeting thought of her over the past several days. She'd even turned off the notifications on her Tech Cupid app because the temptation to set aside work and chat with Claire had been so great. The rational part of Jamie's brain knew that she should take advantage of the chance to drift away quietly. It was the kindest option, freeing up both of them to find what they were really looking for. Someone who lived closer. Someone of the preferred gender. But the thought of actually doing it cut her aching heart like a knife. Jamie closed her eyes, letting her body drift gently with the current as she conjured up an image of Claire in her mind. Her laughing smile. Her dark, shining ringlets. Those deep brown eyes with just a hint of gold.

The hard thump of the tank's glass against her shoulder startled her. Her eyes flew open and she stared out at the sea of tourists beyond the glass. Her gaze landed on one figure in particular. A woman, petite and curvy, walked slowly through the crowd. Her dark hair was pulled into a ponytail and a few soft ringlets floating near her face, which was obscured in shadow.

Claire? No. Claire was on the opposite end of the country. Jamie's sleep deprived imagination was working overtime, though, because she was almost convinced that woman walking beside the glass looked exactly like Claire. The same adorably feminine shape. The same cute, messy ponytail she always wore in Jamie's daydreams. The woman disappeared from view as a dozen kids in matching yellow shirts from a local summer camp edged their way to the front of the crowd. Jamie changed directions with a gentle flip of her fins, trying to catch another glimpse.

The woman reappeared on the opposite side of the tank. Jamie eased her way closer, pretending to examine an outcropping of coral as she floated beside her. Her heart raced as she got a good look at the stranger. It *was* Claire. There was no doubt about it. Jamie's breath caught and she choked against her mouthpiece with a desperate need to cough. Gasping under water was a terrible idea. She could feel her panic growing and experience told her that she needed to get back to the surface as quickly as she could.

Pulling herself out of the water and onto the diving platform, Jamie tugged the mask from her face and gulped the fresh air. Her heart pounded wildly. The diving assistant who helped her out of her equipment gave her a worried look, but Jamie waved away her concern. Bolting down the corridor to the locker room, she shrugged herself out of her wetsuit with one shaking hand while the other hand worked to pull up the Tech Cupid app on her phone. Twelve missed messages from Claire appeared, the last three marked as urgent. *Oh God.* Jamie scanned them at lightning speed, confirming her suspicions.

Claire was in Boston, alright. She had arrived last night.

What am I going to do? Jamie pulled the last of her clothing on over her damp skin before dashing back to her office. She recognized the sound of her office phone ringing as she turned down the final corridor.

"Hello, Dr. Richards?" It was Burt at the security desk. "I'm not sure, but I think there's a visitor here for you."

"You're not sure?" Jamie repeated in confusion.

"Yes, ma'am. There was a Claire Flores here a few minutes ago asking for some guy named Jay, only she wasn't sure of his last name and the only person I could think of that's even close to being a 'Jay' was you. Anyway, I sent her over to look at the dive tank while I tried calling you."

"Yes, thank you, Burt," Jamie responded through the sudden dryness of her throat. "You know, I think she is looking for me. She must have just gotten confused. I'll be right there." Jamie hung up, her brain humming. *Claire was in the lobby waiting for her!* Jamie's heart soared. *Claire was expecting to meet Jay.* Her heart plummeted. *Now what?*

Jamie strode from the elevator to the security desk with every ounce of confidence she could muster. She spotted Claire's outline from a distance and her pulse raced. Claire turned at the sound of footsteps, her nervous smile turning to a look of confusion at the Amazonian woman approaching her.

"Claire?" Jamie called to her. "Claire Flores?"

"Yes," Claire responded, looking puzzled. "Yes, I'm Claire Flores. I'm sorry, but who are you?"

"Jay," Jamie started, then momentarily froze as she realized what she had just said. "You were expecting Jay, right?" *Phew. Close call, you idiot.* "I'm Jay's friend, Jamie. Lee," she added, trying to make her own name sound as different from her alter ego as possible. "Dr. Jamie Lee Richards," she said, extending her hand toward Claire.

"Pleasure to meet you," Claire answered, grasping Jamie's hand with her own.

Tiny shocks of electrical current coursed through Jamie's fingers and up her spine. Remaining steady on her feet required a supreme act of concentration. She hoped she wasn't blushing, but the sudden rush of heat through her body suggested otherwise. And had Claire's own cheeks flushed pink when their fingers touched, or was it just her imagination? Probably imagination, but the mere possibility ignited a more intense burning in her cheeks that Jamie was now quite certain was visible to the world.

"But, where is Jay?" Claire asked.

"Not here," Jamie stammered. It had been obvious that Claire would ask, so she'd cobbled together a decent cover story on the elevator ride down. Too bad she couldn't remember a word of it. Jamie glanced fervently around the lobby of the aquarium, her gaze resting on the new penguin habitat near the entrance. "He had to go to Antarctica. For the penguins," she concluded lamely. *Penguins? Seriously?!?*

"Penguins?"

"Um hm. He specializes in penguins. It was a last minute research trip."

"Oh," Claire replied. Her disappointment was obvious. "I didn't realize. I guess that's why he didn't respond to any of my messages."

"Yes, that must be it. Antarctica's really far away." *Could I sound any stupider right now?*

"Of course. I mean, it's the other side of the world, right? But wait," Claire added, "isn't it winter?"

"Winter?" Jamie repeated. *Yes, winter. It's the southern hemisphere. Of course it's winter.* "Yes. As a matter of fact, that's why the trip was so important." Her brain was spinning now, looking for anything to save herself from this ludicrous lie.

"But isn't that really dangerous?" Claire asked, worried. "And dark?"

"You know, I'm not an expert on Antarctica myself, but I think you're right about the dark." Jamie swallowed hard. This fib was becoming more outlandish with every passing second. She'd better wrap this up and get Claire out of here before it became completely obvious that she was making up every single word. "All I know is, it must be pretty important to him. That's just the kind of guy Jay is. Totally dedicated."

A look of pride lit up Claire's face. "Yes, that sounds just like Jay, right?"

"Absolutely! That's Jay. Totally." Talking about Jay seemed to have distracted Claire from the Antarctica thing. *Thank God.* Maybe Jamie should come up with a few more nice things to say about Jay. "Jay's a really great guy. The best. And he's going to be so sad to have missed you. Are you in town for a while?" *Please say no. I can't keep this up much longer.*

"No. I fly home tomorrow night. I have a job interview later this afternoon," she explained.

Is she trying to get a job here? Tamping down her panic, Jamie seized on the information. "An interview today? That doesn't leave you much time at all to prepare, does it?" Jamie knew Claire was a big planner. Surely that would get her to leave.

"Well, no. I guess it doesn't," Claire agreed, glancing at her watch.

"Well, that's a shame. But look," Jamie added, one

hand on Claire's shoulder to guide her to the door, "if I hear from Jay, I'll let him know you were here, okay?"

"Would you? Thank you so much!" Claire paused at the door and grasped Jamie's broad hand between her own delicate fingers. "It's really been nice to meet you, Jamie Lee."

Jamie squinted into the noon sun as Claire disappeared from view. Relief filled her. That had been a close call. *This is why you shouldn't lie, Jamie Lee.* Funny, she never thought of herself by that name. She'd rebelled against it as a kid, but Claire saying it had turned the name into a sweet melody. It was beautiful when Claire said it.

Beautiful Claire. And now Claire was gone.

Jamie's heart sank like an anchor. She would never see her again. A vast hollowness replacing her earlier relief. She had been so eager to rush Claire out of the Institute that she had taken her one chance to meet Claire in the flesh and wasted it completely. She couldn't believe what she had done. *Stupid, stupid.* How could she have let Claire walk away, out of her life forever, just like that?

They could have gone for coffee at least, or for a tour of the shops down by the marina. Surely a colleague of Jay's should at least offer that little bit of hospitality to his friend from out of town, right? No one would think it was strange. In fact, they'd probably think it was strange not to. Claire was probably thinking right now how rude she had been to rush her out the door like that.

Maybe it's not too late? Claire said she was in town

until tomorrow night. There had to be some way to see her again. Just one more time. After that, she'd be able to say goodbye and move on. Jamie was certain she'd be able to do that, if she could just have one special moment with Claire first.

SEVEN

JAMIE WAITED beside a glowing nineteenth century gaslight at the far end of Charles Street. She'd worn a loose white tank top and colorful Capri pants. Nothing fancy, but she knew it showed off just the right amount of skin and the limited curves that she possessed, and made her legs look about a mile long.

The sun was casting long shadows from the surrounding buildings. Jamie rubbed her hands up and down her bare arms and longed for the familiar comfort of her flannel shirt, despite the sticky mid-August heat. Claire should have arrived almost twenty minutes ago. Maybe she'd changed her mind. *But why would she?* It was just dinner with a friend. Or with a friend of a friend, as it were. It's not like there was any reason for Claire to stand her up.

The moment Claire walked away from the Institute that afternoon, Jamie had truly understood the meaning of the word desolation. The only thing that mattered to her was seeing Claire again. By the time she reached her desk, Jamie had hatched a plan. She logged into her Tech Cupid account and started writing an apologetic note from Jay. He was so sorry for missing her visit and just had to make it up to her somehow. His good friend Jamie Lee—remember Jamie Lee?—would be happy to meet up with her for dinner that night.

Claire hadn't needed much convincing. No one enjoys eating alone in a strange city. With the time and place arranged, Jamie had even attached a photo of Antarctica at night, complete with a vaguely humanoid shape wrapped from head to toe in cold weather gear, waving to the camera. *Greetings from Antarctica!* God bless the Internet and whichever genius invented image searches. She was too proud of her resourcefulness to feel any guilt.

The rumbling of a Red Line train filled the air. Jamie paid little attention, her concentration focused on the brick sidewalk that stretched toward Boston Common, where Jay's message had instructed Claire to park. There was still no sign of her, but just then, a voice behind her called, "Jamie Lee?" She turned, and there she was.

Breathtaking, remarkably sexy, Claire. Her simple peasant blouse framed her curves in a way that was much more modest than the thoughts it was inspiring, and she wore the type of short skirt that would swish and sway mercilessly when she walked. Jamie gulped for air, having forgotten for a moment to breathe. *Good thing I didn't see her coming, or I'd be a melted puddle on the sidewalk right now.* Claire had come from the direction of the T station instead of the garage, which was odd, but it didn't matter. She was finally here. Jamie grinned.

"Claire! You made it. Did you have trouble finding a place to park?"

Claire grimaced. "You can't begin to imagine."

Jamie opened the door with a courtly flourish and the waiter, who had already been given a handsome tip to hold the best spot in the house for them, showed them to a table for two near the window. The restaurant was the perfect blend of casual elegance. There were white linen table cloths, with glass toppers keeping the atmosphere just on the right side of too fancy. There were chandeliers hanging from the ceiling, but the room was brightly lit and there were no candles so it wouldn't be mistaken for romantic. Several pieces of colorful artwork added to the cozy charm. Jamie had chosen the restaurant carefully. As far as Claire was concerned, this was just an evening out with a new friend. But even when she was old and gray, Jamie suspected she would look back on this night as one of the best dates of her life. Even if she was the only one of them who knew that's what it was.

They studied their menus in silence, and after placing their orders, Claire remarked, "I just don't know how Jay does it."

"Does what?" Jamie asked.

"Driving in Boston. It's insanity!"

"Well, I imagine Jay takes the train. I know I do." Jamie smiled at the cleverness of her phrasing. She had the decency to feel guilty for continuing to lie to Claire and was determined not to do it any more than was absolutely necessary. Technically, what she had just said wasn't a lie.

"Yeah, that's how I finally got here, on the subway."

"I thought you were going to drive and park under the Common. I mean," she quickly amended, "I assume that's what Jay probably told you to do."

Did that count as a lie?

"I tried. But the first time around I missed the turn because some guy cut me off without even using his blinker! Then all the streets were one way in the wrong direction. I circled around but I got confused, and I think I passed the same building at least three times. Then I went over a bridge and found a parking garage and asked around until someone pointed me to a sign for the T and said to get off here."

"I'm sorry, but did you say a bridge? Where did you end up parking?"

"I'm trying to remember. Something with the letter K?"

Jamie gaped. "Kendall Square? In Cambridge? How did you manage to get from Boston Common to Cambridge?"

"I have no idea. Maybe it's a good thing that I bombed my interview today. I don't think I'm cut out for living in this city," she said with defeat.

"You don't think it went well at the college?" Jamie was surprised at the disappointment she felt. On the one hand, if Claire moved to Boston it would create a disastrous mess for Jamie personally, but that didn't mean she wanted Claire to fail.

"The competition is fierce, and it just seems like everything about this trip has gone wrong. Jay being out of town, me getting lost tonight... Maybe it's a sign. Do you believe in signs? Jay doesn't. He thinks I'm silly to always be looking for them like I do."

"I, um," Jamie hesitated. Sure, she *might* have implied that believing in signs was unscientific during one of their chats, but it seemed a little harsh to say something like that right to Claire's face. She wanted Claire to like her. "Well, I could see how sometimes it feels like the universe gives you a sign."

Being polite is not the same thing as lying.

Maybe it would be best to change the subject. "So, what do you do in—where is it you're from?"

Pretending not to know wasn't a lie, it just made the conversation less awkward.

"I live in Oregon and teach nineteenth century British literature at Lovejoy College. And you should probably know this about me—I'm obsessed with everything British."

"Really? And yet you're thinking of moving to Boston instead of England?"

"I don't have any professional connections in England, I'm afraid. But I'm starting to think Boston is a close second with the gas lamps and the cobblestones. I had no idea until tonight that parts of the city looked like something straight out Dickens' London!"

"Isn't that a coincidence!" It wasn't a coincidence.

Jamie had chosen Beacon Hill especially for this reason because she knew how much Claire would appreciate it.

"So, you're a scientist, like Jay?"

Jamie nodded.

"My dad was a scientist, too. I'm afraid I didn't inherit any of his aptitude for it, though. It must be very challenging. What do you do for fun?"

"Oh, you know, read, watch movies. Typical stuff."

"So, what's your favorite movie?"

A devilish thought wriggled to the front of Jamie's brain. "My all time favorite is *A Fish Called Wanda.*"

Claire's eyes grew wide. "No way! That's mine, too!"

You know that absolutely counts as a lie, right?

A Fish Called Wanda was an okay movie, but it wouldn't even crack Jamie's top ten. Except, of course, that Jamie already knew it was Claire's favorite. They had discussed it at some length in one of their chats, only that time around Jamie had dismissed her choice and Claire had then defended the film for the better part of forty-five minutes.

"Well, I'm so glad to meet *someone* who appreciates good movies," Claire said smugly.

Jamie knew by the way she said it that she was thinking of Jay. *Ha! Take that, Jay!* The fact that she relished this small victory over her alter ego so vigorously came as a bit of a surprise. The truth was, Jamie felt willing to say just about anything at this moment that would make Claire like her more than Jay. She hated to admit it, but she was jealous. Jealous of herself, which was insane.

Am I honestly attempting to sabotage myself to win a girl?

The check arrived and Jamie reached for her wallet over Claire's protests, but Jamie was determined. She couldn't let Claire pay for this fantasy date that only she knew they were on. But Claire insisted on paying her share. With a flash of inspiration, Jamie played her trump card. "Actually, didn't I mention before? This is Jay's treat. He arranged it all when he emailed me this afternoon. He'd be furious if I let you pay!"

"Oh, how sweet of him! Isn't he just the most thoughtful man? How chivalrous of Jay to do that!" The dreamy look in Claire's eyes stopped Jamie short. She'd been so busy coming up with an argument Claire couldn't refuse that she'd accidentally scored a point for her rival. It was a rookie mistake, one that she'd be sure to avoid next time.

Only there won't be a next time. Soon Claire would go back to her hotel, then back to Portland, and by the sound of it, she wouldn't be coming back any time soon.

As for Jay, Jamie already had a plan for him. After his Antarctic adventure ended, he would be moving far, far away, to someplace where Claire would be certain not to follow, like Brazil. Except Brazil had Rio de Janeiro and that carnival thing. What would stop Claire from just hopping on a plane and heading south? It was a risk. So maybe someplace less appealing than Brazil. Madagascar? No one ever went to Madagascar. Perfect. Plus, they had penguins there, right? Or was Jamie just thinking of that cartoon that Paulie's nieces made her watch with them when they were snowed in last winter? Either way, it didn't matter. Madagascar was the definite frontrunner.

They stood outside the restaurant, lingering for a moment to enjoy the cool evening breeze, which after the warmth of the restaurant now seemed pleasant and refreshing. In the relative darkness of the gas-lit streets of Beacon Hill it was even possible to see a few stars shining overhead in the cloudless sky. Perfect weather, perfect night. *And now it's over.* Jamie turned toward the T station. They could walk together that far, then board trains in opposite directions, and that would be that.

"Jamie Lee? Do you think you could do something for me?"

Anything. "Sure. What did you have in mind?"

"It's just, I've come all this way and I don't want to go home without at least seeing Jay's apartment."

Jay's apartment? *Oh, right.* Instead of coming clean about being a girl, Jamie had inexplicably given Jay a new apartment in Beacon Hill. And why not? He was imaginary so it's not like he had to pay the rent.

"Unless you have to head home," Claire added. She must have taken Jamie's confused silence for reluctance.

She did have a commuter train to catch, but there was still some time, and she wasn't ready to say goodbye. Heading home was the absolute last thing Jamie wanted. "Of course I'll show you. I mean, I don't know the exact apartment, and it's not like I have a key, but—"

"No, I know that. Just the outside. I probably sound like I'm a crazy stalker to even ask, but—"

"Not at all! I get it. Come on," Jamie said, turning to head the opposite direction, "It's this way."

They continued along a narrow side street. There were no businesses here, just rows of brownstone townhouses with window boxes filled with geraniums and tiny front gardens surrounded by ancient-looking iron railings. On one building a climbing vine had a trunk so thick that it must have started its ascent up the side of the house long before either of them were born.

"Just look at all this history!" Claire said, swiveling her head to take it in.

"You really like it?" Jamie asked, uncertain. This was her favorite part of the city, but most people she knew were more impressed by the luxurious glass skyscrapers on the other side of the park. She'd lived in a place like that with a girlfriend once, briefly, and found it to be soul crushing. Not unlike how the relationship turned out to be. Maybe there was something to be said for signs. Although, if she had just used her powers of observation and a little common sense, she would have taken one look at that postmodern apocalypse of an apartment and run the opposite direction. No signs needed.

"I always thought of Portland as being a really modern place. This isn't too old fashioned for you?"

Claire laughed. "Are you kidding? It couldn't be more perfect. But I'm an old fashioned girl. If I do end up moving to Boston, this is where I would live, and not just to be close to Jay. If I could choose anywhere in the city, this would be it." She stopped walking and looked around appreciatively. "You know, Portland has its share of old neighborhoods, too."

"Really? I had no idea." To be honest, Jamie had spent so long cursing Portland for not being in Maine that it hadn't left a lot of time for research.

"Sure! My sister lives in a beautiful antique Craftsman cottage. She and her husband restored it themselves. That's, like, my lifelong dream."

"Restoring an old house?" Jamie asked in disbelief.

"I know it sounds silly, but—"

"No, it doesn't at all. In fact, I've been helping my roommate restore his place for years. It's a Victorian on Cape Ann. It's one of my favorite hobbies." *Damn. Why does everything about Claire have to be so perfect?*

"Jamie Lee?"

Claire's voice came from several feet behind her. Jamie turned, chagrined to realize that the smaller woman was struggling to keep up with her long strides. "I'm sorry. Am I going too fast? I do that sometimes."

"No, it's not that. It's these shoes," Claire replied, embarrassed.

Jamie glanced at the shoes and cringed. She'd noticed them earlier in an isn't-Claire-beautiful-tonight kind of a way, but only now did she register that the heels were at least four inches high.

"I didn't realize how uneven the brick sidewalks would be and my feet are killing me." Claire explained. "Is it much further to the apartment?" It was evident from her tone that she was in pain.

The apartment? Jamie was so wrapped up in conversation she had completely lost track of their original mission and was mostly just trying to extend her time with Claire. "Actually," Jamie said, gesturing toward a row of immaculate brownstones next to an elegant stone church with a towering steeple, "it's one of those over there." They weren't the ones Jamie had initially had in mind, but one fictitious apartment was as good as another, right? Hopefully Claire wouldn't inquire how much it cost to rent these particular units, or she would have to kill off one of Jay's imaginary rich uncles to pay for the damn thing. Claire was suitably impressed. She lowered herself onto the front steps of the house behind them and sat quietly, admiring the view.

"Wow. This is amazing. Thank you, Jamie Lee," she said, gazing up and flashing a radiant smile that made Jamie's heart flutter. "I'm sorry, but is that what everyone calls you? It doesn't seem to suit you. Do you have a nickname or something?"

"Jay—me," she said, quickly correcting herself. "Just Jamie."

"Well, thank you for a wonderful evening, Jamie."

The faintest glimmer of *something* sparked within Claire's eyes in the dim lamplight. It caught Jamie off guard, sending a thrill through her before leaving her completely at a loss as to how to interpret its meaning. If she had been on a real date and a woman looked at her like that, she would have known exactly what it meant. But this was Claire, a thoroughly straight woman who had only agreed to dinner tonight because the man she had come all this way to meet was not available. *It's just wishful thinking*, she concluded. "I guess we'd better head back." Jamie said aloud. *Before my imagination runs out of control.*

Claire glanced at the clock on her phone. "Didn't you say you had an eight-thirty train? Do you think you'll be able to get there in time?"

Jamie nodded. They'd wandered farther from the T than they should have, but there was probably just enough time. She put her hand out and pulled Claire up from her perch on the step. Claire winced as her full weight landed on her tortured feet. She dug her fingernails into Jamie's hand as she fought to steady herself.

"Do you think you can make it?" Jamie asked, looking concerned. "What if you took your shoes off?"

"I thought of that, but the ground is so rough with all this brick. I'm afraid going barefoot would tear up my feet even worse."

Jamie thought for a minute. "I have an idea. Put your arm around my waist." Claire did, and Jamie slipped her arm around her back and under her arm, supporting as much of her weight as she could and using every drop of willpower not to think about how close her fingertips were to the swell of Claire's ample breasts. *That's enough! Do not even think the word 'ample' again.* "Does that help?"

Claire took a cautious step alongside Jamie, then nodded. "Much better. It will be slow, but I think I can make it. Thank you." Claire smiled up at Jamie, then nestled her head against her for the journey.

As they hobbled along, Claire's hand gripping

Jamie's waist, her hip and leg brushing against Jamie's own, Jamie found herself torn between her concern for Claire and the overwhelming sweetness of holding her so close. It was all she could do not to sweep her up like a delicate bird, carry her all the way to the train, and never put her down again. At their current pace, Jamie knew it would take several more minutes to reach the station at the end of the street, but they would make it eventually.

And then Claire would be gone. How was she ever going to let her go?

EIGHT

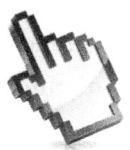

CLAIRE STUMBLED up the last two steps to Jamie's front door, her mangled feet far from recovered even after the drive to Cape Ann.

"You okay?" Jamie turned to Claire. "Maybe you don't really want to come in after all. I mean, my roommate has some friends over, and your feet must be killing you."

Claire studied Jamie's face, trying to puzzle out the sudden change of heart. Concern? Trepidation? Something mysterious lurked behind the woman's cat-like green eyes, but Claire couldn't quite put her finger on it. The realization sent a nervous shiver through her, and for a moment she wondered if she should go inside after all.

"Don't be silly!" she said instead, curiosity overcoming her concern. "I'm dying to see the inside of this house that you've told me so much about. Just promise me one thing."

"What's that?"

"That I can take these shoes off the second you get that door unlocked!" The heels had been a stupid choice, but Jamie was so tall that Claire had felt compelled. Foolish vanity. She was paying for it now, but was it her fault she found the woman's height so—what was the word?—alluring? *No, not alluring!* Intimidating, that was the word she had been looking for. She had no idea where that other word had come from.

Jamie pushed the door open. "After you," she said. "You can kick those torture devices you've been wearing next to the hall tree."

Claire looked to where Jamie's finger pointed and saw a piece of heavy antique furniture that held several coats, some umbrellas, and a large Stetson. It reminded her of the one Jay had worn in his photo. *I didn't realize cowboy hats were so popular this far north.* She stopped beside the hall tree and grabbed Jamie's hands to steady herself as she removed first one shoe and then the other, stretching her toes and sighing audibly in relief as her bare feet came in contact with the smooth wood of the floorboards. She laughed at the sound she'd made, and Jamie joined her. "I just wanted to be taller," she managed to stammer between fits of giggles.

"I don't see why," Jamie replied. "You're perfect the way you are."

Pleasant warmth washed over her at the compliment and she smiled broadly. "Thanks, but tall people never understand. How tall are you, anyway? You must be nearly as tall as Jay."

"Yeah, almost exactly," Jamie muttered, then added more loudly, "Come through here and I'll show you that woodwork in the living room I was telling you about." Jamie strained against the heavy pocket door, which slid into the wall to reveal a large room where maybe a dozen people sat conversing while sipping from glasses filled with fruit slices and red liquid. The rhythm of a nondescript party tune throbbed in the background just loud enough to set the mood. A large man with a shining bald head, trendy beard, and hipster glasses unfolded himself from a chair as they entered and beamed a broad grin in greeting.

"Hello!" the man's deep voice boomed. "You must be Claire! Jamie told me she was bringing home a friend. Welcome! Let me get you a drink." The man stressed both syllables of Jamie's name in an exaggerated way that made Claire wonder just how strong those drinks might be, but she took the glass when it was offered. "Sangria," he explained, "my special recipe."

"Claire," Jamie said, "this is Paul. He's my roommate, and landlord, too, I guess."

"Nice to meet you," Claire replied. "Your house is amazing. But I'm sorry. Jamie said you had a few friends over, but I seem to be crashing a full blown party."

"No worries," Paul assured her, "it's just my usual mid-week sangria party. It's been a long week."

"But it's only Tuesday." Claire took a large swallow from her glass and shuddered as the liquid burned a fiery trail down her esophagus. She wondered if Paul's special recipe required a permit.

"Like I said, it's been a long week."

"Paul and his fellow artist friends here see the world a little differently than the rest of us regular working people," Jamie explained, and Claire giggled.

I must be nervous, Claire thought, *I never giggle.* She sipped her sangria, and this time a gentle warmth replaced the initial burn. It went down more smoothly with practice.

"Sit down, ladies, sit down," Paul invited, gesturing toward the seat he had just vacated.

It was styled like an old fashioned wing chair, only a bit wider, though not as large as a couch, and Claire studied it, puzzled. It looked like something out of *Jack and the Beanstalk*. It made sense, in a way, since both Paul and Jamie seemed like giants to someone who stood barely five-foot-four.

"Paul's precious chair and a half," Jamie explained. "He bought it because he thinks regular chairs are too small for him. You go ahead and sit down. He always thinks you can fit two people in that thing, but he forgets I'm almost as big as he is."

"That's okay," Claire offered, "I don't mind squeezing in. I think we'll both fit." She scooted as far to one side as she could to make room as Jamie eased herself onto the other half. Their legs were pressed together from hip to knee, and between the warmth of that contact and the spreading glow of the sangria she had already consumed, Claire found herself momentarily floating in a pleasant haze.

As the evening wore on, the guests laughed and

chatted as Paul dutifully circled the room, refilling glasses from an earthenware pitcher filled with red wine and fruit. Claire found it alarmingly easy to lose track of how much she'd had to drink as her glass miraculously remained full all night.

She wasn't aware of dozing off until the whole left side of her body was cold. Claire stretched in the chair, which she now occupied solo. She felt chilly and exposed, and wished that Jay would hurry back. She shook her head in confusion. No, not Jay, Jamie. *I came all this way to meet Jamie, where is she?* No not Jamie, Jay. She had come all this way for Jay. The sangria must have been stronger than she thought. She was having a hard time keeping the two of them straight.

"So, you're Jay's new girl?"

Claire looked up in surprise at the voice. A man now occupied the ottoman in front of her, a friendly smile on his face. "Sorry, what's that?" she asked. "How do you know Jay?"

The man laughed. "I think you'd better lay off the drinks, darlin'. I'm talking about Jamie. You arrived together, remember? She lives here? Anyway, are you the new girlfriend?"

Claire shook her head in confusion. "Girlfriend? No. We just met. I don't have a girlfriend. I mean, I'm not her —I'm sorry, I'm not making much sense. Wait, why would Jamie have—Is Jamie gay?"

This time the man laughed so hard his body shook and he slapped his knees. "Good one! That's a good one!

Darlin', I think we're all gay. It's kind of our thing. Hadn't you noticed?"

Claire took a good look around the room. It was all men except her, which she'd noticed in a vague sort of way when they arrived. Looking closer, now she saw something else, too. Most of the men appeared to be *together* in that way that couples do at a party: standing close, holding hands, resting against one another. Kind of like how she had been sitting with Jamie a few minutes ago. *No wonder he thought... But I didn't know!*

"Sorry, darlin'. I just assumed you were Jamie's latest."

"Latest? Why, does she have new girlfriends frequently?" Claire wasn't certain what to make of the jealousy that was bubbling up inside her, but she bristled at the thought of Jamie having a lot of girlfriends.

"Well, she does have a reputation," the man replied. Seeing Claire's eyes narrow, he hastened to add, "Not that she cheats or leads anyone on, don't you worry about that. You can trust her. She just has bad luck sometimes, I think. But you seem like a keeper."

But we're not...oh, never mind. Claire massaged her temples, her head spinning. "I think I had too much to drink...I'm sorry, I didn't even catch your name."

"Malcolm," the man replied. "And, yeah, Paul mixes a mean sangria. There's a secret ingredient in there that gives it an extra punch. He made up a batch once for a party and it kicked off a three day pub crawl that was pretty epic."

Claire laughed and quickly regretted it as the sound reverberated around the inside of her skull. "Well, Malcolm, there will be no pub crawling for me tonight. But there won't be any driving, either, so I might end up crawling home."

"You could always crash here. That's what most of us do. There's plenty of room."

"No, I can't. I have a hotel in Boston I need to get back to."

"Where in Boston?" After Claire told him, Malcolm scanned the room, his eyes landing on a skinny guy in a red shirt who was jangling a set of keys in one hand. "Hey, Adam! You heading home right now? Think you can give Jamie's girlfriend a ride?"

"No, I'm not—" there was no sense arguing the point now. "I don't want to be any trouble. I can take a taxi."

"Don't worry about it," Adam assured her after Malcolm told him where Claire needed to go. "I go right past there on my way home. But I've gotta go right now. I've got an early morning. So, you coming?"

Claire nodded, suddenly overwhelmed with the need to get back to her hotel room, take some aspirin, and go to sleep. She glanced furtively around the room but there was no sign of Jamie. She didn't want to leave without seeing Jamie. "Wait, my car. What am I going to do about the car, and Jamie? I need to say goodbye."

"Don't worry about the car, or Jamie," Malcolm said. "I'll look around for her and explain. She'll understand, and you can think about the car in the morning."

Claire nodded again, too exhausted to argue, then slipped out the door and down the steps to where Adam was parked. The cold leather of the seat sent a chill through her bare skin, and the memory of Jamie's radiant warmth pressing against her filled her with a visceral wave of longing.

I've had way too much sangria.

Something told her she'd have a lot more than her rental car to think about in the morning, but now was not the time to worry about that.

BACK IN THE HOUSE, Jamie filled two empty pitchers with ice as Paul mixed a new batch of his secret recipe from the array of bottles on the kitchen table. Sliding her body away from the soft, warm comfort of a gently sleeping Claire was the most difficult thing she could remember doing in her adult life, and she silently cursed her best friend for needing her help.

"So, how's it going with Claire?" Paul asked with a wide grin.

"A lot better before you dragged me away," Jamie snapped.

"Relax, Girly, I just needed an update. She hasn't caught on about you being Jay?"

"No, not yet. And thanks for reminding your friends to call me Jamie tonight. They didn't think it was strange?"

"They were already drinking when your text arrived. I doubt they gave it much thought. And I saw your Sleeping Beauty out there, all cuddled up next to you, by the way," he teased. "Things will probably go even better after she wakes up, don't you think?"

"No, Paul. I don't think. That should be obvious." Jamie sighed, raking her fingers across her scalp. Her head throbbed from stress, though not from alcohol. Jamie was familiar enough with Paul's sangria to steer clear of the stuff, especially when she had a secret to keep. "I don't think very much at all, lately. I was supposed to have dinner and say goodbye and get on with my life. Instead, I brought her home so my best friend could get her intoxicated, and now I still have to say goodbye, but thanks to you I get to do it with the knowledge of exactly how good it feels to have her asleep in my arms. So, yeah, thanks for that."

"I did it for your own good, Girly! Trust me. I know I said the other day that you needed to move on and all that, but the minute I saw the two of you, I had a feeling. I think she likes you!" His voice sang this particular bit of news. "Why do you think I refilled her glass all night? Now she can't drive home, so she'll have to stay here, and then you can just see what happens."

Jamie squeezed her eyes shut, hoping the action would stop her brain from exploding out of her skull. "That's your plan? Get Claire drunk and see if she turns into a lesbian? You don't just have a few drinks and turn gay, Paul."

"Actually, with this stuff, some people do. Seriously, there was this party last year, and this one really hot model from the shoot—"

"Ewwww! Stop talking right now, Paul." Her head

was already killing her, she didn't need to be nauseous, too.

The kitchen door swung open and Paul's friend Malcolm walked in. "Jamie," he said, "I was just looking for you. Your girlfriend wanted me to tell you that she got a ride home with Adam."

"My girl—you mean Claire? Wait, do you mean she's already gone?" Jamie felt a cold lump of dread form in the pit of her stomach at the thought. "I needed to say goodbye! Jesus, that was the whole point of tonight!"

"Uh, yeah, I think they left a couple minutes ago. No worries, though, you'll see her tomorrow when you bring her car back to her, right?"

Jamie threw her hands up in the air. "Tomorrow? But I was supposed to say goodbye tonight. How did this get screwed up so badly?"

"Why are you saying goodbye to your girlfriend? Is she going somewhere?" Malcolm asked in confusion.

"She isn't my girlfriend, Malcolm," Jamie replied through gritted teeth. The cold in her stomach and the throbbing in her head were pushing her annoyance level to a record high. "And she's never going to be," she added, glancing at Paul. "She isn't even into women, okay?"

"Nah, I don't think that's right." Malcolm answered. "She was definitely into you. My gaydar never lies."

"It's true, Jay," Paul interjected. "Malcolm's uncanny. He just *knows*, like every time."

"Well, not every time," Malcolm replied modestly.

"But usually. Like fifty percent of the time with guys, but I can almost always tell with girls."

"Fifty percent?" Jamie spluttered. "Okay, first of all, gaydar is not a real thing. Period. But second, if it were, what good does it do if it only works half the time? Couldn't you just, like, flip a coin or something?"

"Nah, it's not like that. Plus, it's way more accurate with women," Malcolm countered. "And with Claire, I'm like a hundred percent certain. Maybe more."

"Maybe more?" Jamie muttered. "I guess I know why you're an artist and not a statistician."

"Yeah, well, I may not know statistics, but I do know that with that one, the odds are in your favor," Malcolm said with a shrug. "She was *definitely* into you." Malcolm tossed a set of car keys to Jamie. "Here. I said I'd give 'em to you and tell you she has to check out at eleven." With that, Malcolm rejoined the party in the adjoining room.

Jamie turned to look at her best friend. "Paul, what am I going to do?"

"Easy. Sleep in, skip work, show her the town."

"And what about Jay?"

"You are Jay."

"The other Jay, idiot. The one with the Y chromosome. You know, the one she thinks she's moving here for."

"What were you planning to do before?"

"Have him break up with her and then send him to Madagascar to study penguins."

"You know, Jay, I think those penguins are only in the movie."

Jamie stifled the urge to slap his shiny, bald head. "I don't really care, Paul. I couldn't care less about penguins if I tried."

"Right, Madagascar. Well it's a plan, anyway. So go with it." Paul shrugged. "And seriously, take the day off and spend time with her. See what happens. Your boss owes you a day off, right?"

"Yeah, I guess so." Jamie felt a flutter in her chest that felt strangely like hope. "I just don't know! I was resigned to letting her go. Not happy, but resigned. Am I just setting myself up to be hurt?"

"Maybe, but you won't know unless you try, right? Take tomorrow and make it the best day you've both ever had. Then at least you'll know, right?"

Jamie nodded, remembering that brief glimmer of desire she thought she had seen in Claire's eyes in the lamp light. She felt the flutter again, stronger.

At least I'll know.

She sent a text to her boss to say she wouldn't be coming in, then climbed the stairs to bed. The best day Claire had ever had—Jamie could do that. She knew everything about Claire already from their chats, her favorite foods and hobbies. She had more than enough material to work with in planning one perfect, magical day. Jamie thought about some of Boston's highlights. A restaurant Claire would love. The view of the skyline from the harbor. She could almost picture how Claire's face would light up when she saw it, and just imagining it brought a smile to Jamie's lips. This really wasn't much different from planning her own perfect day. The fact that they had so much in common was the whole reason Jamie'd been so convinced that Claire was *the one*. Was it crazy to hope that there might be a slight chance that it was true?

Jamie rubbed her temples and sighed. Despite her new found excitement, remnants of her headache lingered. Malcolm's remarkable gaydar abilities aside, Jamie wasn't convinced this plan would work. It went against reason. Claire obviously thought she was in love with Jay, so who was Jamie to say otherwise? Claire was a grown woman who should know what she wanted. And she wanted Jay. A sharp stab of jealousy hit her, followed by a drenching wave of shame. Even if Claire *might* consider dating a woman, she'd certainly want it to be the right woman. An exceptional woman. Not someone who would deceive her the way Jamie had. No, there was no way Jamie deserved to win after what she'd done. But at least after tomorrow she'd have a spectacular memory to look back on.

NINE

JAMIE EXITED the hotel elevator on the third floor and stepped into a brightly lit hallway that smelled of cleaning products and fresh laundry. The sound of a vacuum in the distance suggested housekeeping was already busy cleaning the rooms of the early risers. As she approached Claire's door, Jamie could see a Do Not Disturb sign hanging prominently from the doorknob. She put her ear to the door but couldn't hear any sounds within. Jamie rapped her knuckles against the door with just enough force to be heard, yet hopefully lightly enough not to exacerbate the headache that Claire almost certainly woke up with this morning. If she was awake yet, that was.

Jamie heard a shuffling near the door and the sound of a bolt clicking, then the door inched open enough to reveal one squinting eye, and promptly shut again. Claire was awake, and didn't seem very happy about it. Jamie heard the scraping of a security chain and then the door reopened to reveal Claire, fully dressed but wearing a towel on her head, standing in a dark room.

"Good morning," Jamie whispered. "I didn't wake you, did I?"

Claire shook her head, wincing as she did. "Come in," she whispered back. "I'm up, but I couldn't take turning on a light so I showered and got dressed in the dark."

Jamie rummaged in the large canvas tote slung over one shoulder and produced a bottle of pain relievers, which she held out for Claire. "For you," she said. She dug through the bag again, this time pulling out a pair of size six gold pumps with four-inch heels. "And also yours, I believe. You must have left barefoot last night."

Claire grimaced, taking both the pills and the shoes. She set the shoes on the rumpled bed, opened the bottle, and popped a couple pills into her mouth before responding. "I'm so sorry about that. I'm such a lightweight and those drinks went straight to my head. I can't believe I left without my shoes! Or without saying goodbye," she added, her eyes cast downward, clearly embarrassed. She pulled the towel from her head and ran her fingers through the damp curls.

"I almost didn't bring the shoes back," Jamie replied. "Not because I was mad at you for not saying goodbye or anything like that. I just figured you'd never want to see them again after what they did to your feet!" Jamie watched mesmerized as Claire raked her hair into a loose ponytail. Her fingers itched to brush against the soft curls at the base of Claire's neck. She'd stared at them for an eternity as Claire slept against her last night, but hadn't dared to touch.

Claire groaned, "You're right, I don't think I'll ever let those things near my feet again. I wonder if I should just leave them here."

"It would free up more room in your luggage for souvenirs," Jamie suggested.

"I didn't buy any souvenirs," Claire responded with a snort. "I didn't have time to see the city at all. And I head back tonight, so I doubt I'll have a chance." She shook her head slowly. "Oh Jamie, this trip has been a disaster. The interview was awful and I know I don't even have a chance of getting the job. Jay is out of town—no, worse, he isn't even on the same continent. My feet hurt. My head hurts…"

"Because you met some crazy woman who forced you to drink too much and get a hangover," Jamie supplied.

"That's about the only thing that made this trip at all fun," Claire admitted. "Even if I'm paying for it now."

"Fun, huh? Then maybe you'd like to have a little more fun and see some of the city with me before you go?"

"Thanks, but I'm sure you have better things to do than spend the day on the Freedom Trail with your coworker's pen pal. Besides, don't you need to work?"

"As it happens, I have the day off. And give me a little credit. I had something way more interesting than the Freedom Trail in mind for today."

"Oh, really?" Claire asked, sounding intrigued.

"Of course. You do have some decent walking shoes, though, right? And you're up to walking? Like, out in the daylight?"

Claire chuckled. "The pills are kicking in. I think I can manage."

"Great! Then let's get you checked out, drop your bag off with your car, and go see the city!"

The smell of exhaust mixed with the humid air as they walked out of the hotel's parking garage onto Huntington Avenue. Jamie hurried them across the street to the trees and reflecting pool that belonged to the Christian Science center. Dozens of children wearing bathing suits splashed in the fountain while men and women in business suits rushed past, some pausing to gaze at the reflection of the city and sky in the water, or to buy a cup of coffee from one of the food trucks lining the plaza. A massive stone building topped with a dome stood at the far end of the pool and Claire stopped to snap a picture as they passed.

"What is it, a church?" Claire asked, and Jamie nodded. "You're taking me to church? Well, that's certainly unexpected, I'll grant you that."

Jamie laughed, "Not exactly. Yes, this building is a church, but that's not where we're headed. There's a library on the other side of the square with—well, it's hard to describe. But you'll see when we get there."

A few minutes later they were standing on a platform inside a sphere made entirely of glass. On its surface were painted in brilliant colors all of the continents and countries of the world. Claire's mouth gaped open in awe as they walked to the center of the room.

"Look over there!" Jamie said, pointing to a spot on the map. "There's Boston."

"And there's Antarctica," Claire added, pointing straight down. "It's so far away."

Damn it. Jamie was not going to let Jay spoil their day. "Let's find Portland," she said, trying to draw Claire's attention back to the northern hemisphere.

"Wow, your voice is so loud!" Claire laughed and the sound rung back in her ears like a gong. "So is mine!"

"Yeah, the acoustics in here are crazy," Jamie explained, lowering her voice as much as she could. "When you stand in the center, no matter how you talk, it's like you're shouting. And if you stand on one end of the platform and I stand on the other and whisper, you could hear me loud and clear just like I was whispering in your ear."

"Really? Show me!" Claire skipped ahead on the platform until she reached the far side.

Jamie stood at the other side and whispered, "Hello, Claire!" Claire giggled as the message was received, and the sweet sound of it rang in Jamie's ears like her own private symphony.

Back outside in the plaza, the smell of food surrounded them as a crowd of hungry workers lined up outside the trucks for the start of the lunch rush.

"You hungry?" Jamie asked.

"Starving," Claire replied.

"If you really can't wait we could grab something

here, but if you don't mind hopping on the T, I know a really great place."

Claire nodded in agreement, her broad grin a sign that she was relishing the day's adventures and up for whatever else Jamie had in store. They took the T to Government Center and made their way through the midday crowd at Quincy Market. Their numbers thinned as Claire and Jamie approached a narrow cobblestone alley lined with late eighteenth century buildings. Since it was not nearly wide enough to fit a car, walking along this street was like walking back in time.

"It's like an old street in London!" Claire said.

Jamie smiled at her excitement. She pushed open the door to what appeared to be a pub and stepped inside. Claire followed, stopping suddenly. Jamie knew she'd been taken by surprise at the interior that greeted them.

"Mexican food?" Claire asked. "I thought it would be fish and chips or bangers and mash or something. I can't believe it! Mexican food is my favorite."

Jamie, who had learned this in a chat several weeks before, tried to look surprised. "This is probably the best restaurant in Boston," Jamie said. "It's a real hidden gem. They make their own tortillas and homemade tamales and everything."

"Oh my God, tamales? My Aunt Marisol used to make homemade tamales every Christmas. I lived with her after my parents died," she explained. "She was really big on tradition and she would spend days making hundreds of tamales before Christmas. I have to try them. They smell just like hers."

Jamie was thrilled. She had chosen this place because she thought Claire would like it, and because it was close to the next stop on her list. She'd had no idea about Claire's family traditions. "Okay, we'll order the tamales, but let's get them to go. There's someplace else I wanted you to see." They left the alley a little while later with a bag of steaming tamales, chatting as they walked.

"So, how did you become an English professor?" Jamie inquired.

"What, you don't think most girls who grow up with tamales on Christmas end up as English professors?"

"No, I didn't mean it like that," Jamie backtracked, afraid she'd offended Claire with the question.

Claire laughed. "It's okay. My father's whole side of the family is still mystified by me. But my mom's family was from England, and she was a high school English teacher. My dad was a biology professor at Lovejoy College, so I grew up knowing I wanted to teach there." Claire sighed. "After yesterday's interview, I'm beginning to think Lovejoy only hired me out of pity because they remembered my dad."

"The interview couldn't have been that bad. I'm sure you're an excellent professor."

"Thanks, but I'm not even much more than an adjunct, and those are a dime a dozen. And the interview was awful." Claire shuddered. "The woman who met with me kept talking about all the candidates she'd seen, and the fancy schools they'd attended. They'd all done work in England. And here I've only been to London once, and just for a conference. Have you ever been?"

"To England? Uh, yeah. I did my graduate work there," Jamie mumbled.

"That's so funny. Jay did, too," Claire replied. "What a coincidence. Well, I won't lie, I'm definitely jealous. What did you study?"

"Environmental science. There was a university in Norfolk that was doing a lot of cutting edge climate change research."

"I wanted to do a semester abroad, but my aunt said no."

"Was she really strict, your aunt?"

"Yeah, you could say that. She's my great aunt, actually, so she's pretty old. She's really traditional. She took us to mass every Sunday, that kind of thing. She was always reminding me that since my parents were gone, everything I did reflected on how they had raised me."

"That's awful! Talk about a lot of pressure for a kid." Jamie shook her head. Aunt Marisol sounded like a tough old bird. "I don't know, it seems manipulative, like she was just trying to get you to do what she wanted."

"You think so? I never thought about it like that." Claire was silent for a moment. "Manipulative. Yeah, maybe it was. I never realized that until now."

Jamie led Claire into the lobby of a nearby office building and waved in greeting as they passed the security desk. She stopped in front of the elevator bank and pushed the call button. The elevator doors opened and Jamie swiped an access card that she took from her pocket, pressing the button for the top floor. It was clearly labeled Restricted Access.

"Um, Jamie? Where are we going?" Claire asked.

Jamie smiled mysteriously. "You'll see. Trust me."

When the doors opened they stepped out into a glass enclosure, beyond which was a fantasy world of lush trees, flowering bushes, and winding gravel path.

"It's a secret garden!" Claire exclaimed, her smile growing wide with delight.

"Actually, it's part of a rooftop garden initiative to combat climate change. They're all over the city," Jamie explained. "Most of them are working farms that grow organic produce for local restaurants. There's even one at Fenway Park. But this one is my favorite."

Claire looked around, clearly entranced. "But it's so beautiful. And it's completely empty! How did you even know this was here?" She narrowed her eyes at Jamie, looking suspicious. "And why do you have a key card to get in?"

"I was on the advisory committee. I mostly deal with ocean research, but this was a side project that a friend of mine got me into. Anyway, it's not officially open to the public right now, but all the advisers were given keys." As she explained, Jamie sat on a bench under a tree and began arranging their picnic.

"I'll bet you bring all the girls here," Claire said, looking up at Jamie with what could only be described as a coquettish grin.

Jamie wasn't sure what to make of it. *Is Claire flirting?* If it were any other woman, Jamie would definitely consider this flirting, but with Claire she wasn't sure. Claire was straight. At least, she was supposed to be, no matter what Paul and Malcolm said. And she wanted so badly for Claire to be flirting with her that she could easily be imagining it. "So, I guess our friend Malcolm filled you in on a few things last night, huh?" Jamie studied Claire's face carefully. "He confessed this morning that he'd outed me. So, that's okay?"

"Sure, why wouldn't it be? It's the twenty-first century, right? I have a gay cousin. Everyone's cool with it."

"Even your Aunt Marisol?" Somehow, Jamie doubted the sentiment was as unanimous as Claire made it sound.

"God, no!" Claire spluttered, then looked at Jamie sheepishly. "Sorry, that didn't come out well. The cousin's on my mom's side. They're, like, a bunch of hippies who have goats and make their own granola."

"Too bad you didn't go live with them."

"I know, right? But they live in Washington and everyone agreed it would be better for us not to have to change schools. Aunt Marisol lived down the street, so that's who we got."

After they'd finished eating and spent several minutes admiring the view, they rode the elevator back down to the lobby.

"So," Claire said, "it's almost two o'clock and I have about three hours until I have to leave for the airport. What else do you have in store for me? Not that there needs to be anything else," she added quickly. "This has already been the most amazing day I could possibly imagine. I really don't expect anything else."

"Well," Jamie replied, "as it happens, I did have one more thing in mind. Follow me."

The salt was thick in the air as they approached the wharf, and Claire stopped to breathe it in. Jamie was relieved to note the blissful look on Claire's face. She had mentioned sailing once in a chat but it hadn't come up since, and Jamie wasn't certain how serious Claire had been about it. Their next activity would go a lot more smoothly if Claire was really as passionate about boats as she had led "Jay" to believe. Claire gasped when she saw the vintage Soling sailboat bobbing in the water in front of her, prepped and ready for its voyage.

"Is this your boat?" she asked breathlessly.

"I wish," Jamie replied with a chuckle, "but alas, it's just a rental. A fun one, though. I have a membership here, so I can take it out whenever it's available."

Once aboard, they spent a few moments in preparation and it was immediately apparent that Claire was every bit as proficient as Jamie had hoped. Soon they were sailing into the harbor, the city skyline soaring beyond the sparkling water. They zipped around, enjoying the speed and agility of the small craft. Finally, Jamie chose a quiet spot for them to slow down and admire the view.

"This is amazing," Claire breathed. "This morning, I thought I hated Boston and I wanted to go home. Now, I never want to leave."

As if on cue, Claire's phone began to vibrate. They

had been in and out of cell phone coverage on the water and Claire had missed a call. She squinted at the number. "It's a local number. I think it might be the college," she said nervously. "They left a voice mail. It's probably bad news, right? That's why they left a message?"

"Maybe you should listen to the message before you get too worried." Jamie's pulse raced. She hoped for good news, then prayed for bad. Both outcomes were equally desirable, and terrifying.

"I guess you're right. Hold on." She struggled to hear the message over the whipping wind and had to listen a second time. Finally, she slipped the phone back into her pocket and looked at Jamie in a daze. "I got it," she said. "I can't believe it, but they want me back in two weeks for the start of the fall term!"

Claire let out a jubilant yelp and Jamie joined her, each flinging her arms around the other in celebration and jumping up and down, narrowly avoiding tipping the small craft as they did.

In a few short hours, Claire would be flying back to Portland not for good, but just to pack, and then she would return to Jamie and a new job and a new adventure. And if Claire seemed to forget in the excitement of the moment that she would finally get to meet Jay, Jamie was in no hurry to remind her.

TEN

CLAIRE SPUN IN A SLOW, deliberate circle, taking in the growing pile of boxes in her Portland apartment. She planned to pack as much as she could in her car and leave the rest at Theresa's house until she had a better idea of her situation in Boston. Claire had yet to secure an apartment, and Jay was being of frustratingly little help. She had sent him a message as soon as she got home to share the wonderful news, but her excitement had fizzled at his response. He was still in Antarctica and had no plans to return anytime soon. He hardly seemed to care that she was coming to Boston.

He hadn't even bothered to respond to her questions about how he had found his apartment in Beacon Hill, let alone offer her the use of it until his return, as she had secretly hoped he would. It would have been so much more convenient. Claire wouldn't dream of moving in with Jay so soon, but if he was going to be on the other side of the globe, she didn't see the harm in staying in his empty apartment while he was gone.

She had so little time to prepare for the move, and she'd honestly had no idea when she accepted the new position that apartments cost so much in Boston and were so difficult to find. Claire worried that she wouldn't find one in time, or if she did, that she wouldn't be able to afford to live there on a lecturer's salary.

Theresa's footsteps rang out from the kitchen with the exaggerated echo that was peculiar to nearly empty rooms. She'd dropped by after work to take a load of boxes to her house, as well as to take yet another opportunity to lecture Claire on how reckless she was being. If this move was just about living closer to a man she had yet to meet, the way Theresa seemed to think it was, Claire might agree. But it wasn't. Not anymore. The moment Claire heard that message, with the salty wind in her face, the Boston skyline behind her, and the thrill of adventure coursing through her veins, she knew it was a sign. The universe wanted her in Boston, and Claire was not going to argue with the universe.

"Claire," Theresa called out, "what's happening with the stuff in these last two drawers by the stove?"

Unable to recall what was yet to be packed, Claire ventured into the kitchen to take a look. "Honestly?" Claire replied, surveying the collection of spatulas with melted handles and aged potholders of indeterminate color, "I'm thinking trash. If I ever manage to find an apartment, I'll celebrate by buying some utensils that don't look like they've marched through Hell and back."

"Yeah, well, sis, that's some way to celebrate. I've always said you really know how to party," Theresa teased. "And what about the stuff on the fridge, is that trash, too?"

Claire looked lovingly at the photos and memos that covered the refrigerator, held up by one of the largest private collections of cutesy gift shop magnets in the Pacific Northwest. "Bite your tongue! Those magnets are one of a kind."

"Uh huh. Only because the world might explode if there were actually two plastic parrots wearing Carmen Miranda fruit hats in existence at the same time."

Claire just rolled her eyes in response. Her sister could say whatever she liked, the magnets were awesome.

"So, this is Jay?" Theresa asked, pointing toward the photo the parrot was holding. Claire nodded. It was the one Jay had sent from Antarctica. "That's the best picture of him you've got?"

"I have others. I've just, um, packed them already." Actually, Claire had tried putting them up right after Jay sent them, but something about it hadn't felt right. It was like Jay's ridiculously handsome face was constantly staring at her from the photo, demanding an explanation when she failed to swoon.

It was weird, but in those pictures, it seemed like he could almost be just some guy out of a catalog. When Claire stuck them to the scratched enamel of the fridge, they didn't even seem real. Suddenly it'd been like she was back in middle school that time when she framed a picture of a boy that she'd cut out of a magazine and tried to convince her friends it was her boyfriend from summer camp who lived in Idaho.

God, that was so stupid. Why did I do that? She couldn't remember. But anyway, that photo of Jay had come down as quickly as it'd gone up. She liked the one from the expedition, liked that it gave her the overall *feel* of Jay without too many details to make her feel uneasy.

Beneath that one was the selfie of Jamie and her on the harbor that she'd taken right before she left for the airport. Looking at it now, she was reminded of something Jamie had said earlier that day that had been troubling her ever since. "Theresa, do you think we had a lot of pressure on us growing up to act a certain way? You know, to make mom and dad proud?"

"While they were alive? Not at all. But if you mean did Aunt Marisol guilt-trip us every chance she got after they were dead, then absolutely, yes. I mean, I love her, but she could lay a guilt trip on a person like nobody's business. Unfortunately, you got the brunt of it once I left for college."

"But, I mean, there's nothing wrong with trying to make Mom and Dad proud, right? Isn't that a good thing?"

"Sure, if what you're doing makes you happy. But not if you choose everything you do based on what you think they would want." Theresa paused, looking into Claire's eyes. "That's not the way to live. Why are you asking this now?"

"Oh, just something Jamie said to me."

"You mean this Jamie?" Theresa pointed to the photo. "So, you mean this Jamie person was able to figure that out and get you to actually listen to her in one day? Wow, smart and beautiful, huh?" she teased.

"Oh, is she?" Claire shrugged. "I hadn't really noticed."

She had noticed. Of course she had. How could anyone not notice Jamie's long legs and the way her tank top shimmied so suggestively along her curves? Well, honestly, everyone in the restaurant had noticed. It's not like it was just her. Hadn't her sister just noticed? And that was only from a *photo*. It could hardly do justice to the way Jamie's hair had glowed like a halo in the afternoon sun, or the way her slightly crooked front tooth made her smile seem even more perfect.

Theresa snorted. "Sure you hadn't noticed. So, are you likely to see Jamie or Paul or any of those other people you met a lot once you've moved out there?"

"I don't know. I assume so. Jamie gave me her number and told to me be in touch. So yeah. I mean, between Jay working at the Marine Institute and me teaching on the North Shore, I'll probably be up that way all the time."

"But you're still set on finding a place in Beacon Hill?"

"Well, yeah. You should see it. It's like something out of Dickens, seriously."

"Uh huh. And from what you told me about the rents, you're going to end up like one of his raggedy orphans, selling matches on a street corner to live there.

Unless you've heard back from any of the places you contacted yesterday— what about the townhouse?"

Claire groaned. "Oh, Theresa. I can't believe I was so stupid. That listing for the $375,000 townhouse—which I probably couldn't have afforded even with the last of the insurance money from Mom and Dad, plus the loan that you and Larry offered—wasn't actually to buy that cute little townhouse at all. It was to buy the parking space on the street in front of the townhouse."

"People pay that much for a parking space?" Theresa shook her head in disbelief.

"I guess they do in Boston."

"Then, apart from the fact that Jay lives there, and considering he doesn't know when he's coming back and hasn't offered to have you stay in his place while he's gone, why are you clinging to the idea that you have to live in Beacon Hill, or in Boston at all?" Theresa asked. "What about the North Shore? Or, what was the other place—Cape Ann?"

Claire shrugged. "I don't know. Maybe."

"You're leaving the day after tomorrow, Claire, and you have no place to go. You said Jamie gave you her number, right? Why don't you text her and ask for some help?"

Claire squirmed under her sister's relentless gaze. "You mean text her right now, while you watch me like I'm one of your kids to make sure I actually do it? Fine." She grabbed her phone and dashed off a quick text. "There, I sent it. I hope you're happy."

Theresa smiled. "It's a good plan. You'll thank me someday."

Claire glared at her. "Stop staring at me like I'm a naughty toddler who's refusing to eat my vegetables. Jamie's a busy woman. She's not going to drop everything the minute she hears from me and—"

Claire stopped short as her phone vibrated on the kitchen counter, announcing the arrival of a new message. After reading it through twice she looked at her sister and said, "That was from Jamie. She says most of the good places for September 1st were snapped up months ago, even on Cape Ann. But I can rent one of the extra rooms at her and Paul's place until I find something."

Theresa grinned. "There you go! Talk about the universe sending a sign. 'Ask and ye shall receive', as they say."

"I don't know..." Claire replied.

It was the perfect solution. The house was beautiful. In fact, it was exactly the type of house she had always wanted to live in, and it would be an easy commute to the college. The rent Jamie had quoted was so low that all of her budget problems would evaporate in an instant if she accepted. So why did she feel so nervous? "You can stop staring at me because I'm not going to text her back right now. I need to think about it. Haven't you been telling me all week that I'm being too reckless?"

"Yes, but that was different," her sister argued. "That was about a relationship. This is about a roof over your head."

"Be proud, *hermanita*. I am actually taking your advice for once. This is me not being reckless. Now," she added, grabbing a box, "let's put these boxes in your car so you can get home to Larry and the boys. I'll be over tomorrow night for dinner and to say good-bye, and I'll let you know then what I've decided. *After* a sensible night's sleep."

Back in her empty apartment, Claire stared at the pictures on the fridge and tried to make sense of the swarm of butterflies that had migrated to her stomach at the sight of Jamie's text. She studied the picture of her and Jamie. It was, as Theresa had said, a nice picture. *It's not what she said, it's what she was implying when she said it.* And that was without her knowing that Jamie dated women.

Claire was glad Theresa didn't know how shamelessly she had been flirting with Jamie that day. Claire's cheeks burned scarlet at the memory of how she had teased Jamie on the rooftop garden. It hadn't been intentional, exactly, but that comment about Aunt Marisol controlling her had rankled. She'd been looking for a way to strike back, not at Jamie, but at her own repressed upbringing. The thought of being manipulated made her blood boil, though she couldn't for the life of her figure out why it had made her flirt with Jamie that way.

Missy. A name from the distant past echoed in her mind. Claire's breath caught as the memory came flooding back. Of course. The incident with Missy was the reason she had cut out that stupid picture and put it in her locker in middle school. Missy had been a new student at their school that year, her father in the military or some such thing that made them move around a lot. She and Claire were inseparable for a few weeks, until one night when Aunt Marisol had pulled Claire aside.

Her aunt had been so upset. People were talking, she had told her accusingly, saying things about Missy. About Missy and Claire. *Terrible things.* And what would people think? What would they think about Claire's poor deceased mother and father? How could Claire let anyone think this was how they raised her? And Claire had been in tears—she remembered it vividly. Of course she didn't want people to think bad things about her parents. And of course she would stop being friends with Missy, if that's what she had to do.

She'd done exactly that. Claire was shocked to remember it. She hadn't even tried to explain, just stopped hanging out with her, just like that. *Poor Missy.* She must have been so confused and hurt. Claire didn't even know for certain. Missy had moved again the next semester and that was the last time she'd even thought about it until now. But deep down, Claire must have realized that flirting with Jamie would be like twisting a knife into her Aunt Marisol.

So, that explained her behavior. It was a relief to know why she'd done it, but it didn't make it right. Especially since she knew that Jamie might take her seriously. Not that Claire was one of those people who assumed all lesbians had to automatically be in love with her just because she was a girl, or something. But she liked Jamie, and she didn't want her to get the wrong idea. She didn't want to hurt Jamie the way she must have hurt Missy. If she decide to move in with Jamie and Paul, it could only be with strict guidelines in place. No more fancy dinners. No more sailing, or picnics in secret rooftop gardens.

No more flirting.

But what if I'm fooling myself? What if I just really enjoyed flirting with her? Claire brushed the thought aside. It didn't really matter whether she enjoyed it or not. She had a goal to concentrate on. Jay was that goal, and he would be back before too long. In the meantime, she would just have to choose to live by a few rules where Jamie was concerned. She could manage that.

I'll do it, Claire thought. She picked up her phone and sent Jamie a text to accept her offer. Claire felt giddy. In less than a week, she would be moving into her dream house in a charming little village on Cape Ann, with two new friends and a whole new life. How hard could it possibly be to follow a few common sense rules, anyway?

ELEVEN

IT WAS the start of a sunny Labor Day weekend when Claire parked in front of the massive Victorian on Ocean Boulevard. The sound of the engine stopping and the slam of a car door sent Jamie and Paul running to the porch to greet their new roommate. Claire was already unloading boxes, and Paul hollered across the lawn that they would be down in a minute to help.

"Hey, Jay?" he asked in an exaggerated whisper, "What does a lesbian bring to a second da—ouch! Why'd you do that?"

Jamie rubbed her elbow. Paul's ribs were harder than she'd thought. "'Cause you deserved it. It's a dumb joke, Paul. And every single time you tell it, it gets dumber. Besides, you can't call me Jay any more, remember?"

"Sorry! I'll try not to forget. But you have to admit, I called it about the moving thing. Called it the very first day you showed me her profile." Paul smirked.

"Yes. You're a very clever boy. You deserve a cookie."

"You gonna bake me cookies?" His face lit up in a hopeful grin.

"Nope." Jamie slapped her hand playfully against the back of his head. "I'm going to carry Claire's boxes, help her settle in, and take her someplace really nice for dinner. Maybe lobster at that place down by the water."

"Okay, so that's your plan, then?"

"What's my plan? What do I need a plan for?"

"Your plan for wooing Claire, Girly. Should we call it Operation Wine and Dine?"

"Absolutely not. But yeah, it's been working so far, I guess. She sure sends Jay a lot of emails, though."

"I thought Jay was breaking up with Claire."

"He is. He will." Jamie shrugged. "It's just that I was afraid if it happened before she got here, she might change her mind."

"I think she would have come anyway."

"Maybe. When I took her for lunch in the garden I kind of thought... well, I don't know."

"She likes you," Paul said with a singsong lilt.

Jamie shook her head. "I don't know. But if I take her to some nice dinners, go sailing, show her around town, stuff like that... maybe." Jamie hopped down the front steps and crossed the expanse of green grass. "Hi, Claire!" she called out. "Welcome!"

"Jamie! Paul! I'm so excited I finally made it!" Claire attempted to wave but stopped when the box in her arms tipped precariously to one side.

"Here, let me get that," Paul said, coming to her

rescue. "This thing weighs a ton! What do you have in here?"

Claire laughed. "Books, probably. They're mostly books. Some for work, some for pleasure, plus a few cookbooks I couldn't live without."

"Cookbooks, huh?" Paul repeated, his face brightening. "I don't suppose you like to bake, do you, new roomie? Cookies, maybe?"

"As a matter of fact," Claire replied, "I do, and I make awesome cookies. Just not in the scorching heat. But when it gets colder, maybe. It does get colder, right?" Claire added, fanning herself.

Paul chuckled, "Girl, you are going to regret wishing away this heat in a couple of months, trust me."

"Claire, why don't you let Paul earn those cookies you've promised by carrying your boxes inside? I'll show you your new room."

Jamie led the way through the front door and up the staircase to the second floor. "This is where Paul's room is," she said, pointing down the hall. "In fact, this floor is basically his. He's got an office across from his room, and a bathroom and darkroom next to that. His grandmother set it up for him when he first started showing an interest in photography. He doesn't use it anymore since his work is all digital, but if you ever see the door closed, make sure you knock."

Claire nodded, looking around admiringly. "Is that original Lincrusta on the walls in the stairwell and hallway?"

"Wow," Jamie said, "you really know your old

houses, don't you? Yes, it's original. So are most of the light fixtures. Paul found them in the basement and had them restored." She pointed up the stairs. "The stained glass on the second floor landing was salvaged from another house in town that was torn down. There would've been stained glass there originally, but someone had taken it out years ago and replaced it with a plain window."

"Who would do that?" Claire asked, clearly horrified.

Jamie laughed. "I know. I felt the same way, but they did it for the view. You'll see what I mean when we go upstairs." Jamie started up the stairs to the third floor and Claire followed.

"Wow." Claire inhaled sharply at the sight of the vast Atlantic that was framed by the window on the third floor landing. She watched with wide eyes as waves crashed against sharp rocks and seagulls swooped above the spray.

Jamie grinned. "Awesome, right? We're not actually as close as we look. There are two or three streets between us and the beach, but we're on a little hill so you can't see the other rooftops from up here."

"Is that a beach?" Claire asked, pointing toward the water.

"Not really, so don't get too excited. It's rocky and there isn't any access from the seawall. Trust me, if we were as close to the water as it looks from here, and that was a sandy beach down there, Paul would have sold the place for millions and retired to Florida or something."

Claire laughed. "It doesn't matter. The view is spectacular."

"Well, wait until you see the one from your room. It's down here," Jamie said, leading the way. "Mine is behind us, at the far end of the hall, and yours is right through there."

Claire peered through the open door and squealed in excitement. "Really? This is mine?"

She dashed into the center of the room, spinning to take in every detail. The room was semi-circular in shape, with walls painted a soft, buttery yellow and a ceiling of exposed wooden beams. It was furnished simply with an iron bed and a waterfall dresser and nightstand. There was no artwork on the walls, nor was any needed with such a view. All along the curved outer wall, large windows draped in simple lace curtains revealed a coastal panorama.

Claire looked at Jamie, eyes shining. "Are you sure? This must be the best room in the house!"

"The view is amazing, but it has some drawbacks. It's the coldest room in the winter, and no matter what Paul does, the Wi-Fi in here is awful."

"That's okay," Claire responded with a smile. "It'll be worth it. I can't believe I get to stay in the tower room. I've always dreamed of a room like this!"

"I'm glad you like it! Why don't you get settled in and later on I'll take you to dinner at the lobster shack over by the pier." Jamie noticed the smile fade from Claire's face. "What's wrong, not a fan of lobster?"

"No, it's not that. It's just, I've had a really long trip

and I don't think I'll feel up for going anywhere." Claire's reassurance sounded less than convincing.

"Um, sure, of course," Jamie said, feeling deflated. She had been looking forward to another night out with Claire for weeks. She hadn't counted on being turned down, and she instinctively worried that Claire was trying to keep her distance by refusing. "I could make something for dinner—for all of us," Jamie quickly amended, hoping that including Paul would put Claire at ease.

"Well, I guess that would be okay. But I'll go grocery shopping tomorrow, and take a turn making dinner, too. I'm not going to be that roommate everyone hates who takes advantage, I swear. I'm used to being self-sufficient. You'll hardly know I'm here."

Jamie doubted that Claire could be in the same state without her realizing it, let alone the same house, but Claire's words gave her hope. Perhaps the sudden distance Jamie sensed wasn't personal, after all, and Claire was just trying to be conscientious. Besides, there would be plenty of time to spend together once Claire was settled in.

AS THE WEEKS STRETCHED ON, however, it soon became clear that Claire was avoiding being alone with Jamie. There was no other explanation. She worked late almost every night, or else disappeared into her room as soon as she came home. By the beginning of October,

Jamie had to admit that it really *was* like Claire wasn't there.

One evening as Jamie sat at her computer, the Tech Cupid chat window popped open. Jamie's heart skipped a beat at the sight of Claire's smiling avatar.

CLAIRE: *How's Antarctica?*

Jamie knew she shouldn't respond. That was part of her grand plan, after all, to have Jay go away for good. She ignored the message that night and even for the next few days, but the longer Claire remained absent, the more the temptation grew. By Friday night, the crack in Jamie's resolve was as wide as the Grand Canyon. Just a quick response wouldn't hurt, right?

JAY: *Can't complain. You?*

At least Jamie could find out how Claire was doing this way. Make sure she was okay. A brief chat, a few words here and there, was all she would allow herself. And nothing remotely flirtatious. But with a few strict rules in place, she decided that it was worth the risk. Claire was like a drug to Jamie, and she had to get her fix somehow, even if by doing it she was digging herself deeper into the lie.

JAY: *How's your new job?*

CLAIRE: *Not so great.*

Jamie wasn't surprised. Claire worked too hard. She hardly had time to relax. Jamie knew Claire was ambitious in her career, but everyone needed a break sometimes. *Maybe Jay can convince her to take some time for herself,* Jamie thought.

Jay: *I know you want to earn tenure as quickly as you can, but you need rest, too.*

Claire: *I have a confession. I told everyone the position is tenure track, but it's not. I just didn't want my sister to know I gave up a more secure job in Portland to move here. Maybe it was a mistake. Maybe I should have gone to England instead.*

Jamie's heart sank. *Poor Claire.* She'd had no idea about the job. She felt a little thrill at the thought that Claire had shared this secret with her. Then guilt flooded through her. Claire had given up her job security, and it was Jamie's fault. She'd been so excited to find out Claire was moving that she'd never thought to question what she was giving up. Her job. Her family. All to be with her. Or, well, with Jay. But it was almost the same thing, right? Even so, Jamie felt the familiar stab of jealousy where her alter ego was concerned. The temptation to sabotage Jay was overwhelming.

Jay: *England's overrated.*

Jamie grinned wickedly at the words on her screen. Claire was such an anglophile that a sentiment like that was bound to drop Jay a peg or two in her eyes. There was no way she'd want to be with someone who felt that way about her favorite place in the world. Jamie settled against a pillow on her bed and survey her room, wondering if she could find some of the t-shirts and other souvenirs from her grad school days in the UK. After Jay's slight, the sight of them should make Claire swoon.

It was well after midnight when Jamie woke with a

start. She'd dozed off on top of her blanket and shivered in the chilly night air. Her laptop was beside her on the bed. The chat window had been idle long enough that the screen had faded to darkness, extinguishing the only light in Jamie's room. Despite her best intentions, she'd spent much longer than she should have chatting with Claire. Or, rather, reading what Claire wrote. Once she got started, Claire had written enough for both of them. The words had poured onto the screen, and Jamie couldn't tear herself away.

JAY: *HOW ARE YOU GETTING ALONG WITH PAUL? AND JAMIE?*

Even as Jamie had typed the words, she knew she was tempting fate. It was like eavesdropping on a conversation after hearing someone say your name. Nothing good was likely to come of it. But she knew Claire would confide in Jay, and she had to know if Claire was avoiding her. Did she suspect how strongly Jamie felt about her? Did it make Claire feel uncomfortable but she was too polite to say so?

But, no! Claire had written page after page about how great Jamie was. It was enough to make her blush.

Jamie never would have guessed Claire felt like that if she hadn't read it in her own words, but there it was in black and white. It warmed her to know what Claire was really thinking, but at the same time it magnified her own duplicity. She would never have known any of this if she wasn't pretending to be Jay. Jamie sighed deeply. She wanted so badly to be rid of her alias, but until she could figure out how to get Claire to confide in her as herself, Jay would have to stay.

She swung her legs to the floor, searching for a pair of slippers before wandering down to the kitchen for a late night snack. Her stomach growled. Stress always brought out the need for a snack. Passing through the living room, Jamie glimpsed Claire curled up, asleep, on the couch. Her laptop was open on the coffee table, its screen as dark as the one upstairs. A tangle of chestnut curls was splayed temptingly across a throw pillow, as if beckoning Jamie's fingers to play in their silky strands. Jamie sighed, mustering every ounce of self control to keep her hands by her sides.

Claire shifted at the sound of Jamie's sigh, wrapping her arms tightly around herself. It was even colder downstairs than it had been in Jamie's room. Jamie considered waking her, but thought better of the impulse. It would probably spook her. And why wouldn't it? What straight girl wouldn't freak out to realize that her lesbian roommate was staring at her in her sleep, fantasizing about touching her hair? Hell, it would freak her out if she even suspected some girl was doing that to her while she slept. Unless it was Claire. Then it would be kind of hot.

Stop it, Jamie, she reprimanded herself. *Stop fantasizing and walk away. You're about an inch away from turning into a creepy stalker.*

She grabbed a worn quilt from the window seat and placed it gently over Claire's sleeping form, willing her not to wake up because if she did, Jamie knew the raw honesty and desire emblazoned on her face right now would frighten Claire away in a heartbeat, no matter how many nice things she had written about her to Jay.

Jamie ran her fingers across her scalp, digging her nails deep into the skin. She tugged at a fistful of hair, as if the action might yield a solution to this impossible situation. Perhaps if she pulled hard enough, she could yank the thoughts of Claire from her brain and finally have the strength to walk away. She sighed as she slowly climbed the stairs to her room. How was she ever going to get out from under this deception?

TWELVE

CLAIRE SAT on the sofa in the mid-morning sunlight, a cup of coffee warming her fingertips and a faded quilt stretched out across her lap. It was the same quilt she had found tucked around her when she awoke just after dawn, her laptop in sleep mode beside her.

The computer had revived from its sleep a lot faster than she had from hers, displaying her conversation with Jay from the night before with much more brightness and energy than Claire herself could muster. That conversation had been cathartic, yet less than satisfying. She had poured her heart out on the screen about all the things that had been bothering her, and that felt really good. She'd also said more than she meant to about Jamie. *Intelligent. Witty. Beautiful.* Had she really typed all those words? Claire's stomach clenched. Jamie was supposed to be her roommate, not the object of a school girl crush.

No, strike that. Crush was not the right word. Claire

couldn't quite put her finger on what a better word would be, but that one was definitely not it. *Better watch it, or there will be rumors starting for sure.* She could hear Aunt Marisol chastising her inside her head. She could feel her own rebellion brewing, too. No good would come of it.

Think about Jay. Jay's the one you're supposed to have a crush on.

The problem was that thinking of Jay was becoming less helpful lately. Jay was getting on her nerves. Or rather his absence was. He was starting to feel more like an imaginary friend than a potential boyfriend. Sometimes, like last night, it was like she was writing in her diary instead of chatting with a man she was supposed to be in love with.

No, not supposed to be in love with. Am in love with. Am.

It's just that their conversations were so one-sided now. None of this was going the way she'd intended. Not the job, not the move, not the boyfriend. Not the way her pulse ticked up and her stomach fluttered every time Jamie entered the room.

As if on cue, Jamie ambled in from the kitchen, a steaming mug in one hand. She wore a thin gray tank top emblazoned with a faded Union Jack flag. Claire couldn't help but smile when she saw it. Then she remembered the way Jay had dismissed her dream of moving to England in their overnight chat. It was silly, but it bothered her much more than it should have. She'd always thought that it was something she and Jay had in common, and now she felt more than a little disappointed.

Jamie stretched her long arms high above her head, offering a tantalizing glimpse of the outline of her shapely breasts, before settling into the chair across from Claire. The same chair the two of them had shared over the summer, Claire recalled—their bodies welded together from shoulders to toes. The memory caused Claire to squirm, twisting the faded quilt in her hands. She was tempted to fold up the quilt and put it away.

It had suddenly gotten very warm. As Jamie stretched again, cat-like in her sunny chair, the tank top shifted slightly to reveal the smooth white skin around Jamie's belly button, with a tiny freckle that looked like a speck of chocolate. Claire wondered if she pressed her tongue against it, would it taste like chocolate?

Wait, what?

She felt a stab of panic. *Where had that thought even come from?* She needed more sleep. There was something seriously wrong with her brain right now. This was all Jay's fault, with his research trip and his stupid penguins. If he had been in Boston where he was supposed to be, Claire would not even be in Cape Ann in the first place, and would not be blushing over the memory of a chair and being distracted by tank tops that were too small and did not cover what they were intended to cover.

All Jay's fault.

"Did you sleep okay?" Jamie inquired, eyeing the quilt on Claire's lap.

"Oh, um, not really," Claire responded, stopping for a sip of coffee to alleviate her suddenly very dry throat. "Were you the one that gave me the blanket?"

Jamie nodded.

"Oh." Claire toyed with the corner of the quilt, an image in her mind of Jamie holding it in her hands, putting it around her as she slept. Watching her in the moonlight with those feline green eyes of hers.

God, it gets warm in here once the sun comes up. She was deliriously tired right now, incapable of reining thoughts that were rapidly straying into very dangerous territory. Claire knew the safest thing would be to leave the room and go upstairs, but she wanted to stay. She was tired of leaving the room when Jamie came in, of feeling trapped upstairs like a princess in her tower.

"Is that coffee?" Claire asked, pointing to Jamie's mug.

"No, it's tea." Jamie replied.

She held the cup out and Claire could see the string from a tea bag dangling over the edge. She recognized the paper tag as belonging to one of her favorite English brands, Yorkshire Gold. The mug had a fancy crest on it that looked like it belonged to a university.

"Was that from your school?" Claire asked.

Jamie looked at the mug, her lips twitching in a slight smile. "Oh, you mean this?" She nodded. "Yes. It's one of my favorites."

"Did you like living there?" Claire wasn't sure why she wanted to know.

"In England?" Jamie asked. "I loved it."

"Do you miss it?"

"I'd go back in a heartbeat," Jamie replied. "In fact, I bet you would love the town where I went to school. The cobblestone streets and the old churches—"

Jamie stopped mid-sentence as Paul bounded through the living room door. He gave an exaggerated sigh of relief when he spotted Jamie. Jamie looked perturbed.

"Oh, thank God, you're here," he said. "I need your help. Vanessa just called and needs someone to watch the girls, only I have to a photo shoot today. Can I count on Auntie Jamie?"

"Vanessa is Paul's sister, and the girls are her three-year-old twins." Jamie explained. "She's a nurse and sometimes when she gets put on weekend shifts the girls come over here and Paul and I keep them entertained."

"I told her I could do it last week, and totally forgot," Paul added. "That was before the shoot on Thursday got rained out and rescheduled. The shoot's local, just over by the marina, but I can't work and keep an eye on the girls."

"It's fine with me," Jamie said. "You know I'm always up for a day with my favorite girls. But you'd better make sure it's okay with Claire."

"Are you kidding? I love kids," Claire assured them. Wasn't that the whole reason she had moved here, so that she could have the chance for a family of her own? Besides, she'd been missing her nephews terribly lately, and she couldn't think of anything she'd like more than to spend the day with Paul's nieces. *And Jamie.* Claire attempted to quash the roguish thought. It broke the rules.

Screw the rules. She was tired of the rules.

"Are you sure?" Jamie countered. "Abbey and Zooey are adorable, but they're noisy little monsters."

Claire laughed. "I'm positive. In fact, I absolutely insist on helping you watch them. It'll be fun!"

Shortly before noon the doorbell rang. And rang again, several times in quick succession, followed by a woman's voice scolding Zooey to knock-it-off and that-means-now-do-I-make-myself-clear-little-miss?

Claire stifled a laugh as Jamie opened the door to reveal two tiny imps, one dressed as a fairy and the other as a princess, with dark curls similar in color to Claire's own pulled into two puffs on tops of their heads. The girls launched themselves at Jamie, attaching themselves to her legs. A woman in purple scrubs who must have been Vanessa handed over two identical pink backpacks with a grateful smile and imparted a few instructions to Jamie before leaving.

"Claire, this is Abbey," Jamie said, pointing to the princess clinging to her right leg, "and this is Zooey," she continued, this time pointing to the fairy. "Girls, this is my friend, Claire. She's going to play with us today."

Without letting go, the girls wriggled into position behind Jamie's legs before glancing shyly up at Claire, then burrowed their faces into the backs of Jamie's thighs. As Jamie bent to pry her loose, Zooey stood on tiptoes and whispered a question into Jamie's ear. "Oh, no, not my girlfriend, Sweetie," Jamie said.

Claire's cheeks burned as she realized the question this tiny child had obviously whispered in Jamie's ear to speak. She felt completely mortified. And just the tiniest bit irritated. It wasn't like she wanted it to be true, but Jamie needn't have been so quick to set the child straight. It's not like it was a ridiculous conclusion for a three year old to make. The sheer dismissiveness of Jamie's denial stung much more than it should have.

Claire chewed her lower lip, uncertain what to think of that. Then she decided it was better to stop thinking about it and change the subject.

"Jamie, do you think after lunch we could take the girls to the marina?" Claire asked. "It might be fun to see Paul in action. I've never seen a real photo shoot."

"Great idea! Did you hear that girls? We're going to the marina, but only if you eat a good lunch. Now, let go of Auntie Jamie's legs and wash your hands while I make my famous mac-n-cheese." At her words the girls squealed and raced into the kitchen. "Sorry about that thing with Zooey," she added. "She knows that sometimes I have girlfriends, and she's too little to know what's appropriate to ask and what isn't."

"Yeah, I've heard about all your girlfriends," Claire replied. She'd meant it as a joke, but there had been a jealous edge to her voice that she hadn't intended and she could feel her cheeks turning pink.

Jamie raised an eyebrow. "Oh, you have, have you?"

"So, you have a special recipe for mac-n-cheese?" Claire asked, changing the subject.

"Yes, in fact, I do. It comes straight out of a blue box,

in case you were wondering," Jamie confided to Claire as they entered the kitchen.

Claire snickered. "You know, I make a fantastic homemade mac-and-cheese, but when my nephews come over, mine usually comes from a box, too. It's the only thing the boys will eat."

"Oh, yeah? Maybe you can show me how you make it sometime, and then we could eat dinner together."

Claire nodded, biting her lower lip. There was a longing in the way Jamie said it that made Claire's pulse race. *Or maybe that's just my own feelings I'm projecting.* It was also clear from her tone that Jamie was a little wounded, probably from Claire avoiding her, which filled her with guilt.

Above all, the rules were supposed to keep Jamie from getting hurt. Instead, they were having the opposite effect, and they were making Claire miserable, too. *Damn Jay. I wish I had never even heard of Jay or his stupid penguins!*

As Claire was setting places for lunch, Paul bounded into the kitchen.

"Jamie? Claire? Have either of you seen my camera bag?" Paul asked, breathless. "I've looked everywhere. I need to be at the marina in twenty minutes."

"Did you check the mudroom?" Jamie asked.

Paul poked his head into the mudroom. "Ah, there it is! You're a genius." He grabbed the bag and grinned.

"Paul?" Claire asked "I thought I'd finally take you up on your offer to watch you work. You don't mind if we swing by the marina with the girls later, do you?"

"Uhh." The smile faded from his face. "Uh, well..."

"What's wrong, Paul?" Jamie asked. "They've always behaved themselves before."

"Yeah, well. It's just that Blake is one of the models today." He gave Jamie a funny look.

"Blake?" Jamie's eyes widened. "Oh, Blake. Right. That's not going to work, then."

"Who's Blake?" Claire asked, perplexed. Whoever he was, he must be significant.

"Blake is—" Paul began.

"—Paul's ex," Jamie finished. "Really delicate, messy situation. He was a real jerk."

"Oh, Paul, I'm sorry," Claire said, her voice full of compassion.

"Oh, yeah. Thanks," Paul answered. "You know, any other time."

"Of course. I completely understand," said Claire, feeling mildly disappointed. She'd been looking forward to watching Paul work. "Maybe we'll go to a park instead."

Poor Paul, Claire thought as she watched him leave. The way Jamie had reacted to Blake's name, it must have been a bad break up, indeed. The guy must have really done something terrible. Claire couldn't imagine being in Paul's shoes and having to work with a treacherous ex. If anyone ever hurt her like that, Claire would never want to see them again.

Abbey and Zooey gobbled down their lunches in record time and were soon bundled into jackets and ready for the park. It was Claire's first time walking through the neighborhood and she pointed enthusiastically at the beautifully restored homes as they passed. Jamie did her best to fill her in on their histories.

"Wow, you really know a lot about the area! I'm impressed."

"Well, it's a small town, there's not too much to learn. And I've lived here my whole life."

"It must've been so wonderful, growing up in a small town like this."

Jamie snorted. "You mean as the town's only freakishly tall lesbian? The one whose best friend, a boy, also happened to be gay? Oh, and black. Um, yeah, sure, it was really great. I fit in so well."

"Oh, I'm sorry," Claire said, flushing. "I hadn't thought of that. If it was so bad, why do you stay?"

"Well," Jamie answered, "I mean, it's gotten better. The town has changed a lot. Lots of artists and younger people come here to escape the Boston real estate madness. It feels more open minded, so now it's not so bad."

"You're still freakishly tall, though," Claire teased.

Jamie laughed. "That's just because you're so very, very short," she replied, moving closer to nudge Claire with her shoulder.

Claire felt relieved. Her attempt at a joke had broken the ice, and it almost felt like when they first met over the summer.

Maybe it's not too late for us to be friends, she thought. There was a bounce to her steps as they walked side by side, each of them holding one of the girls with their outer hands while their inner hands drifted closer to one another, until they just barely missed touching as they swung back and forth. Claire's fingers tingled with the anticipation of the slightest brush from Jamie's hand. She stiffened at the realization, pulling her hand closer to her own body and away from temptation.

What is wrong with me, that I can't even walk next to this woman on a public sidewalk in the middle of the afternoon without it getting weird?

Claire turned her head, seeking a distraction. Across the busy street beside them was the seawall, and she could just make out the shape of several people climbing on rocks a short distance beyond. She squinted into the bright midday sun for a closer look. One of the figures was a tall, dark man who appeared to be holding a camera. *Paul?* It had to be. And there was someone else with him, tall and blond. *So that's the infamous Blake*, she thought, scowling. Funny, he reminded her a little bit of Jay.

Claire felt a thrill of excitement. She wouldn't have to miss seeing the photo shoot after all. It was like a sign, stumbling upon them like this. She could just dart across the road and take a peek, and Paul would never even know she was there. Besides, she was dying to get a closer look at the evil bastard who'd broken Paul's heart. She started across the street.

"Claire!" Jamie called, her voice sounding urgent.

Claire froze part way across the street and turned toward Jamie.

"What are you doing? Come back here!"

Claire's head swiveled indecisively, looking first at the seawall, then at Jamie. She remained standing, unmoving. The blaring of a horn a moment later brought her back to her senses. She was standing in the middle of the road!

As she sprinted back toward Jamie, her foot caught on an uneven patch of pavement and she went sprawling across the ground. Brakes screeched as an oncoming car stopped abruptly just a few feet from Claire. Within a fraction of a second, Jamie was at her side.

"Oh my God, Claire! Are you okay?" Jamie's voice was frantic as she scooped Claire up and helped her back onto the sidewalk, where Claire crumpled in a shivering heap.

Claire's entire body shook, her pulse pounding from fright. She stared wide-eyed at Jamie and the girls. Both Abbey and Zooey looked terrified, and Claire's heart wrenched at the sight. "I'm sorry. I'm so sorry," she said. "That was so stupid of me."

Jamie reached out and took her hand, helping her stand. Claire winced in pain as soon as her full weight hit her left ankle. "I think I twisted it," she whimpered. "My shoe caught the pavement, and…" Her voice trailed off as she continued to shake.

"Shh. It's okay." Jamie shot a dubious glance at Claire's shoes, a pair of clogs with treacherously thick platform heels. "With those things, it's no wonder." She wrapped her arm around Claire's waist. "Come on, the park is just across the grass here." Jamie's strong arms steadied her as she limped toward an empty space on a nearby bench. "It seems like I do this a lot," Jamie remarked.

"Um-hm," Claire mumbled, her head resting against Jamie's arm. "You're really good at it." *Crap*. That had not come out sounding at all the way she'd intended for it to. It was supposed to sound lighthearted, not like she was moaning in ecstasy. She was obviously still in shock from her near miss in the road. Was it her fault that leaning against Jamie felt so comfortable?

"You know," Jamie whispered, "if you want me to put my arms around you, you don't have to keep hurting yourself. You can just ask." She grinned as Claire stiffened and shot her a glance that was equal parts embarrassment and terror. "Relax! That was a joke, I swear. But seriously," she added as Claire eased herself onto the bench, "we've got to get you some more practical shoes."

Claire gave her a weak smile. "Jamie, I'm so sorry I frightened the girls."

She gave Claire's shoulder a light squeeze. "They're fine. And getting into trouble already. Wait here." She raced off to the playground where Abbey and Zooey were busy dousing each other's heads with generous handfuls of sand.

Settling onto the bench, Claire stifled a yawn. The shot of adrenaline that had sustained her before was fading, and her lack of sleep was catching up to her.

"Amazing how exhausting they can be, isn't it?" a voice from beside her said.

Claire turned to look at the other woman occupying the bench, who looked to be in her early thirties and very obviously pregnant. "You mean kids?" she asked amicably.

"Kids, spouses. Even a simple trip to the park with my family wears me out. This one," she said, gesturing to her swollen belly, "isn't even here yet and he's got me exhausted already!"

"Is this your first?" Claire asked, looking with envy at the woman's bump and the shining gold band on her left ring finger. *She has it all. Probably has a dog, too.* After the way she had been feeling earlier, it was like a sign from the universe, reminding her of her goal. Maybe it was a promise, too, that if she behaved herself, this would be her reward. Or maybe that was wishful thinking. Sometimes Claire wished the universe would be more explicit in its signs. The most recent sign had nearly resulted in having to be scraped off the pavement. She still felt a little shaky at the thought.

"No, that's my son playing over there. He's six."

Claire looked in the direction the woman had nodded and saw a couple of boys of roughly that age bouncing a basketball, a few fathers standing nearby. She wondered which of the men was this woman's husband. Lucky woman, with a husband, a son, and a baby on the way—what more could she possibly want?

Keep your eyes on the prize, she told herself.

"So, are those two yours?" the woman asked.

"Mine?" Claire asked, confused.

"Your kids?"

"Oh, no. I don't have any kids of my own yet."

"Oh. I saw you with those adorable twins a minute ago. They kind of look like you."

Claire glanced over to where the girls were dragging Jamie to an empty set of swings. They did look a little like they could be hers, with their light olive skin and dark ringlets. Her eyes lingered for a moment as she watched Jamie push one swing and then the other in a practiced motion. She smiled, surprised at how effortlessly Jamie interacted with them. Somehow she hadn't pictured Jamie as the type to be good with kids. But she was a natural, and it was clear that she adored Paul's little nieces. Claire'd just assumed that kids wouldn't be part of Jamie's lifestyle.

You mean Jamie's lesbian lifestyle? Oh God, that sounded exactly like something Aunt Marisol would say. The only thing missing was a disapproving little sniff at the end.

"I was about to be really nosy, too, and ask you if you and your wife had adopted them, or—"

"My—no, we're not, um, I mean..."

"Oh, my God. I'm so sorry," the woman stuttered, blushing. "Like that's something you want to talk about with a total stranger. It's just, even the friends who were waiting on principle mostly tied the knot right after the Supreme Court ruling, you know? So now it's all about babies and are you doing adoption or insemination, and which clinic do you go to and blah, blah, blah—I should really shut up now," she said with a laugh.

Claire's mind spun. She looked again at the boy with the basketball and realized that the person with the close-cropped, salt-and-pepper hair, wearing khaki pants and a plain button-down shirt, was not another dad as Claire had assumed, but a woman instead. As if on cue, the woman looked up and waved to Claire's companion on the bench.

"Looks like they're ready to head home," the woman said, grasping her belly with one hand as she eased herself onto her feet. "I'm sorry for being so rude before. I didn't mean to put you on the spot. But believe me, you and your girlfriend are in for quite an adventure if you do decide to give parenting a try." With that, the woman headed across the playground, scooping her wife and son into a big bear hug before they disappeared down one of the neighborhood streets behind the park.

Claire was stunned. That woman with the perfect husband and perfect kids and perfect life was married to another woman? The possibility had never occurred to her.

Claire's mind was still reeling as Jamie squeezed next to her on the edge of the bench a short time later, the twins lagging a few yards behind. She sat quietly as Jamie knelt down to examine her ankle, holding it gently as she rotated it, her expression one of tenderness and concern.

Overcome with curiosity, Abbey and Zooey crowded in to see what Jamie was doing, cuddling up against Claire for a closer look and giving her little butterfly kisses to make her feel better. *Anyone looking over here right now*, she thought, *might mistake us for just another happy family.*

Claire's thoughts returned to the woman on the bench, who had seen her and Jamie and just assumed that they were a couple. Usually Claire took that type of thing as an accusation. Even the hint of a question about Claire's sexuality filled her with the need to defend herself. But today had felt different somehow. Maybe it was the fright from her near miss or the pain from her twisted ankle, but suddenly Claire saw it in a different light. That woman, whose life represented everything Claire feared most, also had everything Claire most desired. Suddenly Claire couldn't quite distinguish if the feelings deep inside her held accusation or promise. It made her too dizzy to contemplate.

Abbey and Zooey wiggled and squirmed, clearly getting bored with sitting.

"Show us a magic trick, Auntie Jamie," Abbey said.

Jamie laughed. "Again? Okay, watch closely."

Claire watched with interest as Jamie pulled a quarter out of her pocket, twirling it along her knuckles several times. With a flick of her fingers and wrist, she made the coin disappear, eliciting squeals of delight from the girls. Then she reached behind Zooey's ear and the quarter materialized between her thumb and forefinger. The girls clapped enthusiastically, then immediately demanded she do it again.

They made their way home soon after. It was slow going, but Claire managed it mostly on her own, only leaning against Jamie's arm now and again for support. Abbey and Zooey walked together a few feet ahead of them, holding hands and kicking at the leaves on the sidewalk.

"That was impressive back there," Claire remarked.

"What? Oh, the magic thing?" Jamie asked. "Oldest trick in the book, trust me." She looked at Claire with an amused expression on her face. "Wait, you did know it was a trick, right, and not real magic? I didn't mean to spoil it for you. I know how you feel about that stuff."

"Yes, I knew it was a trick. I'm not *that* hopeless." Claire blushed a little at being teased. Truthfully, everything about Jamie had struck her as magical today: the way she played with the kids, the way she tended so expertly to Claire's injury. The coin trick was just icing on the cake, but it was a convenient distraction. "Where did you learn it?"

"My grandfather. He did it all the time when I was a kid."

"My nephews would love it. Can you teach me?" Claire laughed as Jamie pulled a coin from her pocket. "What, you're going to teach me now?"

"Sure, why not. The girls don't need us right now. And I told you, it's easy." Jamie rolled the coin slowly in her hand, showing Claire each step of the trick. "Got it?" she asked. She grasped Claire's hand in hers and pressed the coin into her palm. "You try."

A jolt of electricity coursed through Claire's skin where Jamie's fingers touched hers and she giggled. She gave the trick a try, dropped the coin on the ground, and giggled again. "I think I'm going to need some time," she said.

"That's okay. I'm patient," Jamie replied. Her look suggested that she had something more to say, but whatever it was, she held back.

A shiver tingled along her spine as Jamie spoke, and with it came a sense of liberation that was most unexpected. The day had been filled with surprises, both bad and good. But right now, it was definitely good.

THIRTEEN

STEAM BILLOWED from the pot on the stove as Claire shook the last noodles from the box into the boiling water. Her hand brushed Jamie's arm as she reached to set the kitchen timer. She gave her a shy smile and said, "Keep stirring the sauce a couple minutes, then we'll add the cheese."

"That's all there is to it?" Jamie asked in surprise. "I can't believe I've never made homemade mac-n-cheese before. I might have to try making this the next time the girls come over."

"Do you think they'll come over again soon?" Claire inquired eagerly. It had only been a few days since their trip to the park with Abbey and Zooey, but Claire was already looking forward to their next visit.

"At some point, although I don't know how soon. Paul would love to have them over more often, and Vanessa could use the help, but there's not a lot for them to do when they're here, and no extra bedrooms for them to stay over."

Claire's face fell. "That's my fault, isn't it? I took over their room when I moved in."

"No, not really," Jamie assured her. "That room's not ideal, being on the third floor and with just the one bed. Paul thought about doing something better at one point, but he never had the time."

Claire had a flash of inspiration. "What about the old darkroom?"

"What about it?"

"Well, you said Paul never uses it any more, right? It's about the right size for a playroom, and it's on the second floor so if the girls stayed over they'd be close to Paul's room." Claire removed the noodles from the burner as she spoke, whisking the steaming pot toward the colander that waited in the kitchen sink.

"I guess it would work for something like that." Jamie stirred the sauce as she spoke, and Claire sprinkled in fistfuls of grated cheese.

As the sauce simmered, Paul walked in, pausing to inhale. "Something smells amazing," he said. "What's for dinner?"

"Mac-n-cheese," Claire replied. "Hey, Paul? Jamie and I just came up with an idea for your old darkroom."

"Oh yeah?" He looked from Claire to Jamie.

"Yeah, for the girls, actually," Jamie added. "We thought it could make a nice playroom."

Paul's eyes lit up. "You know, it would." He paused for a moment and frowned. "But I doubt I can tackle a project like that any time soon. I'm swamped with work. Everyone wants photos with the leaves."

"Here," Claire said, placing her hand over Jamie's on the wooden spoon, "stir it more like this so it doesn't stick to the pan." She glanced up at Jamie, then at Paul. "Would you let me work on it?"

"Would you have time?" Jamie asked. "It seems like you're always pretty busy with work."

"I wouldn't mind taking a little break," Claire replied. "But I'm not the only one working overtime. Maybe you'd like to take a break, too, and help me?" She glanced down shyly as she spoke, and in doing so spotted the fact that her hand was still guiding Jamie's. She pulled it away quickly and her cheeks grew hot.

"Maybe I would," Jamie replied thoughtfully.

"You know what? I love this idea." Paul said, looking from Jamie to Claire. There was something in his expression that Claire couldn't quite read. "I'll clear the equipment this weekend so you two can get started."

Claire's head was spinning with excitement for the new project. *And working with Jamie.* She brushed the thought aside. Jamie had a lot of experience in renovations and could teach her so much. Claire had a lot to learn, especially if they were going to pull off the idea for a playroom that had started to form in her imagination.

"Hey, Jamie?" Claire asked, "I was thinking, rather than a strictly utilitarian playroom, what about something a little more unusual?"

"Like, unusual how?"

"More old fashioned, to fit in with the house. Do you

remember the nursery in that *Peter Pan* movie that came out a few years ago?"

Jamie grinned. "I loved that movie, and that's one of my favorite rooms. You know, I think we can create something like it with cheap flea-market-type stuff. I know just the place, this little antique store in the middle of nowhere in New Hampshire. You wanna go shopping with me on Saturday?"

Claire's heart fluttered in anticipation. An antique shopping expedition to New Hampshire with Jamie. Was there a better way to spend a day?

LEAVES of rust and orange fluttered from the trees and landed atop crunchy brown piles as Jamie and Claire tramped across a town common in central New Hampshire toward a weathered barn with a hand-painted sign that read 'Antiques'. Claire could hardly contain her excitement as Jamie opened the shop door and the delicious mustiness of the place wafted through.

Inside was a treasure trove of shabby furniture, yellowed lace, and assorted brick-a-brac just waiting to be rescued and restored.

They had equally keen eyes for spotting just the right items for their project, and soon had everything they needed purchased and loaded into the back of Jamie's old pickup truck. Their shopping done in record time, Claire suggested that they explore the town a little before heading home. It was her first trip to

New Hampshire and she was reluctant to see it end so soon.

The sky was gray and a light drizzle of rain had started to fall as they walked back across the common toward the main street. The pungent smell of woodsmoke from nearby fireplaces filled the air. Claire shivered and wrapped her arms tightly across her chest.

"Are you okay?" Jamie asked, taking in Claire's attire. Claire's jacket was stylish but thin, and she wore neither a hat nor gloves, though she had finally taken Jamie's advice and put on a sensible pair of shoes. "It's just going to get colder as the day goes on. Are you sure you don't want to head back now?"

"But I've never been to New Hampshire before," Claire said, her voice filled with disappointment. "Fall's almost over and I've hardly had a chance to enjoy it."

Jamie thought for a moment. "I have an idea," she said. "Here, wrap your fingers beneath my arm to keep them warm, and follow me."

Claire did as she was told, grateful for the tingling warmth as circulation returned to her fingertips. She held tightly to Jamie's arm, trotting to keep up with the other woman's long strides.

Across from the common was a small main street of brick buildings where a sign in an ancient department store window announced the arrival of new winter gear. Jamie pushed open the heavy glass door with her free arm and they were greeted by a blast of warm air against their frozen faces. Huddled beside Jamie, fingers still gripping her arm, Claire looked around at the contents of the country store. There were bins of woolen mittens, hat stands peppered with fleece lined caps, and rack after rack of heavy winter coats.

Claire stood on tiptoe, pulling Jamie downward by her captive arm. "Are you sure about this place? It looks like where a hunter would come to stock up," she whispered in Jamie's ear.

"Awesome, right?" Jamie replied. "This place has everything you need to survive a New England winter. Come on, let's see what we can find to keep you from freezing to death before fall's even over."

Claire dropped Jamie's arm and followed behind her as they squeezed through the narrow aisles. She cast a doubtful glance at a display of bright red plaid coats. "I don't think I can wear something like that," she said.

Jamie laughed. "Yeah, probably not your style. They have trendier stuff, too. Here," she said, pulling a velvety coat of chocolate brown shearling from another rack and holding it up for inspection. "What about this one?"

Claire peeled off her thin jacket and slipped the coat over her shoulders. It was heavy and warm. Standing in front of a nearby mirror, she turned back and forth, smiling at the way the trim fit nipped in at her waist and showed off the curve of her hips. She caught Jamie's eye in the mirror, also looking appreciatively at her curves. Claire looked away quickly, biting her bottom lip in a bashful smile. "Okay," she said, "you have better taste in clothing than I gave you credit for. I'll take it. What else do I need?"

"Gloves, a hat, some shoes," Jamie rattled off.

"Shoes?" Claire asked in surprise. "What's wrong with the shoes I have on? They're very practical. I wore them because of you!"

"Yes, I noticed them," Jamie responded with a grin. "They're perfect. But not for the snow. You're going to want something waterproof, with a warm lining."

"Oh," Claire said, dejected. "I kinda forgot about the snow." Claire hated winter. If it hadn't been for the promise of meeting Jay, she would never have considered moving to New England. Maybe Jay would want to move to Oregon. She should ask him sometime. She tried to recall exactly when they had last chatted. She gave up in defeat and focused her attention on Jamie again. "Does it snow a lot? I'm really not a huge fan of the cold and the snow."

"Really?" Jamie's voice was tinged with sarcasm. "I never would have guessed. Actually, we don't get a whole lot of snow on the coast, except sometimes when there's a nor'easter."

Claire's mood brightened at the prospect of no snow. *No snow on the coast? That's an excellent sign!* Then she remembered the rest of Jamie's statement and her brow wrinkled. "What's a nor'easter?" she asked, feeling concerned.

"It's a type of storm," Jamie explained. "It can bring a lot of wind and snow off the ocean."

"Well," Claire said, smiling hopefully, "maybe there won't be one of those this year."

"Maybe," Jamie answered, though her tone lacked

conviction. "We could get lucky, but you still need to be prepared."

Claire nodded. She dug through the bin of gloves beside her and chose two pairs to match her coat, then turned her attention to a row of boots. "I don't know," she said after studying them for a few minutes. "These are all so clunky and masculine."

Jamie pointed to a pair with thick rubber soles and an oiled leather upper that reached to mid-calf. "These are really good ones."

"I don't know," Claire repeated. "They look like something you'd wear to go duck hunting or something."

"Hmpf," Jamie replied, "thanks. You know, this is exactly the pair I have at home."

"Sorry," Claire said sheepishly. "No offense. I'm sure they're really great on you."

Claire wandered off to check out a clearance bin next to the stairs that led to the store's second level. A gray and red brushed flannel nightgown caught her eye and she stroked it with her fingertips. Her whole back began to tingle as she felt Jamie's presence a hair's breadth behind her. "Oh, I want this. You should feel how soft this is," she murmured, but there was no response. Claire squealed a moment later as she felt something being pulled tightly onto the top of her head.

"If you're not into duck hunting boots, I guess you're going to tell me this isn't your style, either?" Jamie teased.

Claire whipped around, yanking the thing off her head. She laughed when she saw what it was, a fur lined cap with ear flaps like the one that Elmer Fudd always wore in the cartoons. "Hardly," she said, a mischievous gleam in her eye as she faced Jamie. She hopped onto the step behind her, bringing her eyes level with Jamie's, and jammed the hat onto Jamie's head. As she pulled the flaps snugly around Jamie's ears, Claire's foot slipped and she lunged downward, her arms grasping Jamie's neck, her body pressed tightly against her chest as Jamie clenched her arms around her waist to break Claire's fall.

"You fall over a lot, even with practical shoes," Jamie said as she set Claire gently back on her feet.

Claire's heart pounded wildly and she struggled to slow her rapid breathing. Her body felt like it was on fire along every inch that had pressed against Jamie. She focused on a strand of Jamie's cropped blond hair that was poking out from the crooked hunting cap, unable to think of a reply.

"What do you think?" Jamie asked, breaking the silence. "About the hat? Nothing, huh?" she added after a pause. "I think I'm going to buy it, seeing as how it's left you speechless," she said, stifling a laugh. "I'll meet you up at the register when you're ready, okay?"

Claire watched her walk to the front of the store, still shaken. She was completely mortified. *Why do I trip over my own feet every time she's around?* Claire wondered. She wished she could figure out why Jamie made her feel so off balance, if only so she could do something about it before she caused herself any bodily harm. Claire gathered up her coat and gloves and went in search of the register.

At the front of the store, Jamie was putting the hat

back on her head, laughing as she modeled it for the sales clerk. Claire's shoulder stiffened at the sight of the very pretty clerk writing something down on a piece of paper and slipping it into Jamie's hand. *Her phone number? That little hussy!* Claire gave the clerk a cold stare as she placed her purchases on the counter, and took her bag without so much as a smile, feeling sullen.

"My fingers are still cold and that *girl* put my gloves all the way at the bottom of the bag," Claire whined when they stepped out into the biting air.

Jamie held her arm out and Claire laced her hands around it, burrowing her fingers deep into the space against Jamie's side. A little shiver coursed through her as Jamie's arm tightened against her hands, pulling her closer. Claire chalked it up to blustery weather. The leaves on the common, now soggy with rain, squished beneath their feet as they strolled back to the truck arm in arm for the long drive back to the coast.

FOURTEEN

IT WAS the day before Thanksgiving and every inch of Logan Airport was packed with travelers. "Theresa!" Claire called out as she spotted her sister waiting next to a carousel in baggage claim. Her voice was drowned out by the shriek of the buzzer as the metal belt started to turn. Claire tried again, even louder, and was relieved to see her sister's head turn in her direction. Darting through the crowd, Claire arrived at her side just as a stream of bags came down the chute amidst loud clanks and thuds.

"That was quick!" Claire said as Theresa's bag appeared in the first group to make its way around the curve.

"Funny, I was thinking the same thing!" Theresa replied. "I've never seen you move so fast before in my life. Do my eyes deceive me or are you actually wearing practical walking shoes right now?"

Claire laughed, stretching out a foot to better admire

her ballet flats. "I am! Do you like them? Jamie insisted I buy some better shoes. I think she was getting tired of having to carry me home all the time."

"Oh?" Her sister's short response was packed with curiosity.

"I'm just clumsy, that's all," Claire replied, bristling at something in her sister's tone. "And we've been doing a lot of walking, especially at the antique shops and flea markets."

"You've been dragging Jamie to flea markets? Poor girl."

"I'd hardly say I dragged her. She loves antiquing more than I do."

"I find that hard to believe."

"No, seriously. And her eye for finding just the right thing is better than mine, to be honest. But don't you dare tell her I said that," Claire said.

"I look forward to meeting her," her sister replied. "You obviously find her very... talented."

Claire's stomach fluttered nervously at this observation. She knew what Theresa was thinking right now, what she was implying with her seemingly innocent remarks. Why couldn't her sister just be happy for her that she'd made a friend? Why was she so determined to see something that wasn't there? *Thank God she doesn't know Jamie dates women*, she thought. And she would never find out, if Claire had her way. She was thrilled for her visit but would have to keep a close eye on Theresa this weekend.

When they reached the house, Claire raced directly

to the second floor with her sister following close behind. She flung open the door to what had, until recently, been Paul's darkroom. The space was now completely transformed. The walls had been painted pale pink and the ceiling made to look like a blue sky filled with fluffy white clouds. There were two tiny ivory and gold beds with matching canopies of antique crocheted lace. Wooden steamer trunks sat at the foot of each bed, overflowing with assorted teddy bears. A miniature table in the center of the room was set with a tin teapot painted with delicate pink roses, the crystals of a chandelier emitting rainbow sparkles just overhead.

High atop a ladder in the center of the room stood Jamie, dabbing a brush of white paint against a plaster ceiling medallion. Claire let out a squeak when she saw her, surprised to find her home so early. Jamie turned at the sound and set the brush back in the paint can. Claire watched Jamie descend the ladder, shrinking in stature from impossibly giant-like to merely very tall the closer she got to the floor. Her gaze lingered on Jamie's khaki coveralls. The cut and color emphasized her height, and...there was something else. Claire felt a funny buzzing in the back of her brain, like there was something she should remember that was escaping her. She brushed the sensation aside as Jamie held out her paint speckled hand to Theresa, too nervous over them meeting to think of anything else.

"You must be Theresa," Jamie said, extending a paint splattered hand.

"Pleasure to meet you, Jamie," Theresa said. "So this

is what you and my sister have been up to the past few weeks, huh? It's spectacular!"

"Oh, that's all Claire's doing," Jamie replied. "I mostly just use a paint brush."

"Huh, well, that's not how she tells it. She says you're a genius when it comes to this restoration stuff," Theresa said, and Jamie grinned.

The look that passed between them felt conspiratorial to Claire, who cleared her throat loudly from the doorway. She was anxious to to show Theresa the rest of the house. And to stop her from talking to Jamie too much. Her sister's behavior seemed a little strange every time Jamie was mentioned, and something about it made Claire jittery. She didn't want to leave them alone together longer than was necessary.

"Come on, sis," she called, "don't you want to get settled in? I set up an extra bed for you upstairs in my room. Wait until you see the view!"

"Nice to meet you, Theresa," Jamie said, still grinning. "You'll have to tell me all the rest of what Claire said about me later!"

The following afternoon, Theresa, Claire, Jamie, and Paul sat in the dining room, their mouths and forks filled with turkey and all the fixings, the mahogany table and sideboard straining under the weight of all the platters. The house smelled delectably of the meal that Jamie and Claire had started preparing before the sun rose that morning.

"This meal was absolutely amazing," Theresa said, breaking the silence. "So, Jamie, you cook, too?"

"No," Jamie said with a laugh. "And I'm serious this time. This really was all your sister's doing. She planned the whole meal herself and made everything from scratch. I just followed directions."

"Well," Theresa said, looking around the room at all the food, "I can believe that. My sister learned how to cook from our Aunt Marisol, and she always made enough to feed an army. This would definitely give her a run for her money. I'm betting there are at least twenty desserts hiding back in the kitchen right now, too."

"That's a bit of an exaggeration," Claire chastised her sister. "Besides, it's not like you don't do the same thing. I was just excited to finally have a chance to cook Thanksgiving dinner for my big sister. I still can't believe you were able to come!"

"How could I not, *hermanita*?" her sister replied. "You told me you were so homesick you might die if I didn't. Talk about exaggerating, you're obviously doing just fine."

Claire felt her cheeks prick with heat at the memory of that particular phone call. It'd been shortly after she arrived, when she still thought the only way to control herself around Jamie was to hide in her room. She was glad to have gotten over that foolishness and given herself a chance to become Jamie's friend. "It was a rough start. But I'm glad you came, even if I am feeling much better now." Claire pushed her chair back. "But speaking of dessert, I should go get them ready. Paul, are you staying?"

"No," he replied. "I promised Vanessa I'd join her

and Pete and the girls for dessert. In fact, I should head over there now."

Paul pushed his own chair away from the table, standing to give Claire a hug. He did the same to Jamie. When he got to Theresa's chair she put out her hand, but he ignored it and smothered her in a bear hug, too. After Paul left, Claire disappeared into the kitchen to prepare dessert.

ALONE AT THE TABLE, Theresa turned to face Jamie. "Oh good. Now we get to talk, just the two of us."

Jamie's stomach fluttered in a mixture of surprise and alarm. "Sure," she said, keeping her tone as neutral as she could. "What did you want to talk about?"

Theresa smiled. "Relax. Nothing bad. This move hasn't been as easy on my sister as she makes it sound, you know. But she seems so much happier than she did just a month ago, and I'm pretty sure I have you to thank for that, Jamie."

Jamie shrugged, studying the edge of the tablecloth. "That's what friends are for, right?"

"Friends. Hm." Theresa said. "Jamie, since there's no one else in here right now, do you mind if I ask you something?"

Jamie looked at her expectantly. "Sure. Go ahead."

"You like my sister, right?"

"Of course," Jamie said cautiously. "Like I said, we're friends."

"That's not what I meant," Theresa countered. "Not to make this too awkward, but you're interested in Claire, right?"

"Did Claire tell you that I date women?" Jamie asked, surprised.

"Would you be offended if I said it was sort of obvious?"

Jamie laughed. "I suppose it is. I would have been more surprised if you said Claire mentioned it to you. She seems a little skittish about that particular topic."

"The words you're looking for are prudish and terrified. But she was raised by an elderly woman who would have made a great nun, and she's spent most of her adult life immersed in Victorian literature. How else is she going to be?" Theresa shrugged. "But back to my point. It seems to me like you are. Interested in her, that is."

Jamie sighed. It was only natural that her sister would be concerned. "Look, Theresa. If Claire wanted a relationship with me, would I jump at the chance? Absolutely. But she doesn't, so you don't have to worry about that."

"No, Jamie, you misunderstand me—I'm not worried. Far from it." Theresa swiveled her head toward the kitchen door where the muffled sound of a mixer indicated that Claire was still busy with dessert. She lowered her voice. "Claire has gone through a complete transformation since she came here. I haven't seen her this happy in years."

"She must really like her new job," Jamie suggested,

trying to tamp down the excitement that was bubbling up inside.

Theresa snorted. "That crappy job she took as an excuse to move here? Yeah, she tried to fool me about that, but she forgets I know people." Theresa shook her head. "It's not the job. I think it's because of you."

"Me?" Jamie asked, surprised. There was no logical reason to believe that it had anything to do with her. Yet, she couldn't help a sudden surge of hope.

Theresa lowered her voice. "The thing is, I've suspected for a long time that my sister is more attracted to women than she admits. Which she doesn't."

"But what about Jay?" Jamie's tone was bitter. "That's really why she moved here. She says she's in love with him."

"Jay?" Theresa laughed as if to dismiss the idea. "He doesn't exist."

Jamie's eyebrows shot up as an icy chill ran down her spine.

"I mean, obviously he exists, but he might as well be imaginary," she continued. "She's done stuff like this before, you know."

"Like what?" Jamie asked. She slowly let out the breath she hadn't realized she was holding.

"Pretended to be in love. When she was young, my sister put some random boy's picture in a frame and told her friends that he was her boyfriend from summer camp. She spent a whole year in college obsessing over a foreign pen pal, only to chicken out right before they were going to meet face to face. So I know what it looks like when my sister is trying to convince herself she's in love," Theresa concluded. "That's not how it looks this time. This is something new."

Jamie swallowed hard. "But it's the 21st century. Obviously, you're supportive of her. Why wouldn't she just say something?"

"You know our parents died when Claire was nine, right? And we went to live with our great aunt."

"Aunt Marisol," Jamie said with a snort. "Yeah, Claire's mentioned her."

"I'll bet. She had very traditional views, not just about sexuality but pretty much everything. She's also a master of manipulation. She had a way of getting you to do things her way without you even realizing it."

"And she used this manipulation on Claire?" Jamie felt a stab of anger at the thought.

"Constantly. Our parents were pretty open minded. At least that's the way I remember them. But Aunt Marisol used their memory like a weapon. If our aunt didn't like something, she'd say we were dishonoring our parents' memory. And Claire idolized our parents, so she took that seriously."

"So she acts the way she does because she thinks that's what your parents wanted?" It didn't make sense to Jamie. As much as she wanted to please her mother, she'd never lied about who she was to do it.

Theresa nodded. "And eventually she just absorbed a lot of our aunt's prejudices and opinions because it was easier than fighting."

Jamie sat in pensive silence for a moment. "So, what do you think I should do?" she finally asked.

"I think she just needs a reason to finally fight. Maybe you can be that reason."

"What about Jay?" Jamie asked hesitantly.

"Jay." Theresa sighed, shaking her head. "That's right, he's a friend of yours. Is that going to be an issue for you?"

Jamie shrugged her shoulders dismissively.

Theresa chuckled. "All's fair in love and war, right?" Theresa sighed again, "Jay was never part of my plan, you know."

"Your plan?" Jamie sounded surprised.

"Yeah, my plan. The whole reason I gave Claire that subscription to Tech Cupid in the first place was that I read somewhere that it was the hottest new site for same-sex dating."

"It is," Jamie agreed. "But she didn't think that was strange."

"Please. My sister is so naive," Theresa answered. "And they had straight categories, too, so Claire didn't suspect. I just figured once she was in private, her curiosity might lead her in the right direction. I guess I should've known better. She is unbelievably stubborn."

Jamie and Theresa shared a laugh.

CLAIRE STOOD FROZEN IN PLACE, the pie tins in her hands momentarily forgotten as she listened to

Theresa and Jamie talk from the other side of the kitchen door. *My sister had a plan, did she? How dare she!* Claire was livid. *And she thinks Aunt Marisol is the manipulative one?*

Claire's mind was reeling. No wonder she'd been so confused lately. *This is Theresa's fault!* Theresa was the one putting ideas into her head, encouraging Jamie behind her back, making her question her feelings for Jamie when she should have been focusing on Jay. *Jay...*

Claire's stomach tightened into a knot. She hadn't written to him in weeks, not since that night before she and Jamie took the girls to the park, where she had met that woman who had the wife and the son, and then her thinking had gone all topsy-turvy. *Damn it, Theresa. He's going to hate me now. What has your meddling made me do?*

Claire adjusted the pies in her hands and plastered a smile on her face before opening the door to the dining room. She was already formulating a plan to fix this mess, and neither her sister nor Jamie needed to know anything about it. She'd write to Jay tonight, apologize, never see Jamie again— whatever she had to do to make things right—before it was too late.

Her heart sank at the prospect of losing Jamie's friendship, but it couldn't be helped. There was no way she was going to put up with being lied to and having her emotions manipulated by anyone else. Not ever again.

FIFTEEN

"COME ON, JAY," Paul whined. "If you don't finish soon, we're going to miss the show." Paul swiveled impatiently on a chair in the cubicle outside Jamie's office. He'd arrived right after work to go to a movie, and Jamie had already kept him waiting twice as long as promised.

"Sorry, I'm almost done, I swear," she called. Jamie squinted at the spreadsheet containing fifty years of temperature data from the Greenland seas. She sighed. She'd promised to report her findings to Dr. Swenson on Monday. Her eyes ached. She'd been staring at the figures for hours, but it felt like days. Jamie felt strongly that the Institute should hold off on publishing Dr. Matthews' study, but she was going to have to convince her boss. It would mean working the whole weekend instead of spending it with Claire. The timing couldn't possibly have been worse.

Just when Jamie had been ready to give up and admit that any attraction she had sensed from Claire was entirely in her imagination, everything changed. Jamie had gone from pining after Claire while she slept, convinced she would always be out of reach, to waking up in an alternate universe where they cooked dinner together and spent the weekends scouring every out-of-the-way corner of the state for playroom furnishings. It was like all of Jamie's prayers had been answered. It'd been the best month of her life.

Even better, not a single message from Claire had appeared in Jay's inbox for weeks. The whole unfortunate Jay incident was finally behind her.

Or so it seemed, until last week, when Claire disappeared into her room right after dropping her sister off at the airport. Shortly thereafter a pinging noise rang out to announce a new message for Jay. Jamie had no idea what had changed, but she wasn't taking this new turn of events well at all.

Jamie slammed her fist down on her desk in frustration and sent a pile of folders cascading to the floor. "Damn it!"

"Hey, don't hurt yourself in there," Paul said. "Is this just the work deadline that's got you upset, or is it something else?"

"It's Claire," Jamie admitted with a sigh. "She sent another message to Jay this morning. That's three times this week."

"I thought she was done with that. You said she hadn't contacted Jay since the middle of October."

"Well, I thought it was over, too. We were spending so much time together, and she was opening up to me, and I really thought... hell, Paul, her own sister basically told me Claire was in love with me and that she gave me her stamp of approval. I really thought something was finally happening between us."

"But Claire never actually broke it off with Jay. Officially, I mean?"

Jamie sighed again. "No."

"And you never had Jay break it off with her, or tell her he wasn't coming back to Boston, or anything like that? Weren't you supposed to do that weeks ago?"

"Yeah, but...I didn't even think of it. I didn't think it would be necessary. I'll admit, I should have gotten rid of Jay when she moved here, but she wasn't talking to me. I had no other way to know what she was thinking."

"Yeah, that reason sounds a lot more creepy and a lot less convincing than you probably thought it would."

"Fine. You're right. It wasn't my best moment. I should have told her as soon as I found out about the profile glitch, or if not then, at least on the day she walked into the Marine Institute looking for Jay. I don't know why I can't just be honest with her."

"Because honesty would have ruined your chances then. Let's face it though, Girly. You're not the only one who isn't being honest. If she's reaching out to Jay again, Claire's lying to herself, big time."

"I don't even think she likes him that much, so much as, she finds his existence reassuring. Seriously, if I think about how the imaginary Jay has treated her since we met in real life, he's kind of a jerk."

"She wouldn't be the first girl to fall for a jerk," Paul pointed out.

"I swear, I should just kill him off."

"Best idea yet, Girly."

"I'm so afraid she'll end up running back to Portland and I'll lose her forever." Jamie finished re-stacking the folders and set them on her desk with a look of resignation. "Just give me five more minutes, okay? I promise I'll be ready."

Paul shrugged and swiveled around in his chair, passing the time by playing with the computer on the desk where he sat. As promised, after five minutes Jamie switched off her light and emerged from her office.

"Ready to go?" she asked.

"Hey, Jay, come check this out," he replied, beckoning her toward the computer screen.

"What's this?" she asked.

"Something to amuse you. Take a look."

Jamie read the email on the screen. "Oh my God. Paul, that's sick," she said with a chuckle. "I was joking. You're really sick, my friend."

"But you laughed. It's funny, right?" he countered with a grin.

"You think killing off Jay in a blizzard in Antarctica is funny?"

"I only implied he was dead. He could just be missing." Paul smiled. "You want me to print this out for you? Or send it?"

Jamie reread the fake email that Paul had composed while she finished her work. He'd written it on an official Marine Institute template, addressed to Claire's email and everything. It looked very authentic, and the truth was it cheered her up, even if she didn't want to admit it. Part of her really wanted to print it and take it home with her. *A very perverse part.* An even more perverse part wished she could press send and be rid of Jay forever, consequences be damned. She shook her head to clear the impulse. She'd never do that to Claire. She hadn't even been able to ignore Jay's messages for longer than a day because she knew Claire would be hurt by it. *I'm never going to get myself out of this.*

"Come on Paul, stop fooling around. Do not hit print, and whatever you do, do not hit send. Just get rid of it," Jamie demanded. "How did you get onto this computer, anyway? It's supposed to be locked, and we both know you're no hacker."

"Dude left his password on a sticky note under the keyboard. You don't have to be a hacker to break through that kind of security."

Jamie groaned. "I should tell Dr. Swenson about this."

"About Jay?" Paul asked in surprise.

"God, no. Are you kidding me? I meant about my research assistant, Alan, putting his password under his keyboard. It's a violation of protocol."

"Well, *protocol*. La di da. Why do you care? It's not your job."

"No, but it could be. I know you don't really understand lofty career ambitions, but I have a real shot at being the next Head of Research. It would be a huge promotion. And a raise, too."

"Oh yeah? Great! You and Claire can buy your own house and decorate kids' rooms to your heart's content and I can get my bachelor pad back. All your feminine domesticity has put a serious crimp in my sangria parties."

Jamie snorted. "Ha! How exactly am I going to make all of that happen?"

"How about you tell her the truth?"

"You just agreed with me that telling her the truth would ruin my chances."

"The truth about Jay, maybe. But what about the truth about how you feel about her? You said yourself that it's not Jay she cares about. She wants to be in love, and get married, and have a house and a family. Is that what you want?"

Jamie nodded. "With Claire? Of course."

"So tell her. She'll choose you over Jay, I'm sure of it. Of course I can just send her this email and make the choice easier for her..."

"Very funny, Paul. Come on, delete that thing and shut off the computer so we can get to the theater before the show starts."

"Alright," he said, with a final flourish of fingers on the keyboard. "All done. I still say it's a waste of a masterpiece, though."

As they walked toward the theater, Jamie thought about what Paul had said. *Tell her the truth.* Could the answer really be so simple? Surely Claire already knew that Jamie wanted the same things she did. But then again, as far as Claire knew, Jamie loved hosting midweek sangria parties with Paul and enjoyed her reputation for dating lots of women.

A reputation that I know makes Claire insanely jealous. Jamie chuckled to herself at the memory of how Claire had reacted toward the sales clerk in that store when she'd thought Jamie had been flirting with her. It had been all Jamie could do not to skip the whole way back to the truck that day.

Maybe Paul was right. Maybe Claire just needed some assurance that she and Jamie wanted the same things before being willing to open herself up and take a risk. Jamie resolved to find some way to tell Claire the truth about her feelings for her. She just prayed it would work.

SIXTEEN

CLAIRE WALKED along the cobblestones of the Marina Marketplace, admiring the Christmas displays in the shop windows and trying not to focus on the hulking mass of the Marine Institute across the street. The building was closed to the public at this hour, but Claire knew Jamie was probably still working inside. Her heart fell at the thought of Jamie, sitting alone at her desk. She hadn't seen her in almost a week and she felt the absence like a physical pain.

It'd been five days since her sister left and she had retreated back into her tower room, hiding away from Jamie while she tried to fix the mess she'd made with Jay. *It isn't fair.* None of this was fair, especially not to Jamie. None of this was Jamie's fault.

Claire was still furious with Theresa for manipulating her, but when she thought of Jamie, she mostly felt sadness. If only things could be different, if only there was some way that she could still be friends with Jamie without jeopardizing the future that she had always envisioned... but it simply wasn't possible. She'd been able to control her impulses in the past where certain close female friends were concerned, but Claire's defenses were weak when Jamie was around.

She was going to have to find a new place to live. Tears stung the corners of Claire's eyes, and she blinked rapidly to keep them at bay. She loved the house on Cape Ann, loved the tower room and the view, and the new playroom she and Jamie had worked together to create. She'd been looking forward to playing there with Abbey and Zooey after Christmas. She was going to miss them, and Jamie, and Paul. The image of them was so clear in her mind that she almost felt like she could hear the ringing of their laughter in her head.

No, that's not in my head. Claire stopped walking and looked toward the Marine Institute. Paul and Jamie had just exited a side door and were heading straight for where she stood. Claire glanced around furtively but the shops along the street were closing for the night and there was no place to hide.

"Claire?" Jamie called from across the street. "Is that you? What are you doing out here tonight?"

Claire waved at her friends, pretending she hadn't spotted them until just then. "Just doing some Christmas shopping after work, but it looks like everything's closing, so I'm about to head home and grade papers."

"Papers on a Friday night?" Jamie's expression was sympathetic. "Paul and I were just heading to a movie at the little theater at the end of the block. Did you want to come along?"

Claire hesitated, fighting back the urge to say yes. "I really shouldn't. I have so much work to finish."

"Are you sure?" Jamie asked, disappointment evident on her face.

The only thing Claire was sure of was that she wanted to spend the evening with Jamie like she'd never wanted anything before in her life. "I don't know, I—"

"Oh, dang!" Paul interjected loudly, looking at his phone. "I forgot I had that thing tonight."

"That thing?" Jamie asked.

"Yes, you remember the thing I told you about," Paul said pointedly. "I'm afraid I won't be able to go tonight after all, but how lucky that we ran into Claire! I'm sure she can take a couple of hours away from grading papers to keep you company and make sure you're not all alone and friendless. Right, Claire? It would be a huge favor if you got me off the hook, here."

"Well, I guess I can," Claire agreed.

"You really don't have to keep me company if you have things to do, Claire," Jamie told her after Paul left. "I understand."

Claire's emotions warred within her. It was one thing to try to keep her distance from Jamie, and another thing entirely to have enough willpower to walk away now that she was here. The allure of spending the evening with Jamie was just too great, and she quickly gave in. "As long as I have it ready for Monday, I think I can take a few hours off tonight."

A smile lit up Jamie's face. "Fantastic! You've been working a lot lately. You could probably use some time to relax."

Claire sighed. "I honestly could. This job is a nightmare. My schedule's a mess, they have me filling in all over the department. When I was in Portland, I was pretty sure I had a good future ahead of me, but I can't ever see that happening here. And back home when I was stressed, I could at least get out on the water, but it's too cold now to even go sailing."

Jamie thought for a moment. "I have an idea. You don't have your heart set on going to a movie tonight, do you? Because I think there's something you'd enjoy way more, if you don't mind a little bit of risk."

"Risk?" Claire repeated, nervous but intrigued.

"Not a lot," Jamie assured her. "It's not exactly allowed, but people do it all the time. You in?"

"You haven't told me what it is yet."

"And I'm not going to," Jamie told her. "It's a surprise. Are you willing to trust me?"

She knew it was a bad idea. It was herself she couldn't trust. But one look at Jamie's mischievous grin and Claire couldn't say no. "Lead the way."

Jamie held out her hand. Claire hesitated, then decided she was already making such a colossal error in judgment by going with her at all that it didn't really matter. She slipped her gloved hand into Jamie's and allowed herself to be pulled across the street and along the path toward the Marine Institute's side entrance.

Jamie dropped her hand when they reached the door

long enough to swipe the key card from her back pocket. Claire laughed. "Another one of your magic keys?" she teased.

"You'll see," Jamie replied, taking her hand again and starting up the flight of stairs in front of them. They went up three stories, then down a long hallway that ended at a door to a locker room. Jamie opened one of the gray metal lockers and rummaged inside, finally pulling out a fistful of swimsuits. "This is where we keep the extras. Take a look and see if one of these will fit," she instructed. She opened another locker and grabbed her own suit, then headed toward a door at the far end of the room. "There are showers and changing rooms through here," she said.

Claire chose a navy blue one piece that looked about the right size and followed Jamie into the next room. There was a towel waiting for her on one of the changing room doors. She changed quickly, then rinsed in the warm spray of the shower, and emerged, dripping beneath her towel, a few minutes later. Jamie was already waiting for her next to a sign with an arrow that pointed toward the dive platform.

"We're not going diving in that big ocean tank, are we?" Claire asked in surprise.

"Diving? No. That would get me fired. There are at least a hundred forms and insurance waivers you have to sign before you can use the equipment. We're just going for a little swim."

"For a swim in the tank? Not, like, some employee pool or something?"

Jamie laughed. "The Institute's pretty generous, but not enough to put in a private pool for its employees."

"And it's okay for us to go in?" Claire asked, her voice filled with awe as she approached the edge of the platform and peered down into the vast tank of clear water.

"Technically? Of course not," Jamie replied. She was seated on the platform with her feet dangling in the water. "I told you. We're breaking the rules tonight."

Claire's body tingled at those words. *Exactly how many rules am I willing to break?*

She watched Jamie trace circles in the water with her toes. Her long legs glistened with droplets of water from the shower. Claire's gaze traveled slowly upward, taking in the slight curve of Jamie's hips, the bare expanse of her back, her strong swimmer's shoulders and lean, muscular arms.

Claire's breath had grown shallow and it occurred to her to be grateful that Jamie was wearing a very modest suit, as anything more revealing might have sent her passing out into the tank. Drowning during their clandestine swim would almost certainly get Jamie fired. She shouldn't even be looking at Jamie. Not in this way. She was failing miserably at her rules, but not dying and getting Jamie fired should be one rule she could manage not to break.

Jamie lowered herself all the way into the water, flipping her body around with practiced ease to face Claire. "You coming?" she asked, chuckling as Claire attempted to slide from the diving platform while still clutching her towel tightly to her chest with one hand. "It's easier if you leave the towel up there," she pointed out. "Need me to turn around, or something?"

Jamie laughed out loud as Claire tossed the towel aside and, with a look of determination, jumped from the platform into the water. Her head bobbed up several feet beyond the platform, where she tread water for a moment before noticing an outcropping of artificial rock in the center that formed a small island. Claire swam toward it, coming to a rest with her back and elbows against the rock, kicking her legs gently to stay afloat. Jamie joined her.

"So, what do you think?" Jamie asked.

"It's spectacular," Claire answered, looking around appreciatively. "I don't know how I feel about a pool that's three stories deep, but it's so warm and relaxing that right now, I don't think I care."

"Yeah, it's like visiting the Caribbean without ever leaving Cape Ann. And you've already discovered the secret island. Even though the water's deep, if you swim out to the middle, you can rest here all day. It's not that different from sitting in a hot tub, really."

"Do you do that a lot, sit here all day?"

"Uh, no," Jamie responded with a snort. "It's not exactly part of the job description. And when I do get to take a turn, I'm expected to, well, work."

"Still, you're so lucky. Going to work would be a lot easier if I had this there."

"Your job is really that bad?" There was sympathy in Jamie's tone.

"It's just not what I expected. Then again, nothing about moving here is what I expected."

"Do you miss Portland? Your family?"

Claire thought about that for a moment and realized that returning to Portland held little appeal to her. Her family was another matter. Even though she was angry with her, she missed her sister immensely. Her meddling, nosy sister who was usually, infuriatingly, right about most things. Even when Claire didn't want to admit it.

She felt the gentle pressure of Jamie's hand coming to rest on her shoulder. Claire tensed and her mind flooded with a million reasons that she needed to make this stop. But for some reason, it just wasn't as convincing as usual. Maybe it was the soothing effect of the salt water that left her unable to fight. Her body relaxed, her brain no longer thinking, just feeling the reassuring warmth of Jamie's hand.

Claire drew closer, slipping her own arm gently around Jamie's waist, melting against her as she rested her head against Jamie's shoulder. She closed her eyes and breathed slowly and deeply, a delicious shiver running through her as she felt Jamie's fingers slide from her shoulder to the base of her neck, twirling a damp tendril of hair into a tight corkscrew around her fingertip. Claire remained still, her heartbeat steady, allowing herself to be rocked by the peaceful movement of the water. Her ear pressing tightly against Jamie's skin, Claire could hear the sound as Jamie swallowed, and the hitch in her breath just before she spoke.

"Claire," Jamie whispered, "there's something I need

to tell you. I think...I think that I'm falling in love with you."

Claire rested silently against Jamie, feeling strangely peaceful. Her breathing remained steady as Jamie's words washed over her. She thought she'd feel more terrified when the time finally came. She'd known that it was coming, of course. She'd probably known it as she took Jamie's hand on the cobblestone street, and while she watched Jamie's toes drawing circles in the water, and certainly when she leaned into Jamie's embrace.

I could have stopped it at any point, but I didn't. It's no one's fault but my own. But she knew, deep down, that no one was to blame for anything. She'd needed to hear Jamie say the words, ever since she had overheard her and Theresa's conversation in the dining room. Now that she had, Claire had no idea what to do next. But she was very calm about it.

"Have I ruined everything by telling you?"

Claire shook her head no.

"Are you going to say anything?"

Jamie's voice sounded small and nervous, and the uncertainty in it tugged at Claire's heart. Claire tightened her arm around Jamie, squeezing her waist with her fingertips. "None of this is what I expected," she finally said. "It's a lot to think about."

"But it's something you *will* think about? You won't hide from me, or run away?"

Claire took a deep breath in and out. She nodded her head slowly in reply before resting it against Jamie's shoulder again and letting the peace and tranquility of the water wash over her. She listened to the gentle whoosh of Jamie's breath. Closing her eyes, she pictured Jamie's lips, slightly parted, as the air rushed in and out. For a moment Claire let her mind wander, allowed herself to imagine how Jamie's lips would feel against hers, imagined the salty taste of her skin. She shivered in longing, but also in fear. Claire's heart raced and for a moment she was overcome with the urge to bolt, to swim back to the platform and disappear. But she'd promised. No hiding. No running. So she stayed, waiting for her pulse to slow. Knowing that, in truth, there was no place else she'd rather be.

SEVENTEEN

JAMIE LOOKED up from her book as a staccato chime emanated from her phone. Her heart skipped a beat until she saw that it was just the latest update from the weather service and not a new message in Jay's Tech Cupid account. She breathed a sigh of relief. She and Claire hadn't discussed their late night swim since it had happened two weeks before, but as long as there were no new attempts to contact Jay, Jamie refused to be concerned.

True to her promise, Claire had not avoided her. They had gone back to spending the evenings together just as they had done before her sister's visit, often cooking dinner together or putting the finishing touches on the playroom project. The only thing they didn't do was discuss the fact that Jamie was in love with Claire, or what Claire planned to do about it. It was hard for Jamie to live in suspense, but she preferred that to finding out

Claire didn't love her via an email to her evil nemesis, Jay.

A loud stomping from outside the front door brought Jamie out of her musings. The door opened with a blast of cold air and Claire stumbled inside, weighed down by several shopping bags in her arms. Flakes of snow clung to her coat and boots as she placed them next to the hall tree, and Jamie was surprised to realize that the snow had been falling steadily enough throughout the afternoon to coat the landscape outside the living room window in a solid layer of white. Remembering the alert on her phone, Jamie checked the message and saw that a major nor'easter was predicted to arrive within the next twenty-four hours. Today's dusting was just a prelude to the major front that would blow in late on Christmas day.

"Have you heard about the storm?" Claire asked, setting her array of shopping bags down in a pile by the door. "I think it's already starting. I just made it back from the store in time."

Jamie surveyed the pile of bags in amusement. "This is just a squall. It'll let up soon. I'm curious, though. Did you leave anything at the store for the other people?"

"I just wanted to be prepared! I've never been through a nor'easter, you know."

"I know, I know. I'm just teasing you. Come on, let me help you get these into the kitchen." Jamie looped several of the bags over her arm and headed to the other room where she started to laugh as she unpacked the contents onto the counter. "Two dozen eggs, three pounds of butter, a box of fifty votive candles...it's just a winter storm, Claire, not the start of Armageddon."

"I admit, I might've gotten a little carried away," Claire replied with a sheepish grin. "There was a shopping frenzy at the supermarket and I was afraid I'd forget something important and they'd be sold out of it when I went back. I wasn't sure what we'd need, so I just looked in the other carts and bought what they were buying."

"The water bottles and bread might be useful, but the baking supplies? I hate to tell you this, but I think maybe the person with that cart was just getting ready to make some last minute Christmas cookies."

"Oh no," Claire moaned, covering her face in embarrassment. "You're probably right. I was just so nervous about the storm that I couldn't think straight."

"Claire, are you really that worried?" Jamie asked softly, an expression of concern on her face.

Claire nodded. "I know it seems like I'm overreacting. It's just, well, you know that my parents died in an accident, right?"

"Does that have something to do with it?"

Claire nodded again. "They'd gone away for the weekend and were driving through a mountain pass on their way home late at night. A big storm hit. Their car hit a patch of ice and they went off the road and into a ravine."

"Claire," Jamie said, "I'm so sorry."

"Ever since then, big storms always make me nervous, especially snow and ice. Which we don't get a lot of back in Portland, but here..." Claire's voice trailed off with a shrug of her shoulders.

"But you decided to move here, even with our notorious winters. Why?" Jamie's stomach tightened into a knot as she asked. *Please don't say Jay.* If Claire was still stuck on that fantasy after all this time, Jamie had no hope of ever being able to compete.

"It's where I'm supposed to be." She said it simply, like the answer was obvious. "When I came here for the interview and you took me sailing on the harbor, I was looking at the Boston skyline and wanted so badly to stay. And right then, I got the message about the job. It was a sign. I don't argue when it comes to signs." Claire smiled. "I just wish I'd get a sign that we're not all going to die in this storm!"

Jamie's heart leaped at Claire's words. *She didn't mention Jay at all!* She laughed with giddiness. "I don't know about a sign, but I do have an idea to distract you from your insane nervousness."

"Does it involve one of your magical key cards? You seem to have one for every occasion."

Jamie noted the sudden rush of color in Claire's cheeks and wondered if she was thinking about their dip in the ocean tank.

Jamie's body temperature rose a few degrees remembering the feel of Claire's arm at her waist and the faint scent of shampoo when her damp locks of hair rested against her shoulder. She was reminded, too, of the coy look Claire had first stolen her heart with when they sat in the rooftop garden over the summer, because it was almost identical to the way Claire looked at her now. *Does Claire have any idea what that look does to me?* She felt a pang of regret that her current plan didn't, in fact, involve a key. Keys had worked out pretty well for her where Claire was concerned.

"No," she answered, "this time it involves using some of these groceries you bought. There's enough butter here to bake cookies for half the town. We could use some extras to put out when the twins come over tomorrow morning for Christmas, and it'll keep your mind off the storm."

Claire's face broke into an excited grin, "Perfect! Besides, I've been promising Paul for months that I'd bake for him, and I have yet to deliver."

Jamie laughed. "Well, then, there's no time like the present. Besides," she added, "if we do get a storm bad enough to need all these supplies, we'll probably lose power and then the oven won't work, anyway."

"I didn't even think about that," she admitted. "No wonder you're laughing at my storm preparations. I obviously have no idea what I'm doing!"

"That's okay. You're a lot better in the kitchen than I am, so how about you take the lead on the cookies and leave protecting us from the storm to me." Jamie looked into Claire's eyes and the heat inside her cranked up another degree. "How does that sound?"

"It sounds just about perfect," Claire replied softly, blushing as she looked away.

With dough mixed and cookies baking in the oven a short time later, Jamie scraped the remnants of gooey batter from the mixing bowl, licking her fingers in satisfaction.

"What are you doing?" Claire asked, clearly horrified. "You can't eat that!"

"What are you talking about?" Jamie was equally horrified. "This is the whole point of making cookies. Baking them is secondary."

"Aunt Marisol never let me eat raw dough. She said it wasn't good for you."

"Your Aunt Marisol never let you do anything fun. Seriously, I don't even know how you've lived this long without eating raw cookie dough. Here," Jamie said, offering Claire the metal bowl.

Claire looked inside the bowl where Jamie's fingers had scraped bare tracks in the thin coating of dough. With a look of rebellion, she scooped a small glob onto her finger and put it in her mouth. Jamie broke into a grin as Claire's face transformed in a rapture of ecstasy.

"See? I told you. It's the best part." She grinned devilishly. "Makes me wonder about all the other forbidden things you've been missing out on all these years."

Claire studied Jamie's face for a moment, her expression unreadable as her gaze fluttered between eyes and mouth. Suddenly, the bowl was tossed aside and Jamie felt Claire's arms around her shoulders, pressing into her as she raised up on tiptoe to press her lips against Jamie's. As quickly as it had happened, it was over, leaving Jamie's head spinning as Claire looked shyly away.

Were it not for the lingering taste of vanilla from the

cookie dough on Claire's lips, Jamie would have thought her imagination was running wild again.

"Well," Claire said, breaking the silence, "that was one of them." She looked at Jamie with wide eyes, her breath quick and shallow. She looked as surprised at the kiss as Jamie felt, like she couldn't quite believe what she had done.

Jamie pressed her lips together gently, unconsciously trying to recreate the feel of Claire's lips against them. Her arms ached with the desire to pull Claire to her, to kiss her again. "That wasn't really fair," Jamie told her with a sly smile. "You didn't give me any warning. I feel like you might have shown a little more enthusiasm over the cookie dough than the kiss, and I don't like coming in second place. I'm going to need a do over."

"Oh, really?" Nervous excitement added a breathless quality to Claire's words. She inched forward almost imperceptibly as she spoke, a study in contradiction, her chin turned upward as if daring Jamie not to approach, the desire in her eyes begging the opposite.

Jamie stepped toward her, pinning her back against the kitchen counter. She encircled Claire's waist with her arms, easing her gently upward until she rested on the smooth wooden surface of the counter. Their heads now level, Jamie lost herself amid the golden flecks of Claire's eyes, which gazed back at her with equal parts apprehension and attraction. With one finger, Jamie brushed a stray curl from Claire's face, tucking it behind her ear, then raked a handful of dark, silky curls between her fingers and pulled them gently back to reveal the tender flesh behind her lobe. She leaned closer, nuzzling her face against Claire's exposed skin as she inhaled the scent of Claire's shampoo.

With the softness of a butterfly's wings, she brushed her lips along the base of Claire's neck, triumphant at the sudden, sharp intake of breath and involuntary mewling sound she got in response. She felt Claire's body tremble, felt Claire's arms wrap tightly around her, the pressure of her fingertips digging into her shoulder blades, pulling their bodies closer. Jamie dragged her mouth at a languid pace along the raised ridge of Claire's collar bone, flicking her tongue against the hollow of her throat before continuing to nibble with excruciating slowness along the path toward Claire's jaw.

Coming full circle, she nipped Claire's ear lobe with her teeth before sucking it into her mouth, her breath against Claire's ear once more eliciting tiny kitten sounds.

Both hands buried in chestnut curls, Jamie rested her forehead against Claire's, the tips of their noses touching, their breath mixing in shallow, panting bursts. With eyes closed, Jamie could feel rather than see Claire's mouth part, sense the way she moistened her lips in anticipation. Fighting the urge to devour her whole, Jamie brought Claire's lower lip between her own, caressing it with the tip of her tongue. The velvet softness of Claire's upper lip closing over hers sent an electric current coursing through her veins and into her fingertips, making them ache with the need to pull Claire closer. She resisted, sensing that she needed to go slow, instead allowing her lips to slip away from Claire's with the most exquisite gentleness. It was Claire who pulled her back, eyes shut tight, fingers massaging her short blond hair as she kissed her again, harder and deeper than before, lost in the newness of exploration.

It could have lasted forever if the front door had not slammed shut, announcing Paul's return. Claire stiffened at the sound, her eyes flying open as she instinctively pulled away. Her expression registered surprise but not, Jamie was relieved to find, any signs of regret. But her embarrassment was obvious, and Jamie quickly helped her slide back down to the floor. She smoothed Claire's hair and her own into place and had just grabbed a few utensils to pretend to put away when the kitchen door swung open and Paul entered the room. He stopped short mere inches from Claire and gave the air an exaggerated sniff.

"What have you ladies been up to in here?" he asked, his voice booming.

Claire jumped in surprise and tried to answer, but could only make a squeaking noise in response. Paul clapped a large hand on her shoulder and Claire froze, looking very much like a deer in headlights. One very, very guilty looking deer.

"Are you finally making those cookies you promised me?"

Claire tried to answer but this time even the squeaking sound refused to come out, so Jamie jumped in to rescue her.

"Yes, Paul, we're making you those cookies. But

they're for tomorrow and you have to share with the girls," she scolded. "Now, let poor Claire go so she can run upstairs and take care of something. Remember, Claire, that *thing* you were just telling me about needing to do?" she asked pointedly.

Claire nodded and scurried out of the room without a word.

"What was the thing she needed to do?" Paul asked after Claire left.

"I don't know, Paulie. Probably similar to the *thing* you needed to take care of a few weeks ago when you skipped out on that movie with me."

"Oh," Paul replied, then, with dawning realization he repeated, "Ohhh. Wait a minute. Did I just interrupt something here?" He pointed between Jamie and the spot from which Claire had just escaped.

"Yes, Paul. You interrupted us making cookies. Claire's nervous about her first big winter storm. I was trying to distract her."

"Yeah, I'll *bet*," he said with a smirk.

"Yeah, well, that's all *you* are going to hear about it." The timer on the stove beeped and Jamie grabbed an oven mitt. "Seriously, Paulie, don't say anything about it to her, okay?"

Paul nodded. "I swear." He swiped a cookie from the spatula before Jamie could slide it onto the cooling rack. "But, I'm taking this as compensation."

"Paul," Jamie said in a warning tone.

"I know, I know. Not a word. Geez." He popped the cookie into his mouth, then let out a yelp of pain.

"I was just going to tell you to be careful," Jamie said, shaking her head. "The chocolate chips are hot as molten lava when they come out of the oven."

After Paul left, Jamie stared at the counter where Claire had sat and felt a fresh wave of heat crash over her. She could hardly believe it had happened.

I kissed Claire.

And Claire had kissed her back, and not just a little. Jamie's knees went weak at the memory of Claire's fingers raking across her scalp, her teeth nipping at her lips. *Should I go upstairs and talk to her about it?* Jamie wondered, but then thought better of it. Claire probably needed some time alone to recover, and if she stayed in the kitchen, Jamie could just about manage to allow her that space. Her self control might not be up to the task without both flights of stairs that currently separated them. She could be patient, though. For perhaps the first time since the moment Claire had walked into the Marine Institute asking for Jay, Jamie felt completely confident that everything was going to turn out just fine.

EIGHTEEN

"COME ON GIRLS," Vanessa's voice rang out from the foyer. "Mommy and Daddy are waiting!"

Claire straightened up from giving Zooey a piggy back ride and let her slide gently back to the floor. "You heard your mom, kids. Time to go."

"Yeah, kiddos, time to go," Jamie chimed in from the hallway, poking her head through the playroom door. "But first, what do you say to Claire for this super special Christmas present?"

"Thank you, Auntie Claire," the girls said in unison, clamping her legs into a vice-like squeeze before racing each other out of the room and down the stairs.

"Merry Christmas, Abbey and Zooey!" Claire called after them, her heart full to bursting at the way they had started calling her *auntie*. She couldn't remember feeling so happy on Christmas, not since before her parents had died. Even back home with Theresa and her family, Claire usually felt a little like an outsider. But today's celebration, with Jamie and the people who were like family to her, left her feeling complete. It'd been a perfect holiday.

Claire could feel Jamie's presence behind her without turning to look. She sensed the heat of Jamie's body against her back, smelled the spicy scent of her sandalwood soap. She could hear her steady breathing and almost feel the warmth of it against her neck, as she had felt it yesterday in the kitchen. The memory made her tremble, and she knew Jamie was standing so close that she would notice. Claire realized with some surprise that it didn't embarrass her that Jamie might know the effect she had on her. She wanted her to know.

They hadn't talked about what had happened between them, but it was all Claire could think about during the night. It had filled her dreams while she slept. She had struggled all through the ritual of opening presents with Jamie, Paul, and Paul's family, and then playing with the girls in their new room. It was all she could do not to dissolve into a big, sloppy grin at any moment. The site of the freshly baked cookies arranged on a tray that morning had overwhelmed her to the point of needing to leave the room. All she could think about was Jamie, and kissing Jamie. Wanting to kiss her again. She turned her head toward Jamie almost unconsciously, and was surprised at the gentle brush of lips against hers, like an answer to an unspoken prayer.

"What was that for?" she asked, her voice quiet and shy. She wondered if Jamie had read her mind.

"I thought I saw mistletoe," Jamie said innocently.

"I didn't hang any mistletoe in the playroom." Her words came out more defensively than she had intended, but Jamie had been teasing her all week for over decorating.

"Oh, my mistake." Jamie's expression turned devilish. "You should have, though, don't you think?"

"Oh?" Claire said, pretending not to know what was on Jamie's mind.

"Of course. I think there needs to be mistletoe in every corner of the house."

"Well, I might have done that, if I'd realized you were going to need an excuse." Claire gave Jamie a coy look, experiencing a little thrill at her own boldness. It was as if the kiss yesterday had opened a flood gate of naughty impulses Claire never realized she'd had.

Right now, she wanted to see exactly what she could make Jamie do, and figure out how that power was wielded. Like, she'd only just thought of kissing Jamie a second ago, and Jamie had kissed her. Did she make that happen somehow? Could she get her to do it again? Maybe a little less chastely this time? As if on cue, Jamie's arms were around her, their bodies pressing close as their mouths tasted one another greedily. When they broke apart, Claire's head was spinning.

"Sorry," Jamie said with a little grimace. "I shouldn't have done that here, where Paul might walk by and see us."

Claire knew Jamie was trying to be considerate, but was shocked to realize that she didn't even care who saw them, who might know. At this moment, all she really cared about was not stopping. She wanted Jamie's hands touching her, her mouth devouring her. She wanted Jamie to stop being so careful with her and push her against the wall and...Claire swallowed, hard.

Maybe it was a good thing that Jamie couldn't really read her mind. This was all so new, and she wasn't certain where her imagination was going to take her, or that she was altogether ready to go there. *Seriously, Claire. Get a grip. You're in a child's playroom!*

In the past, she'd only known about passion in the abstract. It had never flooded her senses before, never driven all thought from her mind. With the one guy she'd been with, she'd never really wanted to be touched. It was something she had put up with and hoped she might find more enjoyable eventually. She'd never had her skin tingle just to stand near someone before, or felt her body ache from the absence of contact. But that's how it was with Jamie, ever since the kitchen yesterday. Even before that, if Claire were honest. Maybe from the very beginning, only she'd worked so hard to pretend not to notice.

"I'm going to go help Paul clean up. Go upstairs and look on your bed when you get a chance." Jamie added with a secretive smile. "I left something there for you."

"But, you already gave me a present this morning," Claire protested. Jamie had given her a rare first edition of poetry by Edna St. Vincent Millay. The poet's work was a little outside her usual nineteenth century tastes, but Claire looked forward to expanding her horizons. Receiving such a thoughtful gift from Jamie had been one more perfect moment.

"Well, this is just something extra." They had reached the stairs and Jamie paused halfway down. "I didn't think you'd want to open a box of sexy lingerie in front of the children," she said with a wink.

Claire froze.

"I'm just kidding, Claire," Jamie added with a laugh. "Stop looking so terrified."

Claire let out the breath she hadn't realized she was holding and scurried up the stairs to her room, mortified. She had just discovered the limits of her new found bravado, and those horizons hadn't expanded quite as far as she had thought. *Surely Jamie doesn't expect...* fantasies were one thing, but Claire wasn't ready to contemplate doing what a gift of lingerie suggested.

Claire wasn't old fashioned about sex. She just rarely thought about it. It wasn't interesting. But for the past twenty-four hours, sex was about all she could think about. Every time she closed her eyes. Every time something brushed against her skin. It was like every inch of her body had woken up at once, ravenous, and only Jamie could satisfy the hunger. Claire's body burned for Jamie's touch, but her brain wasn't ready to give in so easily. If sex with Jamie was anything like kissing Jamie, Claire knew there would be no going back. The future she had always dreamed of would never look the same after that. Her experience with the family at the park had taught her that she might get a lot of what she wanted in a life with Jamie, but it wouldn't be all. It wouldn't be what had always mattered most. She would never be able to recreate the life her parents had lived and had taken away. That dream had been a part of her for too long to just walk away.

Then there was the question of Jay. *What do I do about Jay?* True, it'd been weeks since they had written. They'd never even met. Could there even be any romantic expectations on Jay's part? *Surely not, right?* But Claire fretted nonetheless. She felt like she'd made Jay a promise and she hated to break her word. Of the many infuriating, yet mostly accurate, things she had overheard her sister say to Jamie on Thanksgiving, one troubled her more than any other. She couldn't accept that her relationship with Jay had been all in her mind.

Whatever else, that initial spark had been real. That's why she felt so confused. There *had* been something there at the start. So where had it gone? Because, if she was honest, it didn't seem to be there any more. Perhaps the relationship had been more one-sided than she had realized. Or maybe it was a warning of her own fickle nature. Maybe she was the type to blow hot and cold, to be in love one minute and out the next. Maybe next week, the flame that burned inside her at the thought of Jamie would be just as dead as the spark she'd felt for Jay. And then where would she be? Perhaps it was better just to wait it out, assess the situation once the embers had cooled.

Claire spied the package on her bed, wrapped in Christmas paper and tied with a bow. Even knowing Jamie had been joking, Claire recoiled, afraid to see what was inside. Still, she really did want to know what Jamie had gotten her, and eventually her curiosity won out. She picked up the package. It was not in a box, and flopped a little in her hands. *Could be lingerie.* She giggled nervously, then tore a corner of the paper and peeked inside, spotting a scrap of gray and red fabric. She brushed the tip of her finger along what was the softest thing she'd ever felt. She tore the paper away completely to reveal a long flannel nightgown.

Claire laughed, suddenly understanding Jamie's joke. Technically, this nightgown *could* be considered lingerie, but it was probably the least sexy thing in existence. Claire loved it. She held it up to her chest. It reached from neck to floor, with sleeves that buttoned at the wrists and a collar that closed snugly at the throat. Not an inch of her would be exposed to the cold winter air. *This is exactly like the one I saw in that little store in New Hampshire*, she realized with a start. How had Jamie known? She'd barely mentioned it at the time, and Jamie hadn't even been paying attention. *She was too busy flirting with that sales girl.* A pang of jealousy shot through her at the memory.

There was another reason to be terrified. Jamie was experienced. She'd had a lot of girlfriends, several she'd even lived with for a while, though none that had lasted very long. *Jamie* was the fickle one. What if this was just a fling for her, and in a few weeks she would move on? Or just a bit of a challenge to see if she could get a straight girl to fall for her.

I might not even be the first. Jamie was so charming and funny and gorgeous that surely any woman couldn't help but fall for her a little bit. *It might not even mean*

I'm a lesbian, Claire realized. *Maybe this is just what Jamie does to people, and it has nothing to do with me at all.* How could Claire be certain? It's not like she had enough experience with men *or* women to have any clue how this was supposed to work.

Maybe I should just stick with Jay. Except eventually he'd return to Boston and she'd have to deal with him in person. Jay, whose model-like good looks made her so uncomfortable that she'd hidden his pictures in a drawer. *How's that going to work out?* The more she thought about, the more she wondered if she should've ignored all of the signs and stayed in Portland from the start. *Love is too confusing. I should stick to books.* Where was a clear sign when you needed one? She clutched the nightgown to her chest, feeling muddled.

Claire stood in front of her bedroom window, looking at the sea. The water was wild and churning, a perfect reflection of her agitated mind. The wind was whipping up the waves and making the tree branches flail and shake. Claire could feel the chill of the air coming through cracks around the wooden window sashes as they rattled in their frames. She shivered. She would appreciate that flannel nightgown tonight. It was only late afternoon but the sky was dark with storm clouds so that it felt like night. As Claire watched, flakes of icy white snow began to swirl outside. A streetlight flickered a few times as it struggled to turn on against the dark. The sputtering, on and off, was a stark reminder that they could lose power at any moment in the coming storm. Claire's apprehension grew.

NINETEEN

"JAMIE?" Claire whispered tentatively in the darkness outside Jamie's room. "Jamie, are you in there?" The rustling of blankets told her that she was, but the single candle in her hand did little to help her see. There were no lights in the house, nor out on the street. As far as Claire could tell, they'd lost power all up and down the coast. It was sometime in the middle of the night, but that was all she knew. Her cell phone had stopped charging and the battery was dead, so the power must've been out for a while. And with it, the heat. Claire's room, with its large, drafty windows that faced the brunt of the storm, were glazed with thick ice and the space held all the warmth of a meat locker.

"Jamie?" Claire's voice was louder now, more desperate.

"Claire?" Jamie responded, finally roused from her sleep. "What's wrong? What time is it?"

"I don't know, the power's out. There's ice everywhere and I'm freezing," Claire whimpered.

"Is that a candle you're holding?" Jamie asked. "I put some of those votive candles you bought on top of the mantle over there. Why don't you light a few so we can see?"

"You have a fireplace? Can we get some logs from downstairs and start a fire to keep warm?"

"Not if you don't want to burn the whole house down. It's not safe to use, but once you get the candles lit, you can warm up under the covers."

Claire nodded, lighting the last candle and setting the one she had brought in with her next to the others. When she crawled into bed next to Jamie, her body was shaking from the cold.

Jamie wrapped her hands around Claire's icy fingers. "My God, Claire. You really are freezing! Slide over closer so you can warm up. You can put your feet under my legs." Jamie yelped when Claire took her up the offer. "Oh, geez, they're cold." She wrapped her arms around the still-shivering Claire and pulled her tightly against her, tucking her closely against her chest. "Are you okay?" she asked, almost as if Claire were a child. "Is it just the cold, or is the storm scaring you?"

"It's so loud," Claire said finally with a sniff of her frozen nose. "I wasn't expecting that. Snow in Portland is really quiet. But the wind and the ice against my windows woke me up, and then I realized how dark it was and it freaked me out. I hope it's okay that I came in here."

"Shhh," Jamie soothed her. "Shhh. Of course it's okay." She ran one hand lightly along Claire's back, caressing the woolly softness of her flannel gown. "Hey," she said with a laugh, "you opened your present. Do you like it?"

"I love it," Claire said, smiling in the semi-darkness. "I saw one like it that day we went shopping in New Hampshire and really wanted it."

"I know, you little goose. When do you think I bought it?"

"What, then? How did you get it out of there without me knowing?"

"I didn't. I got the store's number from the woman at the register and called them later to have it sent to me."

"Wait, *that's* what the clerk handed you, the *store's* number? I thought she was giving you *her* number."

Jamie laughed. "Oh you did, did you? Is that jealousy I detect in your voice, Miss Flores?"

"It's—no, I just—fine, maybe it is," Claire sputtered.

"Hmm, well. Jealousy's good." Jamie kissed Claire's forehead. "I'm not complaining."

Claire shifted her body at the feel of Jamie's lips against her skin, the storm momentarily forgotten. She tilted her head to claim Jamie's mouth with her own. They kissed deeply, their hands roaming more freely in the dark room than they had in the daylight. Claire's back arched as Jamie's palm connected with the swell of her breast, her fingers tracing circles around her hardening nipple through the layers of the flannel nightgown.

Claire moaned in pleasure at the unfamiliar sensations Jamie's touch elicited. "And here I thought I was going to be safe wearing this granny nightgown."

Jamie moved her hand away the next instant, holding it up like a barrier between them. Claire whimpered, missing the warmth of Jamie's touch. She grasped Jamie's fingers, guiding them back toward her breast.

"Claire," Jamie pleaded, pulling her hand back again. "You should go back to your own room. If we keep this up, I won't want to stop."

"Maybe I don't want you to stop," Claire whispered.

"Claire, please. I'm serious."

"So am I," Claire answered firmly, and was startled to realize that it was true. The thought of ending up in bed with Jamie had terrified her just a few hours ago. She'd been so convinced her feeling would fade, or Jamie's would. So what had changed?

"Claire, I don't want you to stay just because you're frightened from the storm."

Is that the only reason? Claire wondered. *No.* She was sure it was something more. She was filled with a confidence no storm could explain. She felt Jamie's fingers twisting the lace on the cuff of her nightgown. *The nightgown*, she realized. Jamie had made such an effort to get it. No one had ever done something like that for her before. And she'd done it at a point when there was no reason to think they would ever be more than friends. That simple gesture had convinced Claire that she was special. That she was loved. Even without speaking the words, she knew. Jamie loved her. That's why everything felt so different now. Jamie loved her, and she loved Jamie. The realization filled her with both exhilaration and peace, more than she'd ever known was possible.

"Jamie, I'm not scared." She took Jamie's hand and brushed the fingers against her lips. "I don't want to stop, and I don't want to be anywhere but here." Claire turned Jamie's hand over and kissed the palm, then placed it back to where it had been atop her breast.

No need for more encouragement, they came together in a flurry of limbs and lips that left them breathless and scrambling for air.

"Do you still feel cold?" Jamie asked between gasps of breath.

Claire giggled. "I think that might be the *least* of my concerns. If we keep this up, I'll burst into flames."

"Okay," Jamie declared, raising up on her knees and draping the duvet on top of her head like a hood, "then I'm taking this."

"Wait, what?"

"All I've got on is a pair of shorts and a sports bra. Meanwhile, you're covered head to toe in flannel. It's putting me at a disadvantage, in more ways than one."

"So you're stealing the covers?" Claire pouted. "I'm rethinking going back to my room after all."

"You'll get them back later. First, I'm going to do something about this nightgown."

"I thought you liked my nightgown."

"I just think I'd like it better if it were on the floor right now. Hold still."

Jamie scooted to the foot of the bed, leaving Claire

on her back in the dim candlelight, desperately wondering what was coming.

"Oh, look! I found toes under here," she teased, grasping Claire's feet. "Much warmer now, too. Good."

She pinched the edge of the flannel gown and raised it a few inches to expose Claire's ankles. She caressed one with each hand, slowly massaging up to the calves and knees, inching the nightgown up as she went. Claire squirmed in anticipation as Jamie lowered her head, still covered by the duvet, and planted a gentle kiss on the inside of each knee. Desire building, Claire tried to slide her legs apart, but Jamie put one hand on the outside of each thigh beneath the flannel gown and held them firmly together.

"I told you, hold still."

Her hands occupied, she wriggled the hem up as far as she could manage with it clenched between her teeth.

"Very creative of you," Claire said, laughing.

She could just make out the expression of Jamie's face in the candles' glow, and her amusement changed to a tingle of anticipation at the intensity reflected there. She tried to imagine what Jamie had planned for her next, but her brain was already too overloaded to think. Her pulse raced as Jamie placed the tip of her tongue in the hollow between Claire's knees and, with excruciating slowness, ran it along the cleft between her smooth thighs, stopping just short of the purple silk of her panties. Claire gulped down air in short gasps, clenching her fists in the sheet beneath her to keep still as Jamie had demanded.

Jamie sat up on her knees and looked steadily into Claire's eyes. "I'll admit, I was half expecting granny panties to match the gown."

"I'm full of surprises."

Jamie shimmied the gown most of the way up Claire's back. She positioned herself on her knees astride, settling with gentle pressure atop Claire's pelvis and spreading the blanket over as much exposed flesh as she could to ward away the chill. Secure in her new vantage point, she flattened her palms on the smooth skin of Claire's abdomen, pressing in slightly at the curve of her waist, and splaying her fingers to cup the swell of her hips. Readjusting her body, Jamie angled her head so that she could press a line of kisses from Claire's navel to the little valley between her breasts.

Instinctively, Claire stretched her arms above her head, allowing Jamie to liberate her from the inconvenience of clothing at last. The gray and red flannel gown landed in a heap on the floor beside the bed.

"See?" Jamie said, pointing to the floor. "Look how nice it looks there."

"Funny," Claire replied, glancing at the floor. "I never would've thought to try it on in the store that way."

"Well, now you know for next time."

Claire shivered, the skin of her newly bare arms turning to gooseflesh in the chilly night air.

"Cold?" Jamie asked.

Claire nodded, then flashed a wicked grin. "I know how to fix it though."

It was as if being free of the gown unleashed a primal

need in Claire. She pulled Jamie to her, wrapping every inch of her body around Jamie's with a force that she'd never experienced before. Her hands grasped and legs wriggled in a flurry, attempting with every movement to bring their bodies closer. She grasped more tightly, needing to feel Jamie's weight on her, but Jamie pulled back, leaving her fuming in frustration.

"Patience, darling," Jamie chastised her. "We still need to get these off."

Leaning back on one elbow, Jamie slipped the fingers of her free hand beneath the elastic of the purple panties. With her fingertips she traced the line between bare skin and soft down. Claire shivered, though not at all from the cold. Jamie's hand slid down further, cupping her firmly. Claire drew a ragged breath, pressing her body more fully into Jamie's eager hand. She felt Jamie's fingers spread her gently apart. She shifted her own legs wider in response, savoring the experience of Jamie's fingers exploring her hidden folds. Jamie shifted her weight onto her now, freeing her other hand to caress and tease one of Claire's hardened nipples. Claire's breath became impossibly shallow and she worried fleetingly that she might pass out before finding out what Jamie had planned for her next.

As Claire heaved for air, Jamie lowered her mouth to the other breast and flicked it with her tongue. As this new sensation shot through her, for a moment Claire forgot completely how to breathe. Jamie closed her lips around her, sucking Claire's nipple deeply into her mouth. At the same moment, Claire felt Jamie's fingers slide lower between her legs, plunging deep inside. She gasped, every inch of her vibrating with pleasure. She felt herself clench around Jamie's fingers as pinpricks of light exploded behind her closed eyes.

She finally remembered to open her eyes again and breathe, but could manage little more than to stare shakily into Jamie's eyes.

"You're so beautiful," Jamie said softly.

Claire grinned goofily, unable to think of a response. But then a shadow of disappointment flickered across her face.

"What's wrong?" Jamie asked in concern.

"Nothing," Claire assured her. "It's just... I didn't expect to be finished so soon."

Jamie laughed. "Finished? Don't be silly," she said. "That was just the warm up, little goose."

Claire giggled as Jamie reached down again and gave the purple panties, now rumpled and soaked beyond all recognition, a practiced tug and sent them sailing to join the nightgown on the floor. Jamie grasped the lower edge of her sports bra and prepared to tug it over her head when Claire called out in protest.

"Wait a minute. Don't I get to do all that stuff that you did, to get you undressed, too?"

Jamie shrugged. "I suppose. But, do you really want to take so much extra time?"

Claire grinned broadly. "No."

In seconds, Jamie's bra and shorts joined the growing heap on the floor, but the feverish need that had consumed Claire moments before flickered to uncertainty.

"Jamie?" she said in a small voice. "You know I have no idea what I'm doing, right?"

"You've managed remarkably well so far. I think you'll be able to follow along."

Lost in sensation, she did what Jamie did, touched the way Jamie touched, mirroring her every action until she could no longer tell where she ended and Jamie began. They had merged into one, every movement bringing exquisite pleasure, each desire fulfilled the instant it was known, until finally, exhausted, they drifted off to sleep, their bodies still entwined.

TWENTY

THE ROOM WAS bright with sunshine when Jamie awoke, with the exaggerated brilliance of light bouncing off fresh snow. Her body felt relaxed and satisfied along every muscle and sinew. Jamie rolled over in the warm sheets and reached for Claire. Her hand came away empty. Sitting up in bed, Jamie realized that the room, too, was empty. Breathing deeply, she could just detect the scent of bacon wafting up the stairs from the kitchen. After the exhilaration of last night, she felt momentarily deflated. She had intended to make breakfast, but Claire must have beaten her to it.

At least if the stove was working, it meant that the power had come back during the night. Though the method she and Claire and found for staying warm was infinitely preferable, Jamie had to admit that central heat had its place. And hot food. Her stomach rumbled at the thought of breakfast and she chuckled. Both she and Claire had burned off quite a few calories. They deserved the chance to refuel. And then? Well, the college was on winter break and Jamie would have the day off work because of the severity of last night's storm. *We might as well both head back to bed...*

Jamie entered the kitchen and looked for Claire, but only Paul was there.

"Did you make breakfast this morning?" Jamie asked incredulously.

Paul shook his head. "No, Claire made it before she left."

"Left?" Jamie scanned the frozen landscape in confusion. Every surface was encased in ice. The roads would be treacherous, and half the coast was probably still without power. "In her car? Where on earth could she be going on a morning like this?"

Jamie's heart raced. *Oh, God. Is she freaking out about last night?*

Paul shrugged. "She didn't say."

"What exactly did she say? Anything?" Jamie raked her hands fiercely through her tousled hair.

"She asked if I wanted bacon," Paul replied, cocking his head to one side and looking perplexed.

"Shit. I was afraid something like this would happen after last night."

"After what happened last night? You mean the storm?"

"Um. No." Jamie's expression was one usually reserved for children who were not very bright.

Paul nodded in sudden comprehension. "Ohhh.

That's what happened last night. Well, that explains all the humming this morning," he said with a chuckle.

"Humming?" Jamie repeated.

"Sure," Paul said. "Claire was making breakfast when I got down here, humming a happy little tune."

Jamie tugged at her hair, deep in thought. Claire had come downstairs happy and humming. That didn't sound like a woman filled with regret. *So, this isn't about last night?* Jamie's heart lifted at the thought. But if not that, then what could it be? What possible reason could there be for Claire to rush off like she had, and without telling either Paul or Jamie why?

The morning ticked by. At almost noon, Claire had not yet returned to the house, nor had she called to let them know what was going on. Jamie was starting to worry.

"Paul, tell me again what happened this morning. From the beginning."

"I told you, she was scrambling some eggs when I came downstairs. She asked if I wanted some, and some bacon. I said sure. She made me a plate."

Jamie sighed, exasperated. "Okay, skip ahead a little. I don't think this has anything to do with the breakfast menu."

"Fine," Paul said, putting his hands up in the air in defense. "You said to tell you everything...A few minutes later she checked her email, then said she had someplace she had to go. That's all I know."

"Wait, you didn't mention an email before," Jamie said.

"I didn't?" Paul replied. "I thought I did. So, yeah, she checked her email."

"And then?" Jamie prompted.

Paul tapped his chin in thought. "She checked her email, got real quiet for a minute, put on a coat, and left."

"Where did she check her email?"

"What? Why is that important?" Paul asked.

"I don't know. It's probably not," Jamie said, frustration setting in. "But it's the only clue we've got. So where did she check it, on her phone?"

"No, she'd brought her laptop down the other day because the Wi-Fi was acting up in her room. She checked it there." Paul gestured toward the dining room.

Jamie spotted Claire's laptop on the dining room table, still open, though the screen was dark. *Please don't ask for a password*, Jamie thought as she pressed a key and the computer hummed back to life. She was in luck. Claire's email appeared on the screen, still open to the last one she had read. An icy stab of panic hit Jamie in the gut.

"We have a problem."

Sometime in the early hours that morning, a very official looking email had arrived in Claire's inbox to inform her that a certain researcher on expedition in the Antarctic had disappeared from base camp.

"I don't get it," Paul said when he finished reading. "I know I deleted that. How did it get sent?"

"Like I would know!" Jamie's voice betrayed the agitation she felt. "It's not like I'm any more of a computer expert than you are. Maybe it didn't get deleted from the trash, or something got reset after the storm. All I know is that Claire read it, and now she's gone."

"Okay," Paul said, "I get that she would be upset. But why not just talk to us about it? Why leave?"

"Oh, God, Paul," Jamie groaned, suddenly remembering her conversation with Claire in the kitchen. "She'd be more than upset. I had no idea when you wrote this, but the way you describe what happened to Jay—the blizzard, the ice, the vehicle going off the road—it's almost exactly what happened to her parents. It's how they died."

Paul looked stricken. "Oh, God, Jamie. I didn't mean for that to...I didn't know."

"I know you didn't. I just wish she had said something before she left. We might have been able to come up with a way to diffuse this. But knowing Claire, she's gone back into her hiding mode."

"But, she'll come back," Paul said reassuringly.

"Claire's in a delicate state, out God knows where on dangerous, icy roads, and won't answer her phone." Jamie's voice cracked and her eyes stung with tears. "If anything happens to her, it's my fault. What am I going to do?"

"Well, you could log in to Jay's account and send her an email."

Jamie wiped her eyes and turned to look at her friend. "Okay..."

"Have Jay tell her that it was all a mistake and he's fine. While you're at it, he could mention that he's moving to that island with the penguins. What was it, Borneo?"

"Madagascar. But Paul, that's brilliant!" Jamie's face brightened. "Not the Borneo part, but having Jay send an email. I should have thought of that. Sometimes I forget that I'm him." She retrieved her phone from the other room and pulled up the Tech Cupid app. "Shit. The site's down."

"They're based near here," Paul said. "It must be because of the storm."

Jamie nodded. "I'll keep trying. I just wish she would come home."

IT WAS WELL after dark when Claire's car skidded back into the icy driveway on Ocean Boulevard. Jamie met her at the door, gathering her into her arms before she even had a chance to take off her coat and boots.

"I was so worried," Jamie said as she covered Claire's ruddy cheeks with kisses.

"I'm sorry," Claire said, her voice sounding as frozen as her body.

Claire stood obediently in place while Jamie stripped away her wet clothing, then shuffled into the living room and let Jamie wrap her in a quilt, the whole time saying not a single word. Her expression was distant and hollow, as if in shock. Bundled next to Jamie in the oversize chair, Claire finally came undone, crying until her whole body shook while Jamie held her tight.

"Claire," Jamie begged, "please talk to me. Where have you been all day? Why did you leave?"

"There was an accident..." Claire sobbed.

She proceeded to tell Jamie about the email she had received from the Marine Institute that morning, informing her of Jay's tragic accident. "You hadn't heard yet?" Claire asked through ragged breaths. "I thought your work might have sent out an announcement to everyone, since Jay's a colleague."

Jamie arranged her expression in a way that she hoped conveyed spontaneous shock and concern. She'd practiced it several times throughout the afternoon. "That's gotta be a good sign, right? Since they haven't, there could be more to the story."

"He went off an icy road," Claire whimpered. "What more is there?"

"They could've found him, safe and sound, and the update just didn't make it through yet," Jamie reassured her.

In fact, Jamie spoke with a confidence in her voice that suggested that this was *exactly* what had happened. Inside, she cursed the Tech Cupid website for still being down. She should have been able to send that email from Jay to Claire hours ago. "You still haven't told me where you've been all day," she added.

"The local police station, state police, the Red Cross. Anywhere I could think to go that might help."

Jamie swallowed hard. Just how many people had been dragged into this mess?

"I tried going straight to the Marine Institute, but they were closed," Claire added.

Thank God they were closed, or I would have had some serious explaining to do.

"Of course they were closed. There's an inch of ice on all the roads. Claire, driving around out there today, you could have been..."

"Killed, too?" she wailed, breaking into a new fit of sobbing.

"Claire, you don't know that. I'm sure he's fine," Jamie snapped. Her breath caught at the wounded look Claire gave her. Jamie hadn't meant to sound impatient, but she was getting more than a little tired of Jay and all the trouble he was causing her. "I'm sorry, Claire. I've just been so worried about you."

"This is all my fault, Jamie." Her tears flowed freely and it was clear she starting to lose what little control over her emotions she had gained. "If I had just remembered to set up a Christmas chat with him, he might not have been out there. How could I forget?" Claire sniffled. "It was Christmas. I'm supposed to be his *girlfriend*. How could I have done something so terrible?" Her tears flowed freely for several minutes while Jamie watched, helpless.

Finally, Jamie stiffened with resolve. *I don't like where this guilt trip is going. How long before she decides this all could have been avoided if she were into guys, the way she's 'supposed' to be?* Jamie cleared her throat to speak.

Claire looked up at the sound. "It's my fault," she

whispered. She stared at Jamie with swollen eyes that failed to focus. "If I hadn't gotten that fever, they wouldn't have come home until morning. The storm would have already passed by."

Whatever Jamie had been about to say stuck in her throat at Claire's words. She was no longer thinking of Jay, she realized. She was thinking of her parents. Jamie's heart broke for the way Claire must have blamed herself ever since she was a child. Jamie pressed Claire tightly to her chest.

"My little darling, none of this is your fault," Jamie said gently.

It's completely my fault, but I'm going to fix it, I promise.

"Why don't you go to bed and get some rest—you look exhausted," Jamie said. "You want me to keep you company tonight?"

Claire shook her head vigorously.

"I didn't mean it like that," Jamie added. "I just thought—"

Claire shook her head again. "I should probably just be alone."

"Of course," Jamie said with a sigh. "I understand. I'm going to head up now. I have to be at work early tomorrow."

"Jamie, could you do me a favor?"

"Anything."

"Would you ask at work tomorrow and find out what's going on?"

"Of course I will," she promised, though with any

luck that email from Jay would be sent well before morning.

"The email was from someone named Alan. Alan Doehring, I think. Do you know him?"

"Mmhmm," Jamie mumbled.

Do I know him? Of course she knew him. Alan was her research assistant. It was his *stupid* computer that Paul had been goofing off with when he wrote that email in the first place. Alan, with his *stupid* password on his *stupid* post-it note under his *stupid flipping* keyboard.

Claire headed to bed, but Jamie remained awake, checking the Tech Cupid site every few minutes. She intended to stay up all night if she had to in order to catch the Tech Cupid site the moment it came back online. *Might as well*, she grumbled, *since I'm sleeping alone tonight anyway.*

The site was still down the next morning, but Jamie wasn't ready to panic. Cursing at Alan had given her a flash of inspiration and she had come up with a plan B during the night. Since the original email had been sent from there, she would just go to work early and get onto Alan's computer before anyone arrived. It should be easy enough to find the template Paul had created, modify it, and send Claire a new message from Alan saying Jay was safe.

It was an easy fix, as long as Alan hadn't taken their little chat about computer security to heart. Chances were pretty good that he had simply moved his password from under the keyboard and put it in his desk drawer. The whole mess would be fixed before lunch.

On her way to the front door, Jamie saw Claire asleep on the couch, still wrapped in the quilt from the night before. Her computer was open nearby. Poor thing. She had probably fallen asleep hoping to hear from Jay. *This scene looks very familiar*, Jamie thought. The only difference was that last time, the thought of running her fingers through those tangled curls had been a fantasy. Now it was a memory so vivid that it nearly took her breath away. She tucked the quilt in around Claire's resting form, brushing a few stray curls from her face before kissing her lightly on the forehead. Claire continued to sleep. *Time to go put everything right*, Jamie thought. She wanted nothing more than to put this behind them and for Claire to fall asleep in her arms tonight.

TWENTY-ONE

DAMN IT, Jamie thought as she rounded the corner near her office. Alan was already at his desk, hard at work. *What is he doing here this early?*

"Morning, Alan," she greeted him in a cheery voice that she hoped masked the frustration she felt.

The young man spun in his chair, his face turning pink. "I didn't know anyone else would be here so early."

"Yeah, well, the storm put me behind schedule so I thought I'd get an early start today. But I thought you were caught up on your latest project."

"Er, well..." Allen fidgeted uncomfortably in his seat.

Jamie glanced at the computer and saw the familiar Tech Cupid log in screen, with the equally familiar message that it was currently unavailable. Jamie's eyebrows lifted in surprise. Tech Cupid was almost exclusively a gay dating site. She'd had no idea her research assistant was gay, though she felt like it was the kind of thing she should have known. She wasn't sure what that implied about her observation skills.

"What's that?" she asked, feigning innocence.

Alan fidgeted some more. "It's a, er... it's a dating site, for... well..."

Jamie took pity on her assistant as his face flushed crimson. "I know all about Tech Cupid, Alan."

His face filled with panic. "I swear, I never go on during work hours, but sometimes I come in early to take advantage of the faster Internet connection. I guess I won't be doing that anymore, though."

"Don't worry about it, Alan, I'm not going to tell anyone your secret. Any of your secrets," she emphasized. "You can do whatever you want on your own time, as long as your work gets done."

"Oh, no, it's not that... I mean, thank you..." he stuttered. "But, no, it's just that now Tech Cupid's gone, I probably won't bother with any others for a while."

"Gone?" Jamie repeated, her heart pounding.

"That's the rumor. One of my buddies works in the same building as them and he says they closed up early on Christmas Eve and everybody was leaving with boxes and stuff." Alan shrugged. "Not a huge surprise, I guess. They had some serious data glitches this summer, screwed up thousands of profiles. I guess there were lawsuits, and the legal fees bled them dry. Too bad, though. I met some really hot guys on there." His eyes widened when he realized what he had said.

Jamie gave him a reassuring smile in response, but could think of nothing more to say. Her head spun wildly over this latest development. Without Tech Cupid, there could be no message from Jay. Hell, without Tech Cupid, there *was* no Jay. He didn't exist anywhere else. He didn't have his own email address or anything else because Jamie had never intended for him to be a real person. Maybe she could create an address now, but given Claire's current state of mind, she'd probably contact the FBI to have it authenticated. Getting onto Alan's computer was now her only shot. Maybe she'd send him out to buy coffee for rest of the research assistants, her treat. That would give her plenty of time to get on his computer while he was out.

Her office phone buzzed. *Dr. Swenson.* Apparently the whole office was in early today. She picked up the phone. "Hello?"

"Jamie," her boss said, "I'm so glad you're in. There's a strange situation that's come up and I need your help."

Jamie hung up the phone and trudged down the hallway toward her boss' office. *Just what I need. Another problem to fix today.*

Her boss looked up as Jamie entered. "Jamie, there you are. Here's the situation. While the Institute was closed yesterday, we got about a dozen messages from some woman...let's see, Claire Flores, I think?"

Jamie nodded, hoping the panic she felt inside didn't show on her face.

"Frankly, they were pretty bizarre," Dr. Swenson continued. "She was rambling about one of our employees getting into an accident in Antarctica, and demanding to know what we were doing to rescue him."

"That *is* bizarre," Jamie managed to reply.

"The name she gave, Jay, isn't anywhere in our system. Plus, why would we even have someone in Antarctica? We've never had any research down there. The whole thing was pretty ludicrous."

"Yeah, that's really strange," Jamie said, trying to keep herself from fidgeting, or grabbing her hair and yanking it out by the handful in a nervous fit. "Why exactly are you telling *me* this?"

Please don't say you've connected me to Claire.

"I know, I know. It's not your job. But you did such an amazing job handling the Dr. Matthews' incident, I felt you were the only person I could trust with this. I'm sure it's nothing to worry about, but do you think you could make a few inquiries today? Nothing official. We do *not* want the Board to hear about this."

"Absolutely. I'll take care of it."

Thank God. That means they don't know yet.

"And Jamie? There was one more thing I wanted to talk to you about. I've been considering your recommendation to go back over all of the data sets before submitting Dr. Matthews' meta-data analysis for publication. I was against the idea at first, but now I think you're right. I was worried about missing the global climate summit, but publishing a flawed study would be far more damaging to our reputation in the long run."

Jamie smiled, feeling pleased. "Thank you, Dr. Swenson. In fact, it may not take as long as I thought. I may have found something. I have a theory that some of the temperatures were taken with older equipment and never converted from Fahrenheit. If that's the issue, it won't take nearly as long to fix as I estimated."

"Spectacular work, Jamie! I just want to let you know that when they ask for recommendations to fill Dr. Matthews' position in January, I'll be submitting your name. I can't think of anyone better for the job."

Jamie floated back to her office on a cloud of praise and relief. *Head of Research.* She couldn't believe it was really happening. Being named the head of research at the Cape Ann Marine Institute at age thirty-four was a huge accomplishment. With the raise she'd be getting, she and Claire could get a house of their own. Jamie could afford to take her on a trip to England. She smiled at the image of the two of them, walking arm in arm along the winding streets of Norfolk where Jamie had gone to school. *Claire is going to be so thrilled!*

Only first, Jamie had a mess to clean up. As she rounded the corner, she saw that Alan's desk was empty. Now was her chance. If anyone asked, she was doing a surprise inspection for IT. She flipped the keyboard over first. No password. *Good boy, Alan.* It would've made it easier for her, but part of her was pleased that he had taken her warning seriously. An assistant director needed to be taken seriously, after all.

She checked the middle drawer. Nothing. Then the side drawers. Struck out again. Perhaps she shouldn't have been so stern when she lectured him a few weeks ago. This was an inconvenience. She heard Alan's voice around the corner and scurried back to her office. She'd have to think of some other way to do this. On an impulse, she picked up the phone and dialed the security desk.

"Burt? It's Jamie Richards, up in research. Do you know if there's any way to get a computer password?"

"Dr. Richards, hi." Burt answered. "Uh, I can get access to passwords, yes. Usually we can't give them out to anyone but the owner, though. But say, is this about the special project for Dr. Swenson?"

"Um, yes, Burt. As a matter of fact, it is. So, you think you could get me the password I need?"

"Absolutely. Dr. Swenson told me all about it and said you were in charge."

"Excellent. Good job, Burt."

Sometimes it's really good to be in charge.

Jamie couldn't believe her luck. As soon as she had the password, she could send the email. With a click of a mouse, Claire would stop being upset and she'd have earned herself a promotion and a big, fat raise. It was almost too easy.

Her phone buzzed again. *Claire.* Her heart felt lighter just reading the name on the caller ID screen.

"Claire? How are you feeling, darling?"

"Jamie, oh my goodness, you won't believe it!"

The first thing Jamie found hard to believe was how animated Claire's voice was. *Is this the same person I left bundled on the couch in a huddled mass this morning?*

"Believe what?" Jamie asked. "What is it?"

"Last night, Jamie. I couldn't sleep."

"Well, I'm not surprised," Jamie answered sympathetically.

"I kept thinking about what one of the people at the police department told me yesterday. Do you know it costs tens of thousands of dollars to do a cold weather rescue?"

"That much? Huh." Jamie wasn't sure where this was going.

"And that's just here in the US. Imagine how expensive it's going to be in a place as remote as an Antarctic base camp."

"Uh, I suppose. But that's not something we have to worry about."

"Of course it is! We have to do whatever we can to help Jay. So I went to one of those donation sites—"

"Wait, you did what?" Jamie asked, alarmed.

Please don't make this any more complicated than it already is.

"Yeah, you know those places where you can get strangers to donate money?"

"Claire, I'm not sure—"

"Jamie, that's not why I called," Claire interrupted impatiently. "Just listen. A few hours after I set it up, some blogger put a link to it on his website, and it's gone viral!"

"What?" Jamie squeaked.

"Jamie, I've raised almost one hundred thousand dollars in twelve hours! Oh, hold on. That's the front doorbell. It's probably the reporter who wanted to do an interview. I've gotta go. I just wanted you to know!"

The line went silent. Jamie stared at the receiver,

dumbfounded. Fund raising? *Reporters?!* This was getting out of control.

Her phone buzzed again. *Dr. Swenson.*

"Jamie, can you come here right away? Burt's found something."

Nerves had nearly gnawed a hole in the lining of Jamie's stomach by the time she reached her boss' door. Dr Swenson and Burt from security leaned over some sort of paper on Dr. Swenson's desk.

"Jamie, take a look at this. Burt printed out a screen shot from one of the security camera feeds from a few weeks ago. It's from one of the hallways, after hours. There's a woman I don't recognize in the picture, but Burt says he thinks he saw her here over the summer, asking for someone named Jay, and he thinks he sent her your way. Do you recall?"

"Um, vaguely." Jamie's heart skipped a beat. "Do you think there's a connection?"

"Maybe. I don't know. It's a long shot but at least it's a lead."

"I doubt there's a connection. But good job, Burt," Jamie added. "That's really something, remembering that incident and digging up this picture." The fact that he'd done either was annoying as hell, but Jamie still needed Burt to give her Alan's password.

"Sure thing, Jamie," Burt replied, beaming with pride. "I've got one of my guys pulling images from some of the other tapes from that night. We'll get to the bottom of it."

Back at her desk, Jamie struggled not to hyperventilate. *This is a disaster.* She held the password to Alan's computer in her hand and was about to send him out to run an errand, but it hardly mattered now. They were looking through the tapes. It was just a matter of time before Dr. Swenson received a pile of photos of her and Claire canoodling after hours in the ocean tank. *I'm going to get fired*, she thought. But if she could finally send the email, she might at least get to keep Claire. She could find a new job, but she would never find another woman like Claire.

Her phone buzzed again. *Dr. Swenson.* Jamie groaned. *Time to find out what it's like to be unemployed*, she fretted on the way to her boss' office.

Dr. Swenson motioned her towards the monitor on her desk. "Jamie, just in time. Look at this." Instead of the dreaded security photographs, a local news broadcast streamed on the screen. Claire spoke to a reporter in Jamie's living room. A banner at the bottom of the screen flashed the headline *Local Woman Raises Thousands to Rescue Missing Scientist.* Jamie felt lightheaded. She had assumed when Claire said a reporter had arrived that it was some journalism intern from the local Cape Ann paper, not a camera crew from Channel Seven. She was living in a nightmare.

"It's the same woman from that picture. No doubt about it. This is more serious than I imagined," Dr. Swenson said. "Coming here in the summer, sneaking in after hours, harassing us with phone calls, and now this. I think she must be mentally disturbed." Dr. Swenson shook her head slowly in disbelief. "I wanted to let you know that you're off the hook, Jamie. I need to turn this over to the proper authorities."

"Dr. Swenson, are you sure?" Jamie asked, masking her rising panic. *Claire is going to end up in jail!* "Think of the bad press. The Board is going to be very concerned." Jamie hoped playing the Board card would buy her enough time. "Give me one more day to see what I can do. Discreetly."

Her boss nodded. "So far they've kept the Institute's name out it, so maybe you're right. There's still a chance it could still be handled without the Board finding out. But only one more day. If this woman is dangerous, it's not worth the risk."

Jamie nodded. The clock was ticking, She had twenty-four hours until everything went completely to hell.

Alan was back at his desk. *Damn it. Aren't young people supposed to be slackers? Go home!* Jamie glared at the back of Alan's occupied chair. No matter. He had to leave sometime. She'd come back after dinner and send the email then. Right now, Jamie had to talk to Claire and convince her to tone it down before the story hit the national news.

TWENTY-TWO

CLAIRE LOOKED up from the computer as Jamie entered the dining room. She smiled, and Jamie's heart melted just to see her looking happy again.

"Claire? You look like you're a lot better today." Jamie felt relief at Claire's improved mood. Maybe it wouldn't be as difficult as she had feared to distract Claire long enough to sneak out back to the office and send that blasted email. How she wished she could have accomplished it already! Jamie swooped down to kiss Claire's lips, but Claire swiveled so that she caught her cheek instead. A shadow of doubt crossed Claire's face, hitting Jamie like a splash of cold water.

"Jamie, it's really not a good time for that," she chastised.

"For what? For giving my girlfriend a kiss after being away all day?" Jamie's voice sounded hurt.

"Your girlfriend?" Claire gulped. "That's kind of rushing things, isn't it?"

"Is it?" Jamie could feel her anger building, and beneath that was a prick of fear. *Where is Claire going with this?* "Forgive me for assuming, but I know I don't make a habit of doing the things we did together the other night without taking it seriously. Do you?"

"Well, I—no, of course not. It's just, in retrospect, maybe it was a little too much."

"In *retrospect*?" The very word incensed her. "What do you mean, *retrospect*? I thought we were looking forward now, Claire. Not back."

"It's just that, with what has happened with Jay and all..." Her voice trailed off as if not sure that more needed to be said.

Jamie disagreed with that assessment vehemently. "Jay?" she said, nearly choking on the word. "What does Jay have to do with us?"

Claire sighed. "Isn't it obvious? I was supposed to be with Jay, only I decided to be with you, and damn the consequences, and then *this* happened. It's a sign."

"A sign?" Jamie's eyes bugged. "A *sign*? You and those bloody signs, Claire. You find them when it's convenient and interpret them to mean whatever you want, or ignore them if you feel like it." Jamie raked both hands through her hair, making it stand up on end like a wild woman. "Do you honestly think that God, or the universe, or whatever, would cause a blizzard in Antarctica to wipe someone off the planet just because we spent the night together? I have news for you, Claire. Orgasms do not cause blizzards."

"Well," Claire sniffed, disapproving. "You don't have to be crude about it, you know."

Realizing that fighting wasn't getting them anywhere, Jamie changed tactics. "I'm sorry, Claire. I didn't mean to upset you. You need space, and I'll respect that." She smiled pleasantly. "So how was your day? Did you do anything interesting?"

Claire smiled graciously in return. "As a matter of fact, I did. I've spent the whole day corresponding with donors." Claire pointed to her computer screen. "I can't believe how generous people are. There are literally thousands of donors on this site who've given money." Claire's smile grew wider. "You should see all these wonderful comments, too. This is going to help so much in getting together a rescue team. With the amount of money that's coming in, we should be able to get extra vehicles, search dogs, a whole mobile hospital if they need it!"

Dogs? Vehicles? A hospital!

"Claire," Jamie's voice was stern. "You're getting so far ahead of yourself it isn't funny. This is out of control. You don't even know if anything happened. A rescue? There may not be any need for a rescue, and then what are you going to tell all these generous, wonderful people, huh?"

Claire's goodwill was short lived. "I'm just trying to do something, Jamie," she said with an edge to her tone. "Someone needs to. What about at work today? Did you find out anything?"

"No, and that's why you really need to take a step

back from this," Jamie said in her most placating tone. "No one has heard anything, okay? Until we do, can you just cool it with the news interviews and the donations? This type of thing is going to make the Board nervous."

"The Board?" Claire asked in disgust. "A friend could be injured and dying all alone on the other side of the world and all you care about is the Board?"

"Yes, because I have to, Claire. It's my job to care about what the Board thinks. If they're unhappy, I could lose my job. They need more than speculation."

If they find out about the crazy mess I've created here, I'll be fired for sure!

"Speculation?" Claire squeaked. "I got an email directly from the Marine Institute telling me that Jay was missing. That's not speculation, Jamie. That's fact. And I seem to be the only one doing anything about it!"

"Claire, that isn't fair," Jamie pleaded.

"Your people need to get their acts together if they can go twenty-four hours and not even know for certain if one of their own is missing or needs help." Tears sparkled in Claire's eyes. "I swear, when I called over there it was like no one's even sure if Jay works there! Maybe a new job wouldn't be the worst thing, if that's how much they care about people."

"Claire, come on. Have you considered that maybe they're doing what needs to be done, and you're just overreacting because you feel guilty?" Jamie cringed as the words came out. She hadn't intended to start fighting again, but that's exactly where this seemed to be headed.

"Well, have you considered you're under-reacting

because you're jealous of Jay and you'd be happier if he were gone?" Claire spat back.

Jamie felt as if Claire had slapped her.

"Jamie, I didn't mean it like that," Claire said. "I don't think you really want him to be dead or anything like that. But you have to admit, you've been a little jealous of my relationship with Jay from the beginning."

"Your...relationship? With Jay?" Jamie stifled an angry laugh. "You don't even know if you're really ready to be my girlfriend, even after an entire night of pretty damned mind-blowing sex, but you have a *relationship* with Jay?" Jamie laughed at the sheer absurdity of it. "You've never met him, Claire. You don't even know him. You're obsessed with him, and you're willing to let me lose my job over him, and you've never even seen him in person!" Jamie's voice cracked, her eyes filling with tears. "I'm not jealous of him, I'm frustrated with you for being so wrapped up in a fantasy about someone you don't know that you're willing to risk everything that we have in real life right now!"

"Jamie, stop." Claire begged. "I can hardly believe what you're saying right now! Jay's a fellow human being, and a friend. I don't have to have met him in person to care about what happens to him. Give me one good reason," she yelled, "why I should care about Jay's well being any less than I care about yours!"

"Damn it, Claire—because he doesn't exist, that's why! He isn't real. It's just me. It's been me all along." Jamie's entire body shook. She hadn't meant to do it quite like that, to spill the truth quite so ruthlessly, but she'd reached the end of her patience with the whole Jay situation. Now all she could do was wait in terror for Claire's response.

"I—I don't understand why you're acting like this," Claire replied. "And don't tell me it's just you now. That's for me to decide. You can't just declare that you're the only one who's important, you know." She sniffed, clearly feeling hurt. "I'll admit that I had a lot of fantasies built up around Jay at one time, and I don't blame you for being jealous of that, but that's not what this is. He's still a person, Jamie. It's not his fault how I behaved. He doesn't deserve to be left to die if we can help, right?"

Jamie made a sound somewhere between a sigh and a sob. Claire had completely misconstrued what she had said. But there would be no reprieve for Jamie. She needed to tell Claire the truth. It was too late for anything else.

"No, Claire. That isn't what I meant. I meant that Jay is not actually real. There's no other way I can put this. He's me. Or, I'm Jay. However you want to look at it." Jamie cast her eyes downward in shame, her cheeks burning. "It's just me. I'm the one you've been writing to all along. From the very first time."

Claire shook her head slowly, her brow furrowed in confusion. "No, that can't be. How can that be? You wouldn't make something like that up! Why would you *lie* about something like that?" Anger made her words shrill.

"I didn't mean to. I swear I didn't. It just happened." Jamie's voice was little more than a whisper.

"It *happened*? That's your explanation? It *happened*? That isn't something that just happens, Jamie. That's something you choose to do." Claire trembled with rage. "Why? Did you think it would be amusing to get a straight girl to fall in love with you or something?" Tears spilled down Claire's cheeks and she didn't bother to wipe them away. "Was it a joke to you? Have you just been laughing at me the whole time?"

"What? No! That's not how it was. And I would never have let it go this far if I hadn't known all along that you weren't really straight." Jamie regretted those words even as they slipped out of her mouth.

"Oh, you *knew* that?" Claire said coldly. "That's fascinating. *I* didn't know that I wasn't straight—hell, I still don't know if I know that!—but you knew it this whole time? And that made it okay, because you *knew*, plus you didn't really do it on purpose?" Her face contorted with anger. "Lying is not an accident, Jamie. You don't *accidentally* tell someone you're a man when you aren't."

"I didn't!" Jamie said in protest. "Claire, it was the profile mix up, remember? It told me you were in Maine, it told you I was a guy. I didn't say it, they did."

"Fine. But when you asked if I lived in Maine, I told you flat out that I lived in Oregon. You, on the other hand...you knew about the mistake and the impression that I was obviously under, and you deliberately chose to mislead me." Claire's voice sounded wounded. "You made up an apartment in Beacon Hill, and...Antarctica, and...penguins! You sent me *pictures*, for God's sake. Pictures! Who was that guy in the pictures, anyway?"

"A model from one of Paul's photo shoots," Jamie mumbled.

"A model? Huh," Claire gave a humorless laugh. "I knew it. I knew he looked like he came straight out of a catalog..." Her eyes narrowed. "Wait, does that mean Paul knew about this, too?"

Jamie nodded, closing her eyes against the coming wrath. But there was no outburst, no anger. Claire's face just went blank. She took several deep breaths before looking Jamie in the eyes.

"I was starting to think of you two as my family," she said, her voice hushed. "And you both lied to me." Claire's manner was eerily calm, and Jamie could only assume she was contemplating the depth of their betrayal.

"What, and your own family never lied to you? Oh, wait, no. They just made you lie to yourself." It wasn't that Jamie wanted to provoke her, but the sudden lack of emotion on Claire's face scared her more than seeing her angry.

"No, it wasn't their fault," Claire said in a quiet voice, refusing to rise to Jamie's bait. "They were always honest about what they thought. I was the one who chose to hide my feelings from them, and from myself. So maybe that was a lie I told myself. But how do I even know now? Maybe whatever I thought I felt was just more of your lies."

"Claire, please," Jamie whispered. "I didn't tell you about the gender thing, but that's all!"

"No, Jamie. That wasn't all, because I shared things with Jay that I never told you, and you used that." Claire's eyes brimmed with tears. "You did it from the very first time we met, didn't you? That day when you showed me the city, it wasn't a coincidence that I thought it was the perfect day, was it? You already knew everything about me. This whole time, all you had to do was have Jay ask a question and you'd know what I was thinking…"

"No, Claire…"

"…and I had no idea it was even happening. You used it to manipulate me, to control me, and make me feel things that maybe I didn't feel." Claire's body trembled all over, and Jamie couldn't tell whether it was from shock or fear.

"Please, Claire," Jamie begged, "that's not how it was. I promise you. All I ever did was create the opportunity for us to get to know each other and see what would happen. That's all."

"No, Jamie. It isn't. You don't even see what you've done, do you?" Fighting back tears, she left the room and quickly climbed the stairs.

"Please, Claire," Jamie called after her, "we'll talk about this tomorrow, okay? Please?"

But silence was the only response.

TWENTY-THREE

"CLAIRE?" The door to Claire's room was shut tight, forcing Jamie to wait in the hallway for a response. "Claire, sweetie, please let me in. Please. We really need to talk so we can fix this." There was nothing but silence. Jamie sighed and trudged down the stairs. Maybe she would find Claire there. Her hand shook with anticipation as she pushed the door open, but only Paul was inside. "Paul, have you seen Claire this morning?"

He shook his head. "Nope. Her car was already gone when I got up."

"Gone?" *Damn it, Claire. Where have you run off to this time?*

"Yeah, that was about an hour ago. This was on the counter, though." He held out a folded sheet of paper. Jamie's name was scrawled on one side.

Her heart sank as she unfolded the page and read. It wasn't the 'Dear Jamie' letter she had feared. No, it was a thousand times worse. A letter would have contained emotions, explanations, maybe a few heartfelt regrets. This read more like an instruction sheet for the mail man.

Please ship boxes on bed to Theresa's house. A Portland address was printed neatly below, and that was all. Not even a signature. Jamie bounded back up to the third floor and tore open the door to Claire's room. Her clothing was missing from the closet, and three boxes sat in the middle of the bed. Aside from that, the room was bare. *She's gone*, Jamie realized. *Really, truly gone.*

Jamie was too shaken up to drive, so Paul dropped her off near the marina and promised to collect her after work. Crossing the street, Jamie stopped to stare at the spot next to the shops where Claire had stood the night of their swim. Tears stung Jamie's eyes at the memory. She went through the side door at the Institute to avoid the ocean tank entirely. She didn't think she could bear the sight of it. Passing by Alan's desk on her way into the office, she noted that it was empty. Not that it mattered now. A message on her desk informed her that Alan was out sick today. *You just couldn't get sick yesterday, huh? Thanks a lot, buddy.* For a brief time with Claire, Jamie had started to believe that maybe signs and fate and magic were real. Now she knew the truth. At best, the universe mocked her.

Her phone buzzed. *Dr. Swenson.* The day was off to a fine start.

"Can you come to my office?"

Jamie knew her boss would want an update. What could she say that was true? She was so tired of lying.

She was still thinking about what she could tell her boss when she entered the office. In her preoccupied state, she didn't notice the large pile of photographs in the middle of Dr. Swenson's desk.

"Shut the door, please, Dr. Richards."

Alarm bells went off in Jamie's brain. Her boss had just called her by her last name. That wasn't a good sign. The pile of photographs suddenly registered like a glowing neon sign of doom, and Jamie knew she was done for. *This is the moment when I get fired.*

"I see you recognize these," Dr. Swenson said, pointing to the photos, her expression neutral. "I was concerned about the building security so I had Burt send over the rest of his surveillance tapes after we spoke yesterday. I wanted to see what this mysterious woman was up to all by herself after hours."

Jamie swallowed roughly. "Up to?"

"Yes. Was she a political activist? A corporate spy? You can't imagine how many scenarios I came up with. Imagine my surprise when I discovered that she was not, in fact, alone, but in the company of my top researcher and right hand woman, who had just assured me to my face that she had no idea who the woman in question was."

"Dr. Swenson, I can explain," Jamie began.

"No need. I think I know exactly what's going on."

"You do?" Jamie gulped. *Huh, I doubt it*, she thought. No one would guess something as messed up as this.

"I do. This Claire Flores, she's your girlfriend, isn't she." She said it as a fact, not a question.

Jamie nodded, stunned. It was a good guess, and mostly true. Claire *had been* her girlfriend, for all of about twenty-four glorious hours.

"I'm going to tell you something, Jamie, that not everyone knows. It's not a secret, but it's not widely known in my professional circles. You're not the only person in this room to get caught by her boss with her girlfriend." Dr. Swenson chuckled at the sudden look of shock on Jamie's face. "I see that surprises you."

Jamie was dizzy. Her boss was back to calling her by her first name, and had just expressed her solidarity as a fellow lesbian. That was an unexpected turn of events, to say the least. "I...I hadn't realized," she said somewhat lamely. First Alan, now Dr. Swenson. *Gaydar, my ass.* Apparently half the staff at the Institute was gay and she hadn't had the first clue.

"Well, why would you? I don't talk about my personal life at work. But I'm telling you this now because I understand what it's like to be in your position." Dr. Swenson sighed. "When I first started my career, a very long time ago, the world was a different place. I didn't even get to take my girlfriend skinny dipping in a giant indoor ocean to get myself in trouble. All I did was hold her hand when I thought we were in private, and got seen by someone who didn't know how to mind their own business. And that was that. I lost my job, and when I managed to get another one, I made sure to be much more discreet."

"We weren't skinny dipping, you know." For some reason, Jamie felt compelled to set the record straight on that one issue. It might be the only chance to defend herself, since Jamie was pretty certain that everything else she'd done was completely indefensible.

"Yes," Dr. Swenson replied, nodding. "I've seen the pictures. It was innocent enough, if against the rules. Trust me, you are not the only one to ever do it. I've personally witnessed two members of the Board of Directors in a much more compromising position in that very tank."

Jamie shuddered at the thought.

"Yes, that was my reaction too," her boss said with a snort. "Anyway, I know the added pressure you may have felt, worrying that someone would find out that you were with this mystery woman that night." Her tone was sympathetic. "It wouldn't just be admitting to breaking a rule, it would be outing yourself to your boss and all of your coworkers"

Jamie nodded. "Thank you for being so understanding." It had never occurred to her to care about being outed—she assumed everyone knew—but she jumped at the convenient excuse.

"What I don't get is this crazy story about the missing scientist. Jamie, I'm asking this in all seriousness. Is your girlfriend mentally ill?"

Jamie could tell that Dr. Swenson was genuinely concerned. "No," Jamie replied. "If only it were that simple. The truth is...well, the truth is pretty messy, but I think you deserve to hear it all." Jamie proceeded to tell her everything, from the profile mix up and the surprise visit, to Claire's move east, and even their breakup and

Claire's moving out. Jamie didn't leave anything out this time. "You don't believe me," she said when she finally got to the end of her tale.

Dr. Swenson shook her head. "Oh, no. I believe you completely. No one on earth could make up a story that insane. It has to be true. It does, however, put me in a very awkward position."

Jamie nodded. "I understand that it doesn't reflect very well on my character."

Her boss shook her head. "There's nothing wrong with your character, Jamie. Even after hearing this, I'd still trust you more than anyone else here. The problem is perception." She sighed. "You know first hand the scandal that was hanging over our heads this summer. Without you, we might have been sunk."

Jamie winced. "The irony of that is not lost on me."

"Nor me. Even now, the Board is skittish about our donors. They don't want any negative publicity. It's why the story with Claire was such a big deal. Normally, who would care about one woman with a crazy sounding story about penguins and blizzards, right?"

Jamie chuckled at the characterization despite herself.

Dr. Swenson smiled sympathetically. "But add in a juicy tale about gender mix ups and online dating, and you've got national headlines, with the Institute front and center. Our PR people are going to be working overtime to make this go away. I'm afraid my hands are tied."

Jamie's heart skipped a beat. *So, I'm getting fired, after all?*

Dr. Swenson held out a manila envelope. "This envelope does not contain termination papers." She chuckled. "Yes, I know you figured it would, so I thought I'd just put that out there right in the beginning. What it does contain is a very generous job offer at a sister facility in Newport."

"A job offer?" Jamie inquired. "I don't think I understand. I'm not being terminated—I'm getting a different job?"

Her boss nodded. "Essentially, yes. When I discovered those videos last night, there weren't a lot of options, and none of them involved you being able to stay at the Institute. The Board would have had me fired, too. And it's a real shame, Jamie, because I was serious about you becoming Head of Research."

Jamie nodded silently in acknowledgment. After everything else that had happened, she could barely process this latest loss.

Her boss continued to speak. "As it happens, I went to college with the director in Newport. I gave him a call and he's thrilled with your qualifications. I think it would be a good fit."

Jamie contemplated the unexpected turn of events. She'd been at the Marine Institute for several years. It was convenient to home, but maybe a change would be a good idea. Besides, suddenly everything here reminded her too much of Claire. She'd barely made it into the office today without breaking down. Newport was only a few hours away, and staying here wasn't an option, regardless. Dr. Swenson had made that clear.

A fresh start with a guaranteed job was hardly the end of the world.

Jamie held out her hand and took the envelope. Jamie's hand hovered above the doorknob as she turned to go. "May I ask one favor?" she said. "Whatever official statement goes out, just don't let it make Claire look bad, okay? None of this was her fault."

Dr. Swenson nodded. "I think I can promise that."

TWENTY-FOUR

"NEWPORT, HUH?" Paul said, eyeing the manila envelope in Jamie's hand.

They sat in a booth at a cafe near the marina, the type of place with tables on the deck outside during the summer and cups of homemade chowder to warm you in the winter. Jamie had intended to go straight home until she remembered Paul had dropped her off at work that morning. She'd swallowed her pride and texted him to pick her up. Stopping for food had been his idea. Food was always his first thought, but he made a good point that almost any disaster was best faced with a full stomach. It was still early for the lunchtime rush, so they had the place to themselves and a fantastic view of the water. Jamie choked back a sob as she realized how much she would miss this view once she moved.

"It could be worse," she forced herself to say. "At least Newport is known for their sailing, right?" She sighed. "How did I let this happen, Paul? I keep thinking there had to be a point where I could've stopped it, but looking back, I can't figure out when. Was this just destined to be a disaster from the beginning?"

"I don't think so, Jay."

Jamie cringed. "Could we just stick with Jamie? I don't ever want to hear the name Jay again."

"Sorry," Paul said with a sympathetic smile.

"I can't believe she's gone, Paul. The job situation I could handle, but how am I going to live without Claire?"

"Maybe she'll come around," Paul suggested. "Once she's had time to think about it, maybe she'll come back."

Jamie snorted in disbelief. "You're a hopeless optimist, Paulie. There's no way she'll ever forgive me for this. I lied to her. She has every reason to hate me. I'm a terrible person."

"No you're not. You only did what you did because she wouldn't have given you a chance otherwise. And you guys were great together."

"We really were." Jamie blinked rapidly as her eyes welled with unshed tears.

"So maybe she'll realize it, too."

She shook her head sadly. "She's gone, Paul. She doesn't want to talk to me. I'm never going to see her again."

"Don't think like that, Jamie," Paul encouraged her. "You don't know that. She only left a few hours ago. She might not even be out of the state yet! Try calling her. Maybe she'll come back so you can work it out."

"Do you think I haven't already done that? She won't

pick up when I call. I've texted her at least a dozen times. She finally did answer," Jamie added ruefully, "but only to say that if I contacted her again, she'd change her number."

"Ouch. Okay, maybe she's not ready," Paul conceded. "So give her a few weeks and then go see her."

"You mean fly to Oregon on the off chance she won't slam the door in my face?" Jamie scoffed. "Even if I thought it would work—which it won't—when am I supposed to find the time to do that? I have about two weeks to pack, find an apartment, and move before I start my new job. I don't have time to rush off on a fool's errand, too."

"So you go after you've settled in a little."

Jamie sighed. "Can't. I've only been offered a six month contract at this point, so if I want to make it permanent, I'm going to have to prove myself. That means working overtime, not taking vacation days. There's too much at stake."

"And there's not too much at stake with Claire?"

"Honestly? Probably not. Not anymore. I think I let it all go too far to ever get her back," Jamie admitted in defeat.

Paul reflected for a moment. "Alright," he said finally, "I guess you know best. So, what's this new job supposed to be like, anyway?"

Jamie shrugged. "I'm not even sure. The whole morning has been such a shock, I've barely glanced at the offer."

"That's it there?" Paul asked, inclining his head

toward the manila envelope on the table. "Mind if I take a look?"

Jamie slid the envelope across the table. "Be my guest."

Paul whistled under his breath. "Not a bad salary," he said. "And there's a stipend for relocating, too. That's nice. You may have destroyed your love life, but it looks like your professional life's still intact, if this is any indication."

Jamie smiled a little despite herself. "Yeah, it's a good offer. The truth is, this may end up being a really good move, job wise. This place has tons of global connections, so even if it's not permanent, it could open up some really exciting opportunities." She gave a little laugh. "Ironic, huh? This fiasco may do wonders for my career."

"Uh, Jamie? Your career might not be the only thing." Paul's expression was unreadable.

"What do you mean?"

He pointed to the contract. "Exactly how much of this did you read?"

Jamie gave a dismissive shrug. "A quick skim. Why?"

"So, you didn't read the last page? The one with the mailing address of the Newport Marine Research Lab?"

Jamie shook her head impatiently. "Obviously I must not have. What are you getting at?"

"Jamie, the lab's not in Newport, Rhode Island. It's in Newport, Oregon." Paul's face lit up in a grin. "Newport frickin' Oregon!"

"You're joking."

"I am not joking. It's a sign!"

Jamie stared at the contract in shock. "There is no such thing as signs. When is the universe going to stop screwing with me?"

"Are you kidding me, Jamie?" Paul countered. "The universe just handed you this on a silver platter."

"You're as bad as Claire," she replied in disbelief. "Signs. I wish I could believe in them, Paul. I really do. But I can't. I evaluate the facts. And the truth is, the facts haven't changed."

"Of course they have! You're going to Oregon!"

Jamie shook her head. "So, I'm going to Oregon. So what? That's just geography. Claire still hates me. I still lied to her, and betrayed her trust. She isn't going to forgive me, whether I'm three miles away or three thousand. The only thing this is a sign of," Jamie concluded, "is that the people in Oregon stole way too many of their town names from New England."

"But you'll at least go see her?"

"No." Jamie shook her head sadly. "I don't think I will. It's over, Paul. I've lost her. I deserved to lose her. I need to move on and try to get over this somehow. Where I do that from doesn't really matter."

"You're serious, aren't you?" Paul asked in disbelief. "You're really going to go all that way and not even see her. Will you at least tell her where you are?"

"Why bother?" Jamie shot back, slumping in resignation.

"Why? Because when she comes to her senses and realizes that you don't find the love of your life everyday, she should at least know how to get a hold of you."

"I'm sure Claire will have no trouble finding someone else," Jamie said bitterly. "As for me, maybe knowing that I'm so close and can never be with her is just the universe's way of punishing me. There's no need to punish her with the knowledge, too."

The waiter arrived with their bowls of chowder and Paul was momentarily distracted, giving Jamie a chance to reflect on the unexpected turn of events. *Newport, Oregon? I sure didn't see that coming.* But she'd meant what she said. It didn't change anything. Claire had every reason to hate her. The truth was, Jamie hadn't just lied. As much as she hated to admit it, Claire was right. Jamie had been manipulative. She'd used information that had been shared in confidence with Jay to her advantage. What kind of a person did that make her?

"Promise you'll at least think about it," Paul said after swallowing a mouthful of soup.

Jamie nodded, but it was noncommittal. She'd think about it, sure. Every single day, once she was in Oregon, Jamie had no doubt she would think about it and be tempted. But she couldn't let herself do anything that would hurt Claire again. Jamie loved her too much for that.

Why does the universe have to be so cruel?

TWENTY-FIVE

RAINDROPS SWIRLED in a drizzling mist as Claire plodded up the flagstone steps to her sister's house. *Did it always rain this much in Portland?* It had never bothered Claire before, but in the past six weeks since she returned home, it seemed as if the rain had never stopped. The days were biting and raw, matching her mood perfectly. It took most of her energy just to drag herself to work each morning.

Lovejoy College had been willing to take her back for the spring semester, but her schedule consisted of the least desirable classes and times, meaning she was at the office constantly but only barely bringing in a part-time salary for her trouble. The chance of ever getting back on track professionally felt remote.

As she removed her wet shoes and coat, Claire heard Theresa's footsteps coming toward the front hall.

"Claire, is that you?" her sister called. "I wasn't sure you'd make it in time for dinner. Where have you been?"

"Out," Claire replied sullenly. "I went to the mall to see if anyone was hiring, but now that the holidays are over, there's not much available."

"A second job? You already spend all day at the college! When would you have time for something else?"

"I don't know, Theresa." Claire nearly snarled in response. "But I have to do something! I can't afford to get my own place on what I'm making, and I don't want to live with you and Larry forever."

"I'm sure your schedule will be better in the fall. The department just wasn't expecting you back this semester, that's all." Theresa placed a hand on Claire's shoulder. "I know it may not be what you want, but you're welcome to keep living here as long as you need to."

Claire sighed. "I'm sorry, Theresa. I don't mean to sound ungrateful. I'm just so frustrated and angry. But with myself, not you."

"Are you finally ready to talk about it?"

Claire shook her head. She had steadfastly avoided giving her sister any details since calling her from a rest stop in New York to let her know she was on her way home. She didn't want to talk about it now, or ever.

Theresa sighed. "Fine. At least come sit with us while I finish making dinner, and say hello to your nephews. They've missed you. Of course, they probably thought with you living in their house that they'd see you more than they did when you were on the other side of the country."

Claire felt a stab of guilt. It wasn't her nephews' fault that she had turned into a recluse since returning to Portland. She'd need to make a bigger effort to spend time with them, if only so they wouldn't worry.

"Aunt Claire," Ryan called, his face brightening when his aunt entered the room, "look what I got under my pillow last night!" He held up a gold dollar coin.

"Another visit from the tooth fairy, *mijo*?" Claire replied, trying her best to sound jovial. "You're going to run out of teeth pretty soon! Here, let me see that," she added, reaching for the coin. She held it in her hand, absentmindedly twirling it along her knuckles and then making it disappear with a flick of her fingers and wrist.

"Wow," both boys gasped, impressed.

"Hey, where did my coin go?" Ryan asked, a little worried.

Claire reached behind his ear and the coin reappeared in her hand. "Here you go, *mijo*."

"So cool," Ryan breathed. "How did you learn to do that?"

An image of walking home from the park with Jamie assaulted her memory. She could almost feel the crisp fall air and smell the faint aroma of Jamie's sandalwood soap. It had been at that moment, she realized, when Jamie had first stolen her heart. Jamie had taken it just like Claire had taken Ryan's coin. And then she'd made it all disappear, and Claire would never get it back. She blinked her stinging eyes and a tear escaped, gliding down one cheek.

"Aunt Claire, why are you crying?" Jesse asked.

Theresa whipped around in place at the stove. "Boys, you can finish your homework upstairs, okay? Go on, now. March." She waited until she heard the creak of feet on the stairs before addressing her sister. "What the hell, Claire?" she whispered sharply. "You still won't tell me why you left Massachusetts, and now you're crying in the middle of the kitchen. What's going on?"

Claire's answer was muffled by sobs. She lay her head on her arms atop the table and wept bitterly for what seemed an eternity. Her sister sat beside her in silence, stroking her shoulders and back, soothing her like she would a small child. Finally, when Claire's sobbing had turned to shallow, ragged breaths, Theresa spoke.

"Is this about Jamie?" she asked.

Claire nodded.

"Were you...were you two dating?" Theresa asked with as much delicacy as she could.

Claire nodded again.

"And something happened." This time it wasn't a question.

"She lied to me. That's as much as I want to say, okay?"

"Okay," Theresa said, nodding. "But don't you think you should talk to her, try to work it out?"

Claire shook her head vigorously. "No. The whole thing was a mistake. It never should have happened."

Theresa sighed. "Claire, I saw you two together. It seemed very real to me."

Claire gave a bitter laugh. "Reality had nothing to do with it, trust me."

"Claire, did this have something to do with that emergency with Jay that you tried to tell me about?"

"Jay." Claire snorted in disgust at the name.

"What, he did something to make you angry, too?"

Claire contemplated this silently for a moment. "In a way," she said finally. "He didn't exist, Theresa. You wanted to know the details? Well, there they are."

"I don't understand," Theresa replied.

"Jamie made him up." Claire's eyes flashed with anger as she spoke. "She lied about the whole thing. It was her the whole time. And then she sent me an email saying he was missing, and probably dead."

"What?" Theresa said, clearly shocked. "That's insane! Jamie did that? Why would she do something like that?"

"She said it was all a mistake, an accident. It got out of her control." Claire's shoulders slumped. "And the thing is, I guess I believe her. It just doesn't matter now."

"Oh, Claire," Theresa said, resting her hand on her sister's shoulder. "I'm so sorry. What are you going to do now?"

Claire shrugged. "Just go back to the way things were before, I guess. Hope to get my career back on track eventually, get my own apartment. What else can I do?"

"What about dating again?" Theresa asked tentatively. "I don't mean now, obviously. But at least one good thing came out of all this. You've figured out something important about yourself, right? Eventually, maybe you'll meet another girl you like and—"

"No." Claire was emphatic. "I won't be doing *that* again."

"But, Claire. You've been looking for a relationship

forever. You can't give up on finding love just because of one set back."

"I don't intend to, not forever. Look, I don't know what Jamie did to manipulate me into being with her, but I won't fall for something like that again."

"Come on now, Claire. The one thing you must have figured out through all of this, once and for all, is that you're a lesbian, right?"

Claire's back stiffened. "I don't know that at *all*. Jamie confused me. I have no idea how I really feel. For all I know, it was all just part of her trick."

"Seriously, *hermanita*? How many of those precious signs of yours is it going to take to get through to you?"

"Signs? What do I know about signs anymore, huh?" Claire's voice cracked in frustration. "As it happens, there's a new adjunct in our department who's been very friendly lately. So maybe that's a sign. Maybe he'll ask me out. Maybe I'll go." Her voice held little trace of enthusiasm.

Theresa rolled her eyes. "I see. Well, I don't know what else to say. I should probably get dinner on the table. You eating with us?"

"I've lost my appetite." Claire disappeared down the hallway toward her room.

AFTER THE DISHES were cleared and the kids tucked into bed, Theresa sat alone in the kitchen, reflecting on what Claire had told her. She had to admit, the whole situation worried her. Claire was hurt and retreating into herself. She obviously needed closure with Jamie, and some serious soul searching. Despite what Claire had said, Theresa still held out a glimmer of hope that her sister and Jamie would reconcile. She'd been so positive about them, and she was rarely wrong when it came to matters of the heart. There had to be another side to this story, one that would make the pieces fit together better. Jamie deserved a chance to explain her side of things.

Theresa picked up her phone and found the number for the house in Cape Ann. Resolutely, she pressed the call button, and it was only when a groggy voice on the other end picked up that she remembered the three hour time difference. She cringed when she saw the clock. It was well past midnight on the east coast.

"Hello, Jamie?" she inquired, her voice tinged with guilt. "I'm so sorry. I forgot it's three hours earlier in Oregon."

"What?" a voice answered in a gravelly tone that could only belong to a man. "This is Paul. Did you say Oregon? Is this Jamie?"

"No, no, Paul," Theresa corrected, "it's Theresa. Remember, Claire's sister? We met at Thanksgiving. I was *calling* for Jamie. Is she home?"

"Huh, I don't know. You'd probably have an easier time finding that out than I would," he said, sounding amused. "Jamie took a job in Oregon about a month ago."

"What? She's moved here?" Theresa was confused. Why had her sister never mentioned it? "Does Claire know?"

Paul gave a little laugh. "Are you kidding? No way. Jamie was so convinced that Claire would refuse to see her, she swore me to secrecy. Oops," he added. "I guess I kind of screwed up by telling you."

"Paul, this is nuts. What exactly happened, do you know? What Claire told me didn't make a whole lot of sense."

"Well, it started last summer with Tech Cupid's infamous computer glitch..." Paul recounted everything that had transpired after that. His version contained many of the same elements that Theresa had heard from Claire, but the way he told it made Theresa feel inclined to give Jamie the benefit of the doubt.

"You're sure Jamie didn't try to fool her on purpose?" she asked. "And she didn't send that terrible email about Jay?"

"No," Paul assured her. "She had nothing to do with the email. That was my fault."

"Why would you write something like that?" Theresa asked, her voice scolding.

"I was just trying to cheer Jamie up," Paul said. "I never would have sent it. And I had no idea about your parents' accident, I swear. I'm so sorry."

"Well, what Jamie did was beyond stupid," Theresa commented when Paul had finished.

"But she only did it because she loves Claire."

Theresa sighed. "She really, truly does?"

"No doubt about it. She's miserable without her," Paul replied without hesitation.

"Claire is, too. It's pathetic, really. She cries, and

mopes around, and barely eats. We need to do something."

"Like what?" Paul asked.

Theresa thought for a moment. "Let me call you back in the morning. I need to check my calendar at work, but I think I might have a plan to at least get them to meet. The rest is up to them."

TWENTY-SIX

JAMIE STARED at the one-way sign on the street ahead, then to the GPS that emphatically directed her to turn the wrong direction down it. She strangled a frustrated scream as she continued to drive. "Recalculating route," the device's soothing British voice informed her. *Yeah, you do that. Again.*

She'd chosen that particular accent to help keep her calm, but it wasn't working. She'd been circling the campus for at least fifteen minutes and it was becoming increasingly clear that some evil entity had come through Lovejoy College in the middle of the night and slapped up one-ways and do-not-enters willy-nilly on every street. Either that or her GPS was possessed.

"Satellite signal lost," it told her. Jamie figured the odds were increasingly in favor of demon possession.

She spotted a sign for visitor parking on her right and whipped the car into the entrance, thankful there had been no obstacles to hit in her haste. She took a ticket from the machine and squeezed into the last remaining space between two cars whose drivers had taken the yellow stripes on the pavement as the vaguest of suggestions. Her shirt caught on the car door as she shimmied her way out of the narrow space, and she cursed under her breath. The last thing she needed was a big grease mark on her front when she went to see Claire. Upon inspection, the shirt appeared to have escaped unscathed, but her confidence was shaken. *This is a terrible plan.*

It wasn't even her idea to come to the campus today. It had taken three weeks for Paul to convince her to talk to Theresa, and another couple of days for her to agree to the plan she had proposed. Even now, Jamie still didn't see how it was supposed to work. Nothing had changed. Yet, here she was, hoping Theresa and Paul were right and she was wrong. Her sister said Claire was miserable without her. Well, the feeling was mutual. *Is that going to be enough to erase the past?*

A map at the edge of the parking lot confirmed that she had chosen the parking lot that was as far away from Endicott Hall, where Claire's office was, as was physically possible while still remaining on campus. *Fantastic.* Were she a believer in signs like Claire, she would turn around right now and go home because nothing in her experience so far pointed to a happy ending to the day. But she wasn't, and so she pressed on until the building she sought loomed directly ahead.

She looked at the time and groaned. She should have arrived at ten minutes before noon, picked up the key to

Claire's office from Theresa, and slipped inside to wait for her to return from class. Theresa had arranged to have lunch with Claire a little after noon to guarantee that Claire would be waiting in her office when Jamie arrived. Instead, it was now twenty minutes past the hour and Jamie had almost certainly missed her chance. *I should just go home.*

Just as Jamie was turning to leave, the door to Endicott Hall opened and Claire exited. A handsome, if somewhat nerdy man wearing stereotypical tweed followed closely behind her. Claire froze at the top of the steps as she spotted Jamie, and for an instant Jamie thought her own heart had stopped. The longing she felt for that tiny, curly haired woman sent such a physical jolt through her body that she wouldn't have been surprised to collapse and die right on the spot. But she didn't. Instead, she just stood and stared as Claire muttered something to the man beside her before descending the stairs. Her posture was rigid, her lips set in a thin, tight line across her face. Anger rolled off her like a wave that took Jamie's breath away. *I should have escaped while I could.*

"What the hell are you doing here?" Claire challenged her in a hushed voice. "Why are you at my work?"

"I needed to see you," Jamie replied with as much resolve as she could muster under the intensity of Claire's gaze.

"Fine. You've seen me. Now go back to Boston and leave me alone."

"Claire, please. Can we talk?"

The nerdy professor came up close beside Claire. "Everything okay?"

He was acting protective. Possessive. Jealousy flared in Jamie's chest and she wished that she could strike this man dead with just the power of her mind.

"Yes, it's fine," Claire replied, "but I think I'll have to take a rain check on lunch, Dennis."

The disappointment was evident on his face. "Oh, okay. But I'll still see you tonight?"

"Wouldn't miss it," Claire assured him with a radiant smile that pierced Jamie's heart like a dagger.

"Who was that?" Jamie asked as she watched the man retreat. "New boyfriend? You happen to mention me?" Sarcasm oozed from her words.

Claire's eyes narrowed with rage. "You've got a lot of nerve...come on," she ordered, turning back toward the stairs.

"Where are we going?" Jamie asked, nervousness pricking the back of her neck. She'd never seen Claire so mad. It was strangely alluring, but also terrifying. She looked capable of leading Jamie anywhere right now. Police station. Dungeon. Firing squad. All were equally plausible.

"We're going to my office," she explained through clenched teeth. "That way if I lose it and slap you, it won't be the talk of the department tomorrow."

The clicking of Claire's shoes echoed in the hallway. Jamie realized she had returned to her old, impractical footwear and wondered what that meant. *Was it for what's-his-name's benefit?* She felt another sharp stab, then a wild hope that Claire would stumble in those ridiculous shoes so that she could come to her rescue. Alas, Claire seemed to be maneuvering in them with no trouble on the smooth linoleum floor. *Where's a good cobblestone street when you need one?*

Claire switched on the light with a slap of her palm, shutting the door with a bang once Jamie entered the small office. "So, talk." Claire directed.

"I...I came to apologize," Jamie began, tripping over her words. She loved sweet and gentle Claire, but in control and furious Claire was really...*hot*. She was having a hard time remembering what she had come to say when Claire was standing so close. Jamie stifled a mad impulse to push Claire onto the desk behind her and devour her mouth like she had that day in the kitchen back home. But she was almost certain that approach wouldn't fly right now. *What a pity.*

"You traveled three thousand miles to say you're sorry?" There was skepticism in Claire's tone.

"No, I drove about two hours from my apartment."

"Your...apartment? You live here?" Her words were tentative, breathy. Confusion filled Claire's eyes, and Jamie could almost see the battle taking place within as Claire wavered between anger and excitement. "Why?" she questioned harshly, anger winning out. "So you can stalk me or something?" She took a step backward as she said it, retreating to the safety of the far side of her desk. Claire glanced furtively at the desktop, blushing in a way that made Jamie wonder if she'd had a similar fantasy about ways they could use its surface. Jamie hoped so.

"Claire, come on," Jamie pleaded. "I'm not here to stalk you. I was transferred to Newport for work almost three months ago. It was completely outside my control, and I wasn't even planning on telling you or seeing you, except..."

"Except what?"

Jamie hesitated, not wanting to get Theresa in trouble. This reunion wasn't exactly going the way Claire's sister had hoped, and there was no sense tipping Claire off to the fact that she'd had any part in encouraging it. "Except I really wanted to see you."

"And what you want is always so important, isn't it?" Claire asked bitterly. "What about what I want?"

"What do you want, Claire?" Genuine desperation filled her as she asked. She really needed to know.

"What do I want?" Claire's voice cracked and tears glistened in the corners of her eyes. "What I want, is to have my old life back. I want to be able to feel happy when a cute guy at work asks me out—"

"I knew it," Jamie interrupted, her eyes narrowing into cat-like slits. "You're going out with that Dennis guy tonight, aren't you?"

"Seriously, Jamie?" Claire responded, her own eyes flashing. "You want to talk about Dennis right now? Fine. Let's talk about him. Has he asked me out? Yes, actually, he has."

"And you're going to go." Jamie shook her head in disbelief. "Do you really think that this Dennis guy, or any guy, is going to make you happy?" she asked, her voice rising in challenge.

"No!" Claire spat back, her own volume matching Jamie's. "And do you have any idea how hard that is for me to admit? Do you know how much I want to enjoy his company, or the company of any other man, instead of feeling a twinge of disgust because I know if he puts his hands on me, they won't make me feel the way your hands made me feel?"

Claire sobbed as the tears flowed freely. Jamie reached out, wanting nothing more than to put her hands on Claire now, to soothe away her despair. Claire took a step back, batting Jamie's hand away.

"This is your fault." Claire told her. "Why couldn't you have just left me alone instead of tying my insides up with your lies and your manipulation and ruining everything for me?"

"Me?" Jamie asked incredulously. "Look, I admit that I was dishonest and for that I truly am sorry. It tears me up that I lied to you and hurt you that way. But you can't honestly blame me for anything else."

"You confused me."

"Yeah, well, you confused me, too. Be logical, Claire. It's not like I cast some sort of spell over you! Whatever you felt for me when we were together, and whatever you still feel now, that came from you."

Claire glared at Jamie but did not speak.

"And for the record," Jamie added, sniffing loudly to keep back her own tears, "you kissed me first. That day in the kitchen, you kissed *me*. And you're the one who came to my room, to my bed. I told you to go. You chose to stay." Jamie's voice shook as she spoke. "I may have lied to you in the beginning, but you're the one lying right now if you think it happened any other way."

Claire's eyes were clamped shut, her whole body trembling. "I think you'd better go, Jamie." She took a deep breath and opened her eyes. The look she fixed on Jamie was icy cold.

"Claire, listen to me. It would be an even bigger lie if I said I didn't want you back. I love you. But even if you don't want to be with me, don't be with Dennis."

"That's none of your business," Claire replied stiffly.

"Maybe not," Jamie said quietly. "But you deserve to find a woman who will make you happy, not settle for what you think other people expect for you. You have to be honest with yourself, Claire."

"I *have* to?" Claire answered with an edge to her voice. "You don't get to tell me what I have to do, Jamie. Or what I want. Or what will make me happy." She threw her hands in the air. "Why don't *you* go find a woman whom you can confuse and manipulate with your charm. I'm sure Portland is just full of women who would love the chance to question everything they ever thought they knew about their identities, all thanks to you."

"Claire," Jamie sighed, "I don't want another woman. I just want you."

"Well, I don't want you. I don't." Though whether this last bit was to convince herself or Jamie, it was impossible to tell.

The quiet sound of Claire's sobbing followed Jamie down the hall. She staved off her own tears until she was safe within the privacy of her car, at which point they flowed freely. This had been her last chance to win Claire back, and she had lost. The love of her life was gone forever.

TWENTY-SEVEN

"YOU DID *WHAT?*" Theresa stared at her sister in disbelief.

The evening was warm for March and the sisters soaked in the fresh evening air on the porch, wrapped in blankets and sipping sangria. She might live to regret mixing up a batch of Paul's secret recipe, but Claire needed something a little stronger than usual to dull the agony that had plagued her since Jamie's visit that afternoon.

She'd sent her apologies for missing the midterm review session that evening—which, incidentally, was the only "date" she had ever planned with Dennis, not that Jamie needed to know that. After a good start on the potent liquid in her glass, she unburdened the day's events to Theresa. Much to her surprise, her sister didn't seem nearly as proud of how Claire had handled the situation as she'd expected her to be.

"I thought you'd be glad that it's finally settled,"

Claire responded in confusion. "You said I needed closure."

"Closure?" Theresa laughed. "Honestly, *hermanita*, you can be so dense. Do you really think Paul and I spent a month convincing Jamie to go talk to you just so you could have a little closure?"

Claire's jaw hung open. "You and Paul?"

"Of course, who else? Didn't Jamie tell you? No," Theresa said, answering her own question, "I can see that she didn't. Poor Jamie. She didn't want to go but we finally convinced her that you were in a forgiving mood and wouldn't act—well, exactly the way you acted." She shook her head. "I guess she really does know you better than I do."

"But Theresa," Claire asked, "why would you encourage her? You know I don't want to think about any of that stuff any more."

"Any of that stuff. You mean," her sister countered, "that stuff like how you're still so in love with Jamie that you cry yourself to sleep every night? Or how Jamie's a woman, and you don't want to deal with what that means because it will mess up this neat little picture you're still clinging to of that perfect future you always assumed you'd have?"

"What's wrong with wanting things to be a certain way?" Claire asked indignantly. "Why am I such a bad person because I want a nice, simple life like Mom and Dad had?"

Theresa poured another glass of sangria and took a long sip before answering. "Like Mom and Dad? Well, for one thing, mom and dad didn't really have such a perfect life. Not the way you seem to think, anyway."

"What do you mean?" Claire's stomach tightened into a knot over how her sister would answer.

Theresa took a deep breath. "I mean, Claire, that you've idolized Mom and Dad your whole life. You're so convinced that what they had was perfect that you've never allowed yourself to really ask if it's the truth. You know what, Claire? Even they didn't always want what they had."

"I don't understand," Claire said in confusion, taking a sip from her own glass.

"Don't get me wrong. Mom and Dad had a pretty good life together, okay? I'm sure they loved us. But Mom never wanted to stay in Portland, or teach high school English."

"She loved being a teacher," Claire protested.

"But it wasn't her dream. She dreamed of was being a writer and moving to New York City to live like an artist."

"Then why didn't she?"

"Because she got pregnant in college. And, you know Dad. He immediately stepped up and insisted they get married."

"Wait," Claire countered, not quite certain if the spinning in her head was from the sangria or the unexpectedly intimate revelation about her parents' personal lives. "You're telling me that our parents only got married because they *had* to."

"I'm sure that wasn't the only reason," Theresa

replied. "But it's also not quite the fairy-tale romance Aunt Marisol let you believe all these years, is it?"

"I guess not."

"Aunt Marisol had no idea how to raise children. The only thing she knew was guilt, how to make us feel terrible at how our perfect, sainted parents wept over our every failing."

"Huh," Claire pondered. "You know, she actually told me once that every time it rained, it was them crying in heaven because I'd been bad."

Theresa stared at her, wide eyed. "We grew up in Portland, Claire. It rains almost every day here. *Ay dios mio*," she mumbled under her breath, "no wonder you're so screwed up."

"Hey, I heard what you just said. It's not like I believed her."

"Maybe not, but you still had to put up with stuff like that floating around in your head. It's not what Mom and Dad would have wanted."

"You really think so?" Claire asked, dabbing the moisture that had formed in the corner of her eyes.

Theresa drained the last drops from her wine glass, then set it down on the coffee table in front of her. "Remember, I was in high school when they died, so I was already thinking about college and careers and that type of thing. You know what Mom always told me?"

Claire shook her head in response.

"She told me I needed to follow my dreams. Take risks. Take time to figure out who I was and what I was meant to be. Honestly, I probably wasn't the best example of that for you. It turns out I'm not really much of a risk taker." Theresa shrugged. "The stuff I wanted was pretty average stuff. But I never forgot her advice. I wish she could have given it to you, too. There's so much more you could do if you gave yourself permission to try."

"Like what?" Claire asked, curious what her sister recognized in her that she couldn't see herself.

"You should be having adventures, Claire! Seeing the world, figuring out what you want. It's what Mom and Dad would have wanted for you. Just look at how fearless you were, running off to Boston. Even when I tried to discourage you."

Claire snorted. "Sure. Look how great *that* turned out."

"But at least you tried! And, was it really so bad?" her sister challenged. "It may not have ended up the way you thought it would, but you got to experience a new place, meet new people. Fall in love?"

"Get duped. Have my heart broken," Claire countered.

"At least it was more exciting than anything that was likely to happen to you if you had stayed here. And I still believe that meeting Jamie will turn out not to be such a bad thing in the long run."

"You mean, you think I should get back together with her," she said, her voice flat.

"It's not my place to say, *hermanita*. I think you should do whatever feels right to you. I'm going to try not to have an opinion on it anymore. But even if you never see her again, just the fact that you allowed yourself to fall in love with her at all has to open up a brighter future for you."

"Why? Because it was supposed to make me realize that my life would be perfect if I would just start dating women? That's what you were figuring, right?" Claire sighed heavily. "Only, it didn't really happen like that. I'm still waiting for that lightning bolt of clarity. Right now, I can't picture myself ever falling in love again. Not with anyone. Honestly, I think I'm more confused now than I was before."

"Aha, but just a few months ago, you wouldn't have admitted that you *were* confused. I think that's progress."

Claire rolled her eyes. "Always the glass half full type, aren't you." She held up her wine glass and examined it in the glowing candle light. "My glass, however, is completely empty, and I know from previous experience that one is all I can handle. I should probably go to bed."

"Yeah, me too," Theresa said. "Promise me something, though?"

Claire raised her eyebrows in curiosity.

"Promise me you'll try to find something you've always wanted and take a risk on it, okay? Maybe not love, but something."

"Okay," Claire promised, though nothing particularly risky sprang to mind.

TWO WEEKS WENT by and Claire still hadn't

thought of a way to fulfill her promise when an oversize envelope arrived in the mail for her. Spying a return address from the not-too-distant town of Newport, Claire's nerves jangled in alarm. *Jamie.* Would she open it to find a long love letter? She wasn't sure how she would react to reading something like that.

Her hands trembled as she sliced through the seal with a butter knife and dumped the contents on the kitchen table. She needn't have been concerned. Inside was a nondescript business envelope with a square, yellow sticky note that read 'For You'. Nothing more. Claire's breath hitched as she recognized Jamie's handwriting. A cloud of disappointment settled over her at the impersonal note, even as she reasoned with herself that she hadn't wanted anything more.

The envelope was from a Boston law firm. Claire unfolded the letter within and began to read. According to the letter, once she signed and returned the enclosed documents, all of the funds that had been collected on the donation site for Jay's rescue would be transferred to the Marine Institute. Claire set it down on the table when she finished and breathed a sigh of relief.

She had known this was a possibility, as the Institute's head of PR had contacted her via email in January with the idea. Claire's main desire at the time had been to put the whole sorry mess behind her with as little attention as possible, and the PR person had agreed wholeheartedly. They determined that the easiest course of action would be to transfer the account to the Institute and allow them to figure out what to do with it from there, assuming, of course, that the lawyers and accountants could figure out a way to do it properly. It seemed they had.

Claire examined the rest of the paperwork and discovered that the Institute did not intend to keep the money, but instead would distribute it to a university that was doing groundbreaking research in climate science. Claire smiled at that. It seemed appropriate, and the thought crossed her mind that Jamie would be pleased, too.

Not that I care.

Moving on, however, turned out to be harder than she had anticipated. What she was doing might better be described as getting by. It was just the same old life, day after day, without movement to it at all. Every morning she went to teach the same early classes that no one else had wanted, hoping the next semester would bring a better schedule. Each afternoon she rebuffed another tentative suggestion of a lunch date from Dennis, or one of the other two adjuncts who had suddenly and inexplicably decided to pursue her this spring. *Where were they all a year ago, when online dating seemed like the only option?* The prospect of their company held little excitement for her now.

Claire tried to convince herself that there was no connection between her lack of enthusiasm and how she ended each day, lying in bed with her arms wrapped around her pillow for comfort, resolute in her efforts not to imagine the scent of sandalwood as she drifted into slumber. She hadn't forgotten the promise she'd made to

Theresa to take a risk on some as-yet-undetermined dream, but she had no idea what that dream might be or how she would fulfill it.

One day in mid-April another envelope arrived, this time bearing stamps with the profile of a queen and the proper-looking crest of a very grateful university on the far side of the pond. When Claire saw what was inside, the seeds of a plan began to form, and for the first time in a very long time, a familiar old phrase flitted through her mind.

It's a sign.

TWENTY-EIGHT

CLAIRE STUDIED the complex of cookie-cutter apartments, their gray siding and white trim vaguely nautical, though technically the ocean was a few miles away. She felt her stomach tighten as she glanced down at the crumpled envelope in her hand. She studied the address again, just to be sure. She needn't have bothered. By the time she looked up again, the door to a unit halfway down the row had opened and a tall woman with cropped blond hair emerged. *Jamie.*

Claire's heart fluttered. She was followed closely by a woman of average height, and well above average figure, with a wild mane of deep purple and brilliant blue. A pang of jealousy stabbed Claire in the gut. Not only had Jamie managed to move on in the three months since she had shown up in Claire's office unannounced, but her taste in women had gotten more daring, too.

Or maybe not, Claire mused. It's not like she knew

anything about the hundreds of other women Jamie might have slept with before her. And it's not like it was any of her business who Jamie slept with now. *But really, purple hair?*

Jamie went back inside, shutting the door behind her. Drawing a deep breath, Claire slammed her car door, wondering for at least the thousandth time if coming here was a mistake. But deep down, Claire knew she couldn't leave Oregon without seeing Jamie one last time. To say goodbye. As her anger toward Jamie finally started to subside, guilt and doubt, and several other unpleasant sensations, had wriggled their way into the space left behind. Over time, her sense of Jamie's betrayal shrank in its enormity, and her awareness of her own shortcomings grew.

She couldn't leave without real closure.

There was no denying that Jamie had lied, and lied big, but she'd only ever been motivated by the chance to spend more time with Claire. *Was that really so bad?* And looking back, it was such an obvious lie. The cowboy hat on the hall tree, Jamie's khaki coveralls, the times Paul had slipped up and called her Jay, there had been so many easy clues. For her own part, Claire had been so insecure in her feelings that her attitude toward Jamie had been completely unyielding once she found out the truth. *Is that any way to treat the person you love?* And Claire had loved her. She could finally admit it.

Not that it really mattered now. Claire was moving, and Jamie had moved on to someone new. At least the experience had taught her a valuable lesson. If she was ever lucky enough to fall in love again, Claire hoped that she would recognize it this time, no matter what shape or size or age or gender it came packaged in, and never let it go. She had Jamie to thank for that.

She rapped her knuckles against the smooth steel of the door, which was hot to the touch in the mid-July sun. Then she held her breath and waited for Jamie to answer the door. *Or see me through the peep-hole and decide not to.* But the door swung open a moment later and Jamie stood in front of her, a puzzled expression on her face at the sight of Claire.

"Hi," Claire breathed.

"Hi," Jamie answered, then remained still for a moment as if trying to recall what should happen next. "Did you want to come in?" she finally thought to say.

Claire gave her a tentative smile and stepped in out of the heat. She noted several boxes stacked in the entry. No doubt they belonged to the new girlfriend, Technicolor Barbie. Claire sniffed in distaste at the thought of this other woman moving in, but refrained from making a comment.

Jamie motioned toward the living room. After assessing the Spartan seating options, Claire chose the battered futon. Jamie half-dragged, half-rolled an equally ancient chair from the far side of the room. It was round and deep, with a bamboo frame, in a style that had once been popular in college dorm rooms. Jamie deposited it next to the futon, and joined her. A memory flashed through Claire's mind of her sister Theresa's first apartment in college, which had been at least as run down as this place. After the beautiful house in Cape Ann, this wasn't at all what Claire had expected.

"It came furnished," Jamie offered by way of explanation, as if Claire had spoken her thoughts out loud.

"Oh," Claire replied. "It's nice," she added for the sake of politeness.

Jamie laughed. "It's terrible," she countered. "I won't be sorry to see it go."

Claire wrinkled her brow. "You're going somewhere?"

"Yes, didn't you notice the boxes as you came in?" Jamie answered, sounding surprised.

"Oh, I guess not," Claire fumbled, having noticed them quite plainly, but wondering what she'd missed.

"My contract's up at the end of the month so I'm moving on. There's a new person at work who's taking over the lease. Actually, you just missed her. She came by to drop off some things."

So that curvy thing with the day-glo hair is the new tenant and not the new girlfriend? Claire's heart did a little dance inside her ribcage at the news. *Not that it changes anything*, she reprimanded herself.

"So, what are you doing here, Claire?" Jamie asked, breaking the silence that had settled between them.

The way she asked wasn't accusatory, just honestly curious, and beneath that, a little sad. Claire had come prepared with a whole speech, but now that she was here, breathing in the scent of sandalwood soap each time she inhaled, she couldn't remember a single word.

"I'm sorry," she whispered, her voice catching in her throat. "I'm so sorry," she repeated, reaching her hand out as she spoke and brushing the tips of her fingers absently across the faded upholstery of Jamie's round chair.

"No, Claire. It was my fault," Jamie said sadly.

"But I ran away. I didn't give you a chance to explain. I know it's too late now, but I wish I hadn't done that. I wish I'd been able to trust you enough to at least make an effort to understand why you did what you did."

"You know I never, ever meant for any of it to happen, right? I could never hurt you like that on purpose."

"I know."

"I should have told you about the mix up the minute I figured it out."

"And if you had, you never would have heard from me again." Claire shrugged. "That's the honest truth."

"That doesn't make what I did okay." Jamie clenched her eyes shut and sighed.

"No. But in a way, I'm kind of glad you did." Claire smiled wistfully. "I would have missed out on so much if I had never gotten to know you."

Jamie crossed her right arm over her chest until her hand reached the spot where Claire's rested. She covered Claire's hand in hers and squeezed it tightly. "Come and sit with me?"

"In that?" Claire hesitated. "We might get stuck and never get out. Come sit next to me," she suggested with a shy smile.

"No." Jamie was emphatic. "Sit with me here, in this chair, just like we did the first night we met." She tugged gently on Claire's hand.

Relenting, Claire slid into the space beside Jamie, feeling herself relax and begin to melt against each nook and curve, erasing every empty space between them. Their limbs wrapped around each other with the familiarity of bodies that had been intimate in the past, but with the restraint that comes with knowing their reunion was fleeting. Claire filled her lungs with warm sandalwood and savored the sensation of Jamie's breath tickling her scalp.

"I've missed the smell of your shampoo," Jamie confessed in a voice just above a whisper. "I almost bought some, but I couldn't remember which brand it was."

Claire's shoulders shook with a silent laugh. "I've dreamed about sandalwood soap every single night since Christmas."

They held each other in silence. "I'm leaving in a few days," Jamie murmured. "Our timing couldn't be worse."

"Nope," Claire agreed with a heavy sigh.

"I wish I could kiss you."

Claire raised her head from Jamie's shoulder by just an inch and, banishing the last lingering doubt, turned until her lips brushed against Jamie's neck, then traveled, with the same excruciating slowness with which Jamie had once tortured her, along the length of her jawline. At last their lips connected, gently, almost as if they had agreed in advance to take their time, to savor every moment of this last kiss.

"I could still stay, maybe," Jamie whispered without conviction.

Claire retreated a few inches to better observe Jamie's face. The tears that glistened on Jamie's cheeks matched the dampness she sensed on her own. She shook her head. "It wouldn't matter. I'm leaving, too."

"Somehow it feels like the universe is trying to keep us apart."

Deflated, Claire sank back into the warmth of Jamie's embrace. "Where are you headed, anyway, back to Boston and the Marine Institute?"

Jamie shook her head. "No, not this time. Actually, it's a great opportunity as a researcher at a university. I probably never would have taken a chance on it if I had stayed at the Institute, so I guess I should be thanking you, in a way."

Claire groaned. "Just my luck. Not only are you leaving, but it's my fault."

"Well, you're leaving, too," Jamie countered.

"True," she conceded. "And I have to admit, it's something I've dreamed about forever. And I *definitely* wouldn't have gotten the chance if it hadn't been for you."

"Ouch. So it's my fault you're leaving, too. But, I'm happy for you. Tell me about it?"

"I've been offered a position as a lecturer in the English department in a university near Norwich."

Jamie's head swiveled and she looked at Claire in surprise. "You mean Norwich, Connecticut?"

Claire shook her head. "No, England! It's the craziest thing. Remember all that money that people donated for my admittedly ill-conceived polar rescue operation?"

Jamie nodded. "It ended up being a lot, didn't it?"

"Yeah, like a quarter of a million dollars. Obviously, I couldn't keep it. The Marine Institute helped me out and arranged for all the money to go to an environmental studies research program in Norwich, and overnight I became one of their biggest patrons. I got a handwritten thank you letter from the university president in the mail saying if there was anything he could do...." Claire shrugged. "Well, people say that, right, but in this case I thought, why not just take a risk and ask if there's an open position. And there was! I'm finally going to England!"

Jamie's face was a study in disbelief. "So am I."

Claire's eyes widened. "What? Where?"

Jamie's face broke into a grin, "Norwich. Back to the university where I did my graduate program."

"You're serious?" Claire squeaked.

"Completely. And I'm beginning to think I have you to thank for it in more ways than I knew. I'll be heading up a new project and I was told they finally got the last infusion of funding they needed because of some big donation from the States."

"I can't believe this," Claire said in wonder. "We're ending up in the same place. Again!"

"Clearly it's a sign." Jamie said.

"I thought that was supposed to be my line." Claire laughed. "You're a practical scientist. You can't really believe this is a sign."

"I don't know. Maybe I do," Jamie replied, staring intently into her eyes.

Claire could feel the heat rising inside herself under Jamie's gaze. She swallowed. "Maybe I do, too." She smile devilishly. "But, I don't know. Maybe we should test this theory. That's what a scientist would do, right?"

"How, exactly?"

"Well, let me think." Claire's eyes twinkled. "Have you packed up your bedroom yet?"

"The bedroom?" Jamie asked, raising her eyebrows. "No. Not yet."

"Definitely a sign," she said, fixing Jamie with her best coquettish grin.

"Oh, really?" Jamie teased. "Of what, exactly?"

Claire leaned forward, and nipped her earlobe playfully with her teeth before she whispered, "It's a sign that I won't be leaving here for quite a few hours."

Jamie pulled her close, pressing their bodies together. "I don't want you to leave at all. Ever."

"I don't know about that. The new tenant's going to want her apartment, eventually." Claire giggled. "But I'm not going anywhere until we've made love at least a dozen times," she concluded matter-of-factly.

Jamie arched her eyebrow. "A dozen?"

Claire nodded solemnly. "At least," she confirmed. "I mean, if we're testing a theory, we should be thorough."

"Very scientific of you." Jamie shimmied to free herself from the chair's deep recesses, then grasped Claire by both hands and tugged. "Come on, we've got to get you out of this chair. I've got a plane to catch, after all."

"I thought you said you didn't leave for another three days."

"Right. Well, thorough research takes time." Jamie quipped.

"Jamie," Claire's tone was suddenly serious.

Jamie froze and turned in place, still clasping the hand she'd been using to drag Claire down the hallway to her room.

"We need to get something straight right now," she continued. "When we get to England, our apartment is absolutely not going to have one of those horrible round chairs," Claire finished with a grin.

Jamie laughed. "*Our* apartment?"

Claire nodded, looking expectantly into Jamie's emerald eyes. Her stomach fluttered. Would Jamie think it was too soon to move in together?

"Our apartment will *never* have one of those chairs," Jamie assured her with an equally wide grin.

"Well, I'm glad we're agreed on that," Claire replied.

"Completely in agreement," Jamie confirmed. "Now, would you like to check out the duvet I had in mind? It happens to be on my bed."

Claire's head tilted back with a laugh. "I'm dying to! Lead the way."

She threw her arms around Jamie's neck and covered her mouth hungrily with her own. Not pausing to break the kiss, Jamie lifted Claire's feet off the floor and carried her the last few feet until they tumbled together onto the bed.

TWENTY-NINE

"HEY, CLAIRE?" Jamie balanced a package against her hip as she shook the raindrops off her umbrella and put it in the stand by the door. "It looks like your sister sent another box for you."

Jamie could hear Claire typing in dining nook, where half the table had been turned into a makeshift desk. The apartment they'd been assigned through the faculty housing department was far from ideal, but based on past experience, both she and Claire had been hesitant at first to commit to a more permanent housing arrangement. Just in case. They had been through so much that they had to be cautious. But from the moment Jamie had met Claire had taken their first walk, arm in arm, through the winding cobblestone streets, open air markets, and picturesque Norman churches of their new home, neither could imagine ever wanting to go anywhere else. Or be with anyone else.

Jamie shut the front door behind her and took in the

very utilitarian surroundings of their current dwelling. She couldn't help but be warmed by the little touches Claire had added to brighten it up—Union Jack throw pillows, a pair of red telephone booth bookends, a *Mind the Gap* sign in a frame on the wall. No matter how many times Jamie hinted that no self-respecting English person actually put things like this in their apartments, Claire would not be swayed. Being here, together, was like a dream, she had explained, and sometimes she needed to wake up and see these things around her just so she could actually believe it was real.

It wasn't just that she needed kitschy tourist souvenirs to convince her she was in England. Claire had also covered every flat surface in the apartment with framed photos of the two of them, to remind her that that was real, too. Jamie found it so endearing that she was determined to dry her hands on the *Keep Calm and Carry On* hand towels in the bathroom without uttering a single negative word. To be honest, faculty housing was only marginally better than the undergraduate dorms, so drab that pretty much any effort made an improvement. Jamie suspected that Claire would be a bit more discerning once they had a place to live that was more in keeping with their style.

She touched her fingertips to the business card in her pocket with a secretive smile, recalling the old cottage they had discovered on a recent weekend boating trip along the River Wensum. She didn't want Claire to know yet, but she had made a few inquiries and discovered that it was both available and manageable on their budget if they could do some of the fix-up work themselves.

It was a big step. Buying property ranked right up there with marriage on the list of major life commitments. They'd known each other for more than a year, and Jamie had known from the beginning that she was in love with Claire, but they hadn't really been together very long.

Jamie would wait as long as was necessary, even pass up the little cottage and start looking again later if that's what was required. Just the memory of Claire shaking hands with the president of the university as she introduced Jamie as her girlfriend, her voice confident and steady, could sustain her for months. Maybe years. Jamie wrinkled her nose at the pungent scent of takeaway curry that had invaded their space from a neighboring flat. *On second thought, let's hope it isn't years.*

"Is that the box?" Claire asked excitedly as Jamie set it down on one the table's last remaining free spaces.

Jamie nodded. "Early Christmas present from Theresa?"

"No, just a few things I asked her to send when she had a chance." She sliced through the packaging tape with a pair of scissors and pried the cardboard flaps apart.

Jamie peered in, perplexed, at what appeared to be an entire box filled with the world's largest collection of refrigerator magnets. "You *asked* for these?"

"Of course," Claire retorted, shooting Jamie a look that warned her to criticize at her own peril. "Although, the refrigerator is so much smaller than I'm used to, I don't think they'll all fit. I might have to rotate them seasonally."

"Naturally. Doesn't everyone do that with their magnet collections?" Jamie teased. "Is that all she sent?"

"No," Claire said, digging deeper into the box. "She sent three jars of peanut butter, too."

"The big bulk-size ones? Yes!" Jamie pumped her fist in a sign of victory when Claire nodded. "Take that, Sainsbury's. At least the grocery stores sell the stuff now, which is more than they did a decade ago. But the jars are tiny and cost twice as much as they should. She really sent three?"

"Yeah. Probably softening the blow of all these magnets. You and Theresa seem to have similar opinions on my collection."

"I think they're adorable," Jamie assured her, bending quickly to give her a peck on the lips. "Just maybe not all on display at once, okay?"

"Okay," Claire agreed, pulling Jamie closer for a proper kiss this time. When she finally released her, she gathered the magnets back into the box, then carried the box to the kitchen.

"Mind if I use the laptop? I told Paul I'd be home for a video chat this evening."

"Go ahead," Claire shouted from the next room.

As Jamie settled into the dining room chair, the corner of the business card in her front pocket poked into her upper thigh. Butterflies swarmed in her stomach at the thought of the cottage. *It's perfect for us*. She wanted so badly to tell Claire what she had discovered, but was it too soon? Jamie had ruined more than her fair share of relationships by taking things too quickly. She knew Claire loved her, but would the prospect of buying a house together, in a foreign country no less, be too much? After all they'd been through, the thought of losing Claire now was more than she could bear. *Better to take it slow.*

Jamie flipped open the laptop and the screen hummed to life. The web browser was still open to the last place Claire had been, and when Jamie saw what it was, she froze. *Is this what I think it is?* Her eyes scanned the page again, and she chuckled a little under her breath. *You've got to be kidding me.* For two weeks Jamie had been carrying that estate agent's card around, trying to work up the nerve to broach the topic of getting a house together, and meanwhile Claire was spending her free time looking at this?

"Claire?" Jamie called in as calm a voice as she could manage. "Can you come here a minute?"

Claire poked her head into the room, her eyes widening at the sight of the computer screen. "Don't worry, it's not what it looks like," she said hurriedly. "I can explain."

"Okay," Jamie mused, "so I guess it's not that you've been browsing for baby daddies on a site that promises to be 'Great Britain's premier source for sperm'?"

"No. Um, I mean, yes. I guess I have," Claire stammered. "But it's just an idea. Just research for, um, later. Oh God, you're completely freaked out by this, aren't you? This is why I hadn't mentioned it," she said with a sigh.

Jamie put her hand to her mouth, trying to stifle a laugh. "No, not at all. Okay, maybe a little freaked out. I mean, a baby, Claire? That's—"

"A huge commitment, I know. And you want to take things slowly. I don't expect you to be ready to think about it. That's why I wasn't even going to bring it up yet." Claire paused to catch her breath.

"You want a baby?"

Claire nodded. "I know it's not something we could do right now," Claire assured her. "But eventually, well... yes. And then I remembered a conversation I had with this woman in the park about it and—"

"I'm sorry," Jamie interrupted, "but you discussed sperm donation with a stranger in the park? What kind of park *was* this?"

"You really want to know?" Claire answered, pressing her lips together nervously. "It was that day last year when we took Paul's nieces to the park. That was *the* day."

"*The* day for what?" Jamie asked, puzzled. "Other than inappropriate small talk with strangers."

"It was the day that I first admitted to myself that there was a possibility that I could fall in love with you. That the world might not end after all if it turned out that I wanted to be with you. And that I could maybe still have the life I had dreamed of. A house, kids. But I wasn't sure if that's what you wanted, so I've been a little afraid to mention it."

Jamie started to laugh.

"What's so funny?"

"You were afraid to ask *me* about the future? Claire, after everything we've been through this past year, I've been completely terrified to ask *you*." She reached into her pocket and pulled out the business card, sliding it across the table to Claire. "I've had that card for two weeks," she explained. "I've been carrying it around, trying to think of a way to bring it up without you thinking I was rushing things. I didn't want to scare you off."

"It's a realtor's card," Claire observed.

"It is. It's for the agent who's representing that cottage we passed, the yellow one in that little village near the river. I dropped in and asked about it as soon as we got back from our trip."

"You did?" Claire asked, looking nervous. "And? Did you get to go inside? What did you find out?"

"We could do it. I did go in and it needs a lot of work, but most of it we know how to do. The price is right. We might even be able to lease it first if we need more time to think about it."

"No." Claire was emphatic.

"No?" Jamie's shoulders slumped, disappointed.

"No, not no," Claire hastened to explain. "I mean, no, we don't need a lease. If we can really do it, let's just do it!"

Jamie gave Claire's waist a tug and pulled her onto her lap. "You're sure?"

Claire nuzzled her lips against Jamie's neck, in that

sensitive spot just below her ear that made Jamie's body tingle all the way to her toes. "I'm absolutely positive," she whispered. "I want us to buy a house, and fix it up, and then maybe we can decorate one of the rooms like we did for the girls in Cape Ann, and—"

"What about getting married?" Jamie asked suspiciously.

"Well, I...um, I mean, I sort of assumed, but I don't want to make you feel pressured or rushed or..."

"No, no. I was just...checking. And I suppose you'd want a ring, or something..."

Claire sat up in Jamie's arms, flashing a grin from ear to ear.

"Uh huh. Like I said, I figured I should check. A girl needs to know what the expectations are. So," Jamie said after a moment, "I guess you should tell me more about this website you've been looking at. Although I'm not so certain I trust you. The last time you went looking for someone on the Internet, you couldn't even manage to get the gender right..."

"Oh, yeah? I think I got it figured out." Claire touched her lips to Jamie's in a gentle kiss. "You'd better trust me, because I trust you."

"You do?" Nervousness lingered. "You're sure that after everything, you really do?"

"I truly do. So how about I'll tell you more about that website after you tell me everything about your visit with the estate agent." Claire settled back into Jamie's lap, snuggling in like she was about to hear her favorite bedtime story.

"Okay, so, it's a lot bigger inside than it looks, and there's a bow window with a window seat in the front room that would be perfect for a reading nook." The joy that filled Jamie at that moment colored every description with a rosy glow. "And the woodwork! All original."

"Amazing. Could we get a dog?" Claire asked dreamily.

"Sure, I suppose, if that's what you want...or—"

"A cat." They said it at the same time, then laughed.

"Absolutely, a cat," Claire concluded. "Now, tell me more about our cottage."

They sat together for hours that night, listening to the soft patter of English rain against the window while they shared their dreams for the future. They were thousands of miles and an ocean away from where they had started. What lay ahead was not exactly what either of them had expected it to be just a year before, but somehow they trusted that wherever they ended up would be perfect, now that they would arrive there together.

THE END

A MESSAGE FROM MIRANDA

Dear Reader,

I hope you enjoyed reading Jamie and Claire's story as much as I enjoyed writing it! I was inspired to write this story because I wanted to explore what would happen if a normal, well meaning person found themselves the unwitting perpetrator of a "catfishing" scheme, where a lie they'd had no intention of telling ended up granting them their heart's desire. How hard would it be for an honest person to tell the truth if doing so meant losing what they wanted most?

Telling Lies Online was my first novel, and I really appreciate that you took a chance on a new author.

Best Wishes,
    Miranda

Made in the USA
Monee, IL
31 January 2024